KEEPING SECRETS

WESTON PARKER

BRIXBAXTER PUBLISHING

Keeping Secrets

Copyright © 2020 by Weston Parker

First Edition.

Editor: Eric Martinez
Cover Designer: Ryn Katryn Digital Art

FIND WESTON PARKER

www.westonparkerbooks.com

DEDICATION

*To all the wonderful readers who have supported me in this incredible
journey. I do what I do for one reason. You.*

-Weston

CHAPTER 1

CALLEN

"Encore, encore," the crowd chanted as I set down my guitar and pretended to get ready to leave the stage. I missed the thrill I used to get from hearing thousands of people screaming our name, from feeling the heat of the lights on my skin and tearing up stage after stage with my best friend.

Clark, our frontman, gave the audience his trademark smirk and stepped back up to the microphone. A hush fell over the eight thousand concertgoers in the venue.

"So you want more, huh?" He rocked his head from side to side as if thinking about it before turning around to wag his dark brows at the rest of us behind him. "What do you think, boys? Can we hang around for a few more minutes to give these people what they want?"

Brent shot him a thumbs-up from behind the drum set, twirling his sticks between his fingers with a flourish as he winked. The crowd roared.

Jason and I nodded too, lifting our guitars from their stands and slinging the straps back over our heads. The audience went wild as another light show started and I strummed the intro to one of our more popular songs.

I used to be addicted to this feeling, to the adrenaline of stepping up onstage and the thundering roar of the crowd. It was my greatest dream come true to be able to earn a living playing my guitar and touring with Clark, our frontman as well as my best friend.

We'd started our band, Kraken, together years ago. We'd played any bar or pavement that would have us and eventually recruited the other guys. I'd never really gotten to know Brent and Jason, though.

Despite the hours we spent together on the road, we didn't have one of those big fancy tour buses yet, and most of the time, I was in my vehicle with Winter and Alice while the others followed us, riding together in a minivan.

Even so, I used to feel this sense of togetherness and achievement while we made music together. It was almost like as soon as we got onstage, our minds fused and became one for the ninety minutes we jammed together.

But I hadn't felt that way for nearly eighteen months now.

I hadn't felt much of anything for nearly eighteen months now.

Not since Alice's life was snuffed out far too early and I'd had to learn how to face my new reality. I had to learn how to live for the rest of my life without my wife and how to raise our baby girl without her.

These days, I stood onstage and played like a robot, going through the motions without any emotion whatsoever. I did my job, and then I went back to whatever hotel we were staying in and crawled into bed with my toddler.

Winter was my life now, the only thing I kept living and breathing for. The only joy in a sea of pain.

Spending my nights and as much of my days as possible with a three-year-old wasn't exactly the sex, drugs, and rock-n-roll lifestyle I had thought I would have if the band ever made it, but it was my life. And except for wanting my wife back in it, I was happy with that.

Clark growled the last lyrics of the song into his microphone, his head cocked and his eyes closed. His hand gripped the mic like it was his cock and he was on the brink of an epic orgasm.

Without breaking the rhythm, I watched my best friend as he put on another stellar performance for the crowd. I might not have felt the same about performing as I used to, but he still lived for it. I couldn't see him ever giving it up, even if the band didn't end up making it all the way to the top of the charts.

When the song was done, he dipped into a low bow and smirked at the crowd. As they drowned us in their voices, he threw his hands up into the air and did a victory lap around the stage to wave at the fans one last time before running off it. The rest of us departed with less theatrics.

We just walked off. Perks of not being the frontman.

I handed my guitar off to a roadie waiting backstage and set my sights on my dressing room.

Ignoring the crowds of VIPs, competition winners, and the general humdrum backstage after a show, I kept my head down and weaved my way through the throng of waiting bodies.

I got stopped a few times, forced to take selfies or sign something, but I got away as fast as I could. Always.

I tried to be friendly with the fans when they stopped me, but I'd earned something of a reputation for being the stoic, quiet, intimidating one of the group, and honestly, it suited me just fine. It meant the majority of people backstage swarmed around Clark and the others while only a few diehard fans bothered to approach me.

After I got into my dressing room, I shed my sweaty clothes and grabbed a quick shower, then dressed in clean clothes and picked up my backpack to gather my stuff so I could leave. The muted noise of the music and crowd outside became sharp for a minute, cluing me in to someone entering my supposedly private dressing room.

With a scowl twisting my features, I popped my head out of the bathroom. Clark stood in the center of the room, his arms draped around two women. He smiled when he saw me, and my scowl softened. *Just a little.*

"Hey, man. You ready to go? The after-party tonight is going to be off the charts. This was our biggest show yet. Craig just told me the final ticket numbers confirmed it. Time to celebrate."

I slipped my arms through the straps of my backpack and shook my head. "Nope, sorry. No can do."

Clark's face fell, but then he squared his shoulders to let me know he wasn't giving up.

My best friend had often been rumored to be my secret brother, considering the similarities in our features. Both of us had pitch-black hair and green eyes with tall, swimmer's physiques that were covered in tattoos.

But while we looked a lot alike, our personalities couldn't have been more different.

Especially these days.

Clark was still the life of the party, the outgoing, outspoken one who was willing to hang onto his balls and jump into just about anything. Even if it meant he'd have to figure a way out of it later.

On the other hand, I was whatever the antithesis of the life of the party was. *Loser? Loner? Anti-social?* Whatever it was called, I was it.

I had been categorized by reporter after reporter as being the strong, silent type to counter Clark's outbursts and antics. I loved the guy, and I'd always had his back and always would, but there was no way he was dragging me to this party.

"Come on, Callen. Live a little. We're starting to catch fire with more and more fans, bro. The after-party is a good opportunity to get our faces out there a little more and have some fun while we're at it."

The blondes he had under his arms nodded, looking up at him like he was a messiah. Which to the die-hard Clarkians, as his cult-like fanbase had dubbed themselves, he probably was.

"If we're going to talk about this, we're doing it alone." I gave a pointed stare at his groupies, then walked to the door and opened it, sweeping my hand toward the waiting area. "Well?"

Clark smacked a kiss to each girl's forehead, then slapped their asses playfully. "Go on ahead, my dears. I'll be right there."

They looked crestfallen but did as their hero asked after whispering what I assumed were promises about later in his ears. When I shut the door behind them, he flung himself onto the couch and propped his hands behind his head, spreading his long legs out in front of him.

"Well, at least you didn't physically escort them out this time." He grinned, obviously taking this fact as a win. "The one on the left was for you, by the way. Apparently closed-off douchebag is her type. Name's something with a B."

I sighed and sat down across from him, dragging both of my hands through my wet hair before they settled at the nape of my neck, squeezing as I willed my frustration with him to ease. "You know I can't go to the party, bro. I have to get back to the hotel to Winter. You also know that groupies aren't my thing."

The almost constant good-natured humor that shone from his eyes dimmed. "It's been almost a year and a half that no woman has been your thing."

"I know, but I just... I can't."

His gaze met mine, concern etched into his sharp features. "Maybe it's time to get back in the game, Cal. Alice is gone, and I know you're still hurting, but you can't be celibate forever. Getting with a busty blonde tonight might be just what the doctor ordered."

I rolled my eyes at him. "Getting off with a groupie isn't going to make me feel any better about my wife dying and it sure as hell isn't going to help me with Winter. I'm just not ready for a new relationship."

"You don't need to get into a relationship to have your dick sucked." He sighed, sitting up and dropping his hands to his knees. A mixture of understanding, worry, and determination glinted from his eyes under the bright fluorescent lights. "Just come to this one party with us, man. I meant what I said about it being a good opportunity and I'm worried about you. You can't hole up in your hotel room for the rest of your life. The babysitter's been paid for the whole night, so don't give me that shit about having to get back to Winter. She's fine."

Before I could answer him, the door opened again and Craig came strolling in. His light brown hair was smoothed down and he was probably the only guy in a suit in a three-block radius.

I mean, who the fuck wears a suit to a rock concert?

Our manager did. That was who. While he was our manager and therefore present in an official capacity, the suit still made him look like a total dick. On the other hand, he *was* a total dick, so the look suited him.

"What do you want?" Clark snapped, his carefree demeanor vanishing as his spine straightened. The feeling that Craig was a total dick was mutual. "We're having a private conversation here."

He gave us a narrow-eyed glare and shut the door behind him, with him still on this side of it. He flat out ignored Clark's unspoken request for him to leave. "Yes, well I'm here to have a private conversation with the both of you. It's important."

Clark stood up to his full height, unwilling to be looked down on if Craig insisted on talking business right now. He also moved to my side so we stood shoulder to shoulder, a united front, the same way we'd always faced the world, despite whatever differences we had privately.

"Fine. Talk. You've got two minutes." He thrust his chin into the air and crossed his arms over his chest. I mirrored him, knowing we cut a pretty damn intimidating figure in that moment.

Craig swallowed but didn't back down. "I need you to sign a contract for touring as the opening act for Axe. They're kicking off in Chicago next week, so I'll need you there by then."

"Are you fucking kidding me?" Clark asked, and I practically felt the tension radiating from Clark's body. "The answer's no. We're not doing it. Axe is spiraling, man. We're bigger than them right now. I'm not touring with them for the next few months to help save them. They're dicks. I fucking hate them."

"But—"

I cut Craig off by lifting my hand and jabbing a finger at the door. "Leave. Now. I'll talk to Clark about this and you'll have our final answer in a couple of days. This was the last stop on our tour and we weren't supposed to take off again for at least a year. We'll need to speak to the others, too."

"Everyone knows you two call the shots. It's your damn band. The others are nothing but props, backup." He tried to argue, but he was already walking backward.

I arched an eyebrow and tamped down on the frustration simmering inside me. I hated it when he said shit like that, but he did it all the time. *Hence: dick.*

With another jab of my finger at the door, I turned my back on Craig and dismissed him. He huffed out a breath, but then the door opened and closed, leaving me alone with Clark once more.

"He's such a fucking asshole" he hissed. "I'm not touring with Axe, bro. I don't care what he says or what anyone else says. Just not doing it."

"I'm not saying you have to," I said evenly. "I know you've got big problems with them and I know why. All I'm saying is take some time to cool off. Then we talk to him about it. We've done everything we were contractually required to do. They can't force us to sign this new one, but we also need to be smart about this. Think about the consequences of saying no and figuring out the best possible way to do it."

His cheeks puffed up as he drew in a deep breath and released it as a heavy sigh. "Yeah, you're right. I need to talk to the lawyers about it as well. I know you're smart as fuck, but I need to make sure our asses are covered. If we're going to go head to head with Craig on this, I need to know there isn't some detail buried in the fine print giving them the right to sue if we refuse this kind of request."

We slapped our palms together in agreement, exchanged a quick back-thumping hug, and moved to the door together. "You sure I can't convince you to come to the party? There might be a girl that ends up being your new type you can crawl into bed with tonight."

"I'm not going, but thanks for trying." I meant it, too. I knew I'd been a miserable son of a bitch to put up with the last few years, ever since Alice's diagnosis.

Clark had never given up on me, though.

I appreciated that, but as I climbed into bed with Winter after getting back to the hotel and thanking the babysitter, I also knew there was only one girl I wanted to crawl into bed with.

It was the small little body pressed into mine now. The only one whose dark hair matched mine and had eyes the color of the Mediterranean on a spring day, just like her mama used to have.

Maybe one day I'd be ready to enter into some kind of romantic or sexual relationship with a woman again, but that day wasn't today. And I was okay with it.

CHAPTER 2

TIFFENY

"Did you know that Katrina Lawson is shacking up with Ryan?" Julia asked me, her brown eyes wide and sparkling like they did when she found time to gossip.

I loved my best friend to absolute bits, but I'd never understood her passion for all things sharing. I listened to her, though, because she was my best friend and it was my job to listen.

She was a technician who owned the nail bar next to my small ice-cream shop, so listening to everything she learned while doing her job was an almost daily occurrence. My shop was slow right then, so I didn't mind. It wasn't like my actual job was keeping me busy, unfortunately.

"I didn't know that. I didn't even know they were dating."

To be fair, I was also having a hard time placing who Katrina was and I was pretty sure I didn't know any Ryans, so I probably wouldn't have known they were dating. Why would I?

Julia didn't seem to realize I had no idea who she was talking about, though. She was too busy picking up steam with the rest of the story, passionately immersing herself in it.

"Yup. Ryan's girlfriend didn't know about it either. Isn't he just the worst for cheating on her like that? I mean, Ally's one of the sweetest girls in town and he just moved in with another woman without even breaking up with her first. I can't believe either he or Katrina would do that."

"Cheating on her would have made him the worst, no matter who she was," I pointed out, but even I had to admit that Ally really didn't deserve to be treated like that. At least I knew who she was, so I wasn't a total lost cause after all. "Is she okay?"

I didn't know her well enough to call her a friend, which was also why I hadn't known she had a boyfriend. But she came into my shop after getting her nails done with Julia sometimes and we'd chatted. She really was sweet.

Although I had technically been born and bred here in Myrtle Beach, my mother had shipped me off to boarding school as early as possible. All my life, I'd attended fancy schools to prepare me for the life my parents wanted for me.

I'd never lived up to their expectations, no matter what I did. Eventually, I'd realized that I never would and I stopped trying.

At that point, I'd been about to embark on my third year of law school. Instead of re-enrolling, I'd come back here and used all my savings to buy my little ice-cream parlor. I didn't need a degree to own my own business, and since I had realized I would never make my parents happy, I did something to make myself happy instead.

Of course, that meant I'd only come back to town as an adult and I didn't know nearly as many people as Julia did. We'd met as kids, but she'd never left and had a huge local network because of it.

When I'd returned, she'd welcomed me back with open arms and we'd been friends again ever since. But I wouldn't be able to get all those years I'd been lost to everyone here back.

Julia shook out her fiery red head of wavy curls and pouted. "No, she's not okay. I think we should dismember him with a blunt butter knife as punishment."

A chuckle escaped before I could stop it. Then I put my hand on her shoulder and rolled my eyes. "Whoa there, cowboy. You really have to stop saying stuff like that in public. Some people might think you're being serious."

"I am being serious," my fiercely loyal friend muttered. "He's an ass."

"Yeah, but even asses are entitled to human rights. We're absolutely not dismembering him," I said firmly, even though I knew she wasn't really being serious. Julia wouldn't seriously hurt or maim a fly, never mind a Ryan.

On the other hand, even if she wouldn't dismember him, there was a small chance she'd kick him in the shin with her little foot the next time she saw him. She might be small, but she kicked like a mule thanks to martial arts training for most of high school.

"If the next thing you were going to suggest was kicking him, I'm telling you right now that you can't do that either."

She sighed deeply, clutching her heart as if I'd injured her. "That was what I was going to suggest. How about punching him in the balls?"

"No. No acts of physical violence will be sanctioned." I laughed, shaking my head at her.

Before I could tell her no acts of mental warfare would be accepted either, the bell above my door jingled and signaled the arrival of a customer.

I perked up, thinking that I might be about to make my first sale for the day when I saw who it was.

My spirits dipped again because I knew there was no way Amber was going to buy an ice cream.

She came in at least twice a week to sample some flavors but always left without making a purchase. Although I knew she wasn't about to change that now, I still smiled when I greeted her.

"Hey, Amber. How's it going today?"

She sniffed the sweet air in the shop, shuddering as if the air itself would make her gain weight. "Do you have any strawberry shortbread for me to try? It's a strawberry shortbread kind of day."

"Really?" Julia planted her hands on her hips and lifted her brows at Amber. "Why don't you buy some strawberry shortbread for a change then?"

Amber scoffed. "I shouldn't even be having a sample because of all the calories in it. There's no way I can have a whole cone."

"Then why—" Julia started, but I bumped my hip into hers to shut her up.

"It's no problem. You're in luck. I do have strawberry shortbread. Let me get you your sample." Smiling brightly, I turned to grab one of my sample containers. I added a blob of strawberry shortbread to the thick cardboard base of it and walked back to the counter to hand it over.

"Thank you," she gushed, eating the generously sized sample in two bites and dumping the container in the trash. "See you girls around."

She hightailed it out of the shop with a wave of her fingers. Julia cocked her hip on the counter and faced me. "You have got to stop giving that girl free ice cream. She's never going to buy anything, but she's coming by almost every day now."

"It's not that bad," I said, but when I thought about it, I knew she was right. Amber was coming in a lot more than twice a week, which was how often I used to see her. I sighed before I explained why I couldn't just stop serving her free samples. "She's going through a tough time right now. Her cat is sick and her brother's fiancée is rubbing it in her face that she's getting married and Amber isn't."

"You're too good to her," Julia said, rolling her chocolate-colored eyes. "Surely, they covered the need to make a profit in one of your fancy business classes. Even if they didn't, I know there's a smarty-pants deep down inside of you. I remember how you've never met a test you didn't ace without even needing to study for more than an hour."

I shrugged. "Maybe having the knowledge doesn't mean you have good business sense, but I'm getting by. I'd rather be true to myself while I do it. It's not like I'm looking to build up an empire of ice-cream parlors."

Julia's reply was cut off by another chime of the bell. My heart soared with hope again, only to slam itself back down to the very bottom of my ribcage when I saw Mr. Nicholson walking into the shop.

Our landlord's appearance was never a good sign. He owned the strip mall both our shops were in and he loved to dangle it above our heads that he could evict us at any time.

Joseph Nicholson wasn't much older than we were, but in his early thirties, he'd already started going gray. He dyed his hair a few shades too blond to try covering it up and slicked it back like he was in the nineteen fifties.

His sharp gray gaze landed on us, a cruel smile that never quite reached his eyes inching his way up his thin lips. "I'm glad I found both of you. How are our businesses doing this month?"

I bit back a sigh while Julia's nostrils flared. We despised it when he acted like he owned our businesses just because he owned the mall they were located in.

Joseph was a big deal in town. He'd moved here from New York after making a crap ton of money in investments. He'd apparently decided to spend that money buying up real estate all over our county and loved flashing it around.

"It's fine," I managed to say without any of my hatred of the way he treated us seeping into my tone. "How are you?"

He smirked. "Oh, I'm excellent. There's nothing quite like a day checking in on all of my investments."

Julia's mouth pulled into a very forced smile. It looked like it was so hard to do that, her lips might crack from the action. "We're sure. What are you doing here, Mr. Nicholson?"

No one was allowed to call him by his first name without his permission, which obviously he hadn't given us. We were worse than mere peasants in his eyes. We were *tenants*.

He flicked his hand into the air and waved it around. "The monthly rent for the mall is going up next month. I thought I should give you some notice."

Julia's brow furrowed while my heart sank. I was barely breaking even as it was. Having to make higher rent could force me to close my doors.

Or worse. *Force me to approach my parents for help.*

The very thought of having to crawl back to them, especially to ask for money, made me sick to my stomach. They'd never approved of my business and I had no doubt that if I went to them for help, there would be some awfully fat strings attached to anything they did for me. *If* they did anything to help me at all.

"Is there anything we can do to stop it from happening?" I blurted out the first question that came to mind. All I could think about was finding some way of making the business survive without having to involve my parents.

Unfortunately, in my moment of weakness, I forgot about how lecherous Joseph could be.

Almost immediately, the blood drained from my face as I noticed lust darkening his eyes. They raked over my body, making me feel like there were fire ants on my skin where his gaze lingered. He didn't even try to hide that he was checking out my breasts, his fingers twitching like he was imagining touching them.

A shiver traveled down my spine. Definitely not a good kind of shiver, but he must have mistaken it for interest.

"There's nothing you can do, unless you're willing to renegotiate the terms of your contract over dinner."

Julia's face said it all, her disgust so apparent that I worried she was about to throw up on her shoes. I felt the same way, but I couldn't let him see it or else he'd take my rejection even harder and make it that much more difficult for me to stay on.

"Thank you for your offer, but I'll find some way to make the payments. It's hardly fair that only my contract should be renegotiated."

He narrowed his eyes, the familiar cold cruelty replacing the lust there in an instant. "Very well, ladies. I'll be coming to collect soon. Have a good day now."

Both of us held our breath until he was gone, then groaned when the door shut behind him.

"Damn, he's so gross," Julia said, her lips twisting. "I can't believe he's raising our rent just to try to force you to go out with him."

"I don't think it's that. I think that was just him taking a chance. He's raising our rent just because he can." And I honestly didn't know how or even if I would make it once he did.

CHAPTER 3

CALLEN

"Do I have to go to day-care today, Daddy?" Winter's lower lip trembled and her eyes were misty when I met them in the rearview mirror.

It was our first Monday back home in Los Angeles, which meant back to school for Winter after spending the last couple of months on the road with me.

"Yeah, sweetheart. You do." I pulled into a spot outside the center and unbuckled my seatbelt, twisting around to face her. "What's wrong? Why do you look so sad? Haven't you missed your friends while we've been gone?"

"I don't like it here," she said, her small sweet voice quivering. It broke my fucking heart to hear her sounding so upset. "I don't like the other kids and I don't like my teacher."

Every word out of her mouth was like a physical blow to my chest, but I couldn't let her see it. She was in pain. She needed me to be the adult, to give her comfort and reassurance.

Fuck. Alice would have been so much better at this than I am.

I couldn't afford to think about it too much right then, though. Not if I didn't want Winter to see I was sad, too.

"It will get better, baby. You're probably just feeling this way because you've spent all day with me for so long now. You'll get back into the swing of things soon."

She sighed, nodding as she looked down at her hands folded in her lap. The problem was that I knew it wasn't just that. Winter wasn't happy here. She never had been.

My smart, sweet little girl wasn't throwing a tantrum because she had to go back to school. She was genuinely unhappy.

But I was fucked if I knew what to do about it.

The plan had been that Alice would stay home with her the first few years. She'd been a freelance photographer for the band since we'd become a big enough deal that people would actually buy her pictures of us.

Since it was a position she could always go back to or do part-time, she'd said she wanted to put all her focus on Winter for the first couple of years after her birth. They'd still have traveled with me whenever I had to go on tour and Winter would have both of us there for her.

We had it all planned out. Life was supposed to have been fucking perfect.

Then it was all blown to smithereens when she went to a doctor because she'd started having headaches that wouldn't go away. At first, we'd thought the headaches, nausea, and fatigue were a result of the pregnancy, but it turned out it wasn't that.

After Winter was born, the symptoms didn't go away.

It turned out what was causing them wasn't the pregnancy but a fucking brain tumor. She had advanced-stage brain cancer, the inoperable kind, and eight months later, she was gone.

Eight fucking months. How the hell was I supposed to have prepared for any of this in eight months?

I'd had my entire world ripped away from me and, at the same time, had a little girl to care for. A little girl who was my entire world, even though it still felt like everything that had made up my world was gone.

My passion for music, the rush of performing, my fucking wife.

Yet every time I looked at Winter, I knew I would survive because she was my heart and my world running around right in front of me.

It was all so confusing that I still got headaches when I thought about it.

What it came down to was this. I had no other option than day-care. My parents were long gone, I had no other family she could stay with, and neither did Alice.

Therefore, while we were in town, Winter had to attend a day-care center so she wouldn't be all alone with a nanny at home. Apparently, it was important for her to socialize at her age.

Whenever I went on tour though, she came with me. Since I had no one to leave her with in LA and I wouldn't have been able to leave her for such long periods of time anyway, there was nothing I could do about her being alone then.

It wasn't a perfect arrangement, but it was the best I could do. *Fuck.*

"I'm sorry, sweetheart," I said finally, hugging her tightly when I got her out of her car seat. "You have to go inside now, but I promise to see you later, okay?"

She nodded into the crook of my neck, then grabbed her backpack once I set her down and marched into the center with her head held high. I was so damn proud of her, it felt like my chest might burst.

But I was also going to have to come up with another plan. I wouldn't be able to stand seeing Winter that sad every day. It would break what little of me was left in half.

All the way to the recording studio, I played around with alternative ideas. My mind kept coming back to Alice, though. What she'd envisioned for our baby and the way life was supposed to have been.

Alice had grown up in Myrtle Beach and we'd planned on buying a house there once the baby was born. She wanted to raise Winter in the same place she'd been raised as much as possible. We were going to stay in LA whenever I had to record, go on tour when I had to, but then go home to Myrtle Beach in between.

Stupid fucking cancer.

I screwed my eyes shut and swallowed the lump in my throat as I parked in the VIP lot at the recording studio. The familiar burn of flames licking at my insides only subsided once I had my guitar in my hand, locked away in one of the booths reserved for us.

A song came spilling out of me when my fingers slid across the strings. It didn't take me much longer than a second to realize the lyrics popping up in my head were about Alice's hometown. Myrtle Beach. Where Winter was supposed to have had a home too.

"I called Craig," Clark's voice suddenly boomed through the equipment. "He's meeting us here in a few minutes, so you'd better get your ass out of that booth. The song was sounding good, though. What was it? I don't think I've heard it before."

I shrugged and stowed my guitar on the stand, not answering his question just yet. Craig came into the studio a minute after I joined Clark, a shiny black leather briefcase in his hand.

"I spoke to a few people over at the label," Clark said, jumping in without any pause or pleasantries. "They told me *you* made the decision about us touring with Axe. It's not something they're requiring us to do."

"So what?" Craig set the briefcase down and clicked it open, extracting a thick sheaf of papers. "I made a decision on behalf of the band I manage. Here are the contracts. All your usual riders have been included. Sign them and get them back to me."

"Or what?" Clark's green eyes narrowed, the muscles in his shoulders rigid and tense. "You made a decision without talking to the band, after I told you we weren't going to do it. The label is happy for us to take the time off we were promised and to negotiate new contracts for us for a next album since our current contracts are up."

"You don't sign onto this tour with Axe, there won't be anything for you to come back to whenever it is you wanted to come back." Craig's tone was as sharp as a goddamn samurai sword, but neither of us so much as flinched.

Clark took a step closer to him, and Craig winced, but Clark didn't back down. "I've told you before and I'll tell you again. I will stop recording. I'll never make another album again if it means not going on tour with those assholes."

"What about the rest of your band? Would they let you throw everything away just because you have a problem with some guys in another band you wouldn't even have to spend much time with?"

"I'd have no problem stopping recording," I volunteered. I'd still play, and that was all I needed in my life. I didn't need to record what I played, not anymore. "The others wouldn't have a problem either. They've all gotten offers since people know our contracts are up now that we're done with the tour. They could take any of those."

"You'd really quit?" Craig yelled suddenly, spittle spewing out of his mouth. "You'd destroy everything you've worked so hard for when you're at the top of your careers, over this?"

I nodded silently, but Clark hadn't run out of things to say yet. "I looked into why you were pushing this on us so hard. You were going to get a massive cut of our earnings, more than double what you made before."

Craig paled, but he gritted his teeth and pushed through. "You don't have a choice here, boys. You've authorized me to sign certain agreements on behalf of the band and this was one of them. It's done. All I need you to sign are the finer details concerning what compensation each of you will be getting and confirming your riders."

"It's not done," Clark seethed. "What *is* done is us. You can't force a band to go on tour when there is no band."

My mouth dried up and I felt my stoicism crack. *Is he really doing this?*

Clark's gaze found mine, obviously seeking backup. I nodded because I was with him. I had his back, even with this.

Of course, if Craig knew the truth about Axe, he wouldn't have looked as utterly shocked as he did now. Clark wouldn't have ripped Kraken apart over anything except for this, but this was pushing him several steps too far.

Clark and I had a history with the boys in Axe, and it wasn't a pleasant one.

Axe had hit the bigger leagues a little ahead of us. Their first big hit had come out about a year before ours had. We were pretty neck and neck with them popularity-wise for a while there, though.

But that wasn't the problem we had with them now. It wasn't some friendly competition or having to open for rivals. It was so much worse than that.

We'd known those guys, played a lot of the same festivals, and even sort of became friends.

Clark's sister met them at one of our shows and we'd introduced her to them because why not?

She'd struck up a friendship with their drummer, and when Axe started immersing themselves into the *drugs* part of the sex, drugs, and rock-n-roll lifestyle, so did she. She overdosed on the drugs the boys from Axe had gotten her hooked on not long after.

The other members of Kraken knew the truth, but no one else did. The assholes hadn't even called for help until all traces of Axe ever having been in the room with her had been cleared.

So, yeah, we'd all start over at the pinnacle of what we'd achieved together as a band so far if we had to, but we wouldn't be going on tour with Axe. There was no fucking way.

It didn't matter what it cost us or how hard we'd worked to get here. This was the one thing none of us were prepared to do to make it to the top.

Craig sputtered for a few more seconds, then seemed to realize we were dead serious. With his face a worrying shade of purple, he grabbed his briefcase and stormed out of the studio.

Clark massaged his temples, collapsing into the chair behind him. His eyes were filled with uncertainty when he looked up at me, and his voice was shaky.

"Fuck, I can't believe that really just happened."

I walked to the chair next to his, gripping his shoulder as I sat down so we'd be at the same eye level. "You did the right thing, bro. Really. We're all with you on this."

"Yeah, but fuck, Cal. After everything we've both done to get this far? You must fucking hate me."

"Absolutely not," I said, looking him right in the eye. He needed to see how serious I was. "I need a break from all this anyway. I have to figure out how to get my damn shit back together. Craig forcing our hands couldn't have come at a better time for me."

A deep frown appeared between his eyebrows, concern and sorrow etched into the skin around his eyes. "What will you do? Whatever it is, you know you don't need to do it alone, right?"

"I think I do need to do it alone," I said quietly, squeezing his shoulder before letting it go. "I'm going to go to Myrtle Beach. It's where Alice always wanted us to be in my downtime, and I think Winter might be happier there. I don't know why. I just think that if I'm going to get my shit together again, it will be there."

He nodded, understanding where I was coming from without needing any more of an explanation. He already knew it.

"If you decide to do anything else, let me know?" I asked.

"Of course," he agreed. "Same goes for you."

"Of course." I left Clark a few minutes later, striding out of the studio with a new-found sense of purpose.

This was the right thing to do. I could feel it all the way to my bones.

At some point, I knew shock over Kraken being gone would set in. But as I walked out of that recording studio for what could very well be the last time, I didn't have a single fuck to give about turning my back on recording or on the life I had always imagined.

Before going to pick up Winter later that afternoon, I called a realtor in Myrtle Beach and found a moving company in Los Angeles. Now that I'd made the decision, I wasn't going to spend the next month or two getting things done.

Urgency drove me now, egging me on. Thankfully, the one thing I had in excess was money and I threw enough of it at the various people I had to deal with that doors just opened left, right, and center.

By the time I picked Winter up from school, we were basically all set to go. We had a few days of driving ahead of us, and if we made a road trip out of it and took some time to bond, our stuff would get there before we did.

Winter gave me a huge hug when I arrived, allowing me to carry her to the car and strap her into her car seat without any fuss. I'd already packed the stuff we would need for the next week or so, and excitement over her reaction grew in my chest.

"Guess what, baby?" I asked, turning over the engine and looking back to meet her eyes before pulling out of the parking spot.

"What?" she asked, leaning as far forward as the restraints on her seat would allow.

"You and I are going to get away from here for a little bit. You ready to go on a new adventure with me?"

Her smile lit up her face, making her blue eyes sparkle. "I'm ready, Daddy. Let's go."

Well, then. Goodbye LA, it is.

CHAPTER 4

TIFFENY

"How about this?" Julia asked, dropping her spoon into the bowl of ramen in front of her and sitting up straighter. She looked proud, like she'd been hit by a wave of brilliance. "You hire strippers to bring in more male customers. Females are the primary demographic that visit both of our shops. If we can do something to bring in more men, you'd have your rent covered without a problem."

I laughed, sitting back in my seat in the ramen-noodle joint at the end of the mall we were in. It was our regular lunchtime hangout, cheap enough we could afford it without having to worry about digging too deep into our pockets to get a good meal every afternoon.

"That might have worked if the strippers wouldn't end up costing us more than what we'd make. I don't know how many ice creams I'd have to sell to cover the cost of strippers for a few days, but I'm pretty sure the men aren't going to buy that much ice cream. Or have their nails done, for that matter."

She sighed, but there was laughter in her eyes and a smile on her lips. "Fine. What do *you* suggest for bringing more business to your shop? I'm all ears."

"I've also been thinking about the demographics of who my most regular customers are." I took the bite on my fork, chewing and swallowing it down with a sip of orange soda as I thought about how best to formulate my idea. "Like you pointed out, my primary demographic at the moment is women. Young moms who bring their kids in from time to time mostly."

"Okay." She motioned for me to continue, a spark lighting up her eyes. "So you want to think of a way to expand that market?"

"Kind of. I was thinking that if I could get in a band or some live music, I could bring in more of a younger crowd. The shop could become the kind of place they could come to hang out, sort of like people used to do back in the day."

"You might be onto something there. Not with the band, but with the young mom thing." She scrunched up her nose as she thought, holding up a finger to let me know she needed a minute. Once she had a few more bites of her food, she smiled. "How about going around to schools and local day-care centers? I'm sure they supply ice cream to the kids there sometimes. So why not buy it from you in the future?"

"You think they would?" I frowned.

I'd considered supplying in bulk before. I just hadn't gotten around to doing it yet.

It was a good idea. It would be much easier to make enough money to cover my rent if I wasn't selling cone by cone but tub by tub to people who bought a few tubs at a time. Maybe it was time to reconsider the bulk sales.

I sold tubs of ice cream in the shop but only to customers who were already there and looking to take some home. It wasn't wholesale business the way this would be, and best of all would be that I wouldn't need to lay out a heap of capital on something I didn't know for a fact would work.

If I did it right, I'd be able to meet with local schools and day-care centers before I actually started making the ice cream. I'd know for sure they were taking an order before I spent any money at all on it.

"If I can combine that with some kind of loyalty or incentive program, I might even be able to get more feet into the shop," I said. "Like giving people a stamp card and every fifth ice cream is free."

"If you make it every tenth, I definitely think it can work," Julia said, grinning like mad. "And while those loyal customers of yours are there, they might decide to pop in next door to have their nails done while the little ones enjoy their free ice cream."

My lips drew up higher than they had since Joseph had given us the news. "That's genius. I can't believe we haven't done any of this before."

"Me either," she said, but then she shrugged. "I guess it's because we got stuck in our comfort zones. Why try to drum up more business when you've got enough?"

"Exactly. Maybe Mr. Nicholson's rental increase was the kick in the butt we needed. We've been too complacent."

She pointed her spoon at me. "You know I don't know anyone else who uses words like *complacent* in everyday conversations?"

"That's why you love me so much," I said.

Julia shook her head and struggled to hide her smile. "Girl, you own an ice-cream shop right next door to where I work. You don't need to look any further than that to know why I love you so much." She winked, then sighed when she saw the time as she glanced down at her watch. "Damn. My next appointment is in five minutes. We can keep brainstorming ideas later, but I have to go."

"Go. I'll get the check and see you later." Julia and I ate there so often that we never bothered arguing over the check or insisting on paying our own portions anymore. It took way too much time and energy. I knew she'd pick up the check next time.

After paying and heading back to my shop, I immediately pulled up a list of all the day-care centers and schools in the area on my computer. Painstakingly rummaging through them and visiting their websites to get a feel for each, I narrowed it down to three places to try first.

Calling every school in the county and trying to set up and get to meetings with all of them would result in me having to close the shop too often. Besides, this was a targeted effort. I was bound to yield more results this way than just cold calling every school around.

The first place on my list was an elementary school who put me through to their cafeteria. I waited with bated breath but was let down after I'd explained my idea. "I'm sorry, ma'am. We've already got someone who supplies our ice cream. Leave me your contact details and I'll call you if we ever need someone else."

Disappointed, I rattled off my number and wondered if I'd been overly optimistic before. Realistically, I knew people could get their ice cream from many places. My shop was attractive to some because the ice cream was handmade and I was always playing around with new flavor combinations in addition to the usual, but schools didn't need much more than chocolate, strawberry, and vanilla.

Any one of the suppliers they already used could supply a couple of tubs of that. Unfortunately, they could also do it at a better price than I'd be able to offer.

I couldn't give up just like that, though. I had to keep trying. The fate of my shop depended on it.

The possibility of having to approach my parents for help made me feel like I was trying to breathe underwater. It was completely suffocating.

One of the reasons I loved my shop so much was because it was mine. I'd decided on the type of business I wanted. I'd found and leased the space. I'd designed the logo myself and spent months sourcing all the producers I bought from.

I didn't want anything more from it than what it was. I only needed to make enough money to keep going and to be able to cover my expenses. I wasn't an empire builder and I didn't want to be one.

Under my parents' guidance and control, they would try to turn it into the next big thing. They'd brand it, franchise it, and do it all under the guise of giving me what I want: to have my own ice-cream shop.

Sighing as I clutched my phone, I dialed the second number on my list. I got a similar reaction from them, but the lady I spoke to was much kinder about it.

"Why don't you try some of the private schools in the area, dear? They might be interested in more exotic flavors and their students might actually give a damn about it being handcrafted."

I smiled into the receiver. "I'm planning on looking into that next actually. Thanks so much. Enjoy the rest of your day."

"You too, sweetheart." The woman hung up, leaving me mulling over what she'd said. I really had thought about it between the walk from the restaurant and the shop, but I'd decided to stick to this part of the plan first.

The private schools had more money but with more money came more drama. If I needed to, I'd take that route.

If I could avoid it, though, I wanted to try. Not only because I knew the crazy kinds of demands kids in those schools could make but also because it felt like that was dipping a toe into my parents' pool.

It was a little too close to their circles for comfort, but it was an option I was willing to leave open. If push came to shove, I'd start calling them tomorrow. While I'd rather not call them, I'd still rather get a private school as a client than having to call my parents or be forced to close up shop.

The last place I had on my list for the moment was a day-care center not too far away. It was in a nice, family-friendly neighborhood that wasn't overly swanky but where people definitely lived comfortably.

The center was on the outer reaches of the geographic area I thought I should be targeting if I was going to try to pair it with an incentive scheme, but it wasn't too far away. The strip mall we were in was only a few miles away from them.

It was probably too far to randomly bring a child for some ice cream, but it was close enough to bring a child who already loved the ice cream and might get some kind of reward for coming here. I still had to figure out what the reward would be, so I wouldn't mention it yet, but I really was hoping to increase the traffic in the shop itself at the same time.

"This is Tomorrow's People," a professional-sounding voice said. "Anna speaking. How may I assist you?"

"Hi. I'd like to discuss your menu and catering with someone please? I'm not a parent. Don't worry. I'm a potential supplier."

"Ah, you're going to want Ms. Austin then. She's our manager. Just a minute."

True to her word, I was on hold for no more than a minute before another women's voice came over the line. I explained my idea to her, then held my breath as I waited for her answer. If she rejected me, I didn't know what I would do.

"That sounds like a wonderful idea," she said. "Would you be able to come in for a meeting later this week to discuss it? We're always looking for new and innovative ways to give our center that little edge above the competition, and this might just be it."

I punched the air in victory and felt a massive smile creeping onto my lips. "Yes, I'd love to come in to meet with you. When would you be available?"

Ms. Austin and I quickly hashed out the details, and when we hung up, I released an incredulous laugh into the air. *I've done it. I've really gone and done it.*

Fine, it was only a meeting, but I knew this could be just what I needed to save the shop. I would have to make sure that I did whatever it took to turn this meeting into a resounding "Hell yes."

CHAPTER 5

CALLEN

Winter's warm body was still curled up beside mine when I woke up the first morning in our new house. She had her own room but had gotten so used to sleeping in my bed on tour that I'd felt her come crawling into bed not long after I'd come to bed.

I didn't mind it, though. The tour, constantly moving from place to place, and then moving again so soon after we'd come off tour had been a huge upheaval for her. Eventually, we'd transition her to sleep through the night in her own bed.

Although if any of the literature I'd looked up was anything to go by, she'd be crawling in with me for a long time to come. It meant more cuddles for me, so I really couldn't complain.

Soft, early morning sunlight streamed through large windows and skittered across the ocean beyond the beach. It was a breathtaking view to wake up to.

When I'd contacted the realtor, I'd asked him to find me a beach-front property, and he'd come through. Winter loved the beach and had been thrilled at the prospect of daily walks along the shore when we had arrived.

Our entertainment area outside was separated from the beach only by a copse of trees, a small sand dune, and the infinity pool overlooking the azure blue waters of the Atlantic. The house itself wasn't ostentatious or overly large like the one we'd left behind.

It was a modern but cozy three-bedroom house with a study I was going to convert into a space for me to play, a garage, and a nicely sized backyard. There was already a jungle gym on the bright green lawn and the pool was covered for Winter's safety.

The movers had unpacked all our large furniture and the basic stuff for the kitchen, but the rest was going to be up to me. There were still a lot of boxes left for me to slog through, and the house was less than unpacked, but it still felt more like a home than the place we'd left behind ever had.

A light breeze rustled through the leaves of the tall Wax Myrtle trees the city was named after. I lay back in bed, just watching the wind and crash of waves to the shore. There was something about being here that was soothing to my soul.

Winter stirred, the biggest smile on her face as soon as she opened her eyes. It looked like it wasn't only my soul that was feeling happier and more at ease here.

"Good morning, Daddy."

"Morning, sweetheart." I propped myself up on an elbow and leaned over to kiss her forehead. "Are you hungry?"

She nodded, rubbing her eyes with her tiny fists. "Do we have food here?"

"Yeah, I think we should." I'd arranged with the realtor to stock the fridge, but I didn't have the slightest clue where to even start looking for everything I'd need to make a good breakfast. There was also the small issue of me being a terrible cook.

With everything that had happened after Alice's passing, I'd tried to fit in making an effort to learn. It hadn't gone super well for me thus far, but maybe that was another thing I could work on while we were here.

Ten minutes later, I stood in the center of the kitchen with my hands on my hips, and I gave the fuck up. "How about we go get something to eat somewhere else?"

Winter giggled, her head bouncing up and down as she sat on the countertop watching me. "I think that's a good idea."

"Hey, you can't say I didn't try." I grinned and playfully poked her in the ribs before lifting her off the counter and setting her down on the floor.

"You tried," she replied dutifully between giggles, her arms winding around her waist to stop any further poking as she ran out of the kitchen ahead of me.

After getting Winter dressed and settled with a puzzle in the living room, I had a quick shower, and when I was done, I found her standing in front of the bay window looking out over the ocean. I ruffled her hair as I came to stand next to her. "What do you think? It's pretty here, huh?"

"So pretty," she agreed, letting out a soft sigh. There was a smile on her lips when she looked up at me. "I like it here."

"So do I, baby. But we still have to eat. So what's it going to be?"

She opened a fist I hadn't realized had been balled up, presenting me with a ponytail holder. "Pancakes, but pony first."

I took the band from her and motioned for her to turn around. Yet another item on the long list of things I hadn't been prepared for was the practical challenge of being a single father to a little girl. I'd never had to make a ponytail or a braid before in my life, but I was slowly reaching expert level.

Pulling her soft hair into a ponytail high up on top of her head just the way she liked it, I took her hand when I was done and led her to the car. I'd seen a diner a few blocks back when we'd driven into our neighborhood yesterday and I figured they had to do pancakes, so I went there.

Winter and I got settled in a booth and ordered pancakes and a milkshake for her, coffee for me. The waitress gave me a curious look, lingering a little while after taking our order. I didn't think she recognized me, though.

Since I wasn't Kraken's frontman, I didn't get recognized very often. Lead guitarists weren't usually the public's focus very often.

The waitress winked, letting me know she wasn't looking for my autograph but for something I couldn't give her. I gave a small shake of my head and the corners of her lips pressed in before she took off to get our order in.

I wondered if I'd ever feel that spark of interest when I looked at someone again. I didn't know if I even wanted to. But those were all things I could figure out with time. Time which I now had.

Turning my attention back to Winter, I gave her my best stern look. "This is our last day of pancakes and milkshakes for breakfast. Tomorrow morning, we're back to our usual routine."

"Yes, Daddy." A smile tugged at her lips. "If you can find oats in the kitchen."

"I'll find the oats. Don't you worry. I just need time to get acquainted with our new kitchen. Speaking of which, we're going to look at a new day-care for you today. How's that sound?"

"Good." Excitement flashed in her blue eyes and she bounced on the seat. "Do you think I'll make friends at the day-care?"

"Yes, baby. I think you'll make friends." I didn't really know why she hadn't made any before, but I had a good feeling about Myrtle Beach, and that feeling extended to Winter settling in well.

The fact that she was excited to go look at a day-care center and not sad about it was already a good sign. A better sign was that when we got to the brightly painted day-care center, I could practically see Winter falling in love with it.

The manager I'd spoken to the day before, Ms. Austin, met us at the front entrance and took us on a tour of their facilities. By the end of it, I was a goner for the place too.

"So do you think Winter will be joining us here?" she asked as we started circling back to where we'd started.

"Absolutely," I said without hesitation. "Where do I sign?"

She smiled. "Let's go get you the paperwork from my office. You can take it home with you and just bring it in when you drop your daughter off in the morning. You did say she'd be starting as soon as tomorrow, right?"

"Right," I agreed.

"Then let's get you signed up." She grinned and motioned me down a corridor I assumed was the administrative wing.

As we walked up to the manager's office, there was a woman sitting in one of the waiting area chairs. Since we were walking down the corridor leading to said waiting area, I had a full view of her face.

I was surprised I even noticed her, but then again, I'd had to have been blind or dead to not notice her. She was beautiful, the kind of woman you noticed if you had a pair of eyes, balls, and a working dick. Even if it hadn't worked in a long-ass fucking time.

Deep blue eyes stared off into the distance while her fingers fidgeted in her lap. I couldn't help but look at her as we approached the office. I tried—I did—but every time I looked away, it was like there was a magnet in her and the other side of it was lodged in my eyeballs.

Okay. One minute. Look, then leave. That's it.

Surely, admiring a beautiful woman couldn't be a betrayal of Alice's memory.

As Clark had pointed out to me time after time, I was still alive. Alice had believed in grabbing each day by the horns. She wouldn't have wanted me to live the way I was now.

It didn't mean I was getting into a relationship, but it did make the guilt gripping my heart in a vise for just having noticed the woman ease up.

Look. Don't touch.

Sucking a quiet breath as I gave myself permission to do it, I let my eyes roam freely and took in what really had to have been the most stunning woman I'd ever seen, aside from the one I'd made my wife.

The bony groupies Clark liked to get down and dirty with had never turned me on. Nor had the full but fake lips or the balloons implanted into their chests.

This girl, however, had everything that did turn me on. *You know, back when I still used to get turned on, anyway.*

Loose black curls tumbled down her back and, in the front, hugged a sizable pair of breasts that didn't look as perfectly round or perky as implants did. The neckline of the flowing, paisley-patterned dress she wore wasn't low, but those weren't the kind of tits that were easy to hide. Not from a self-professed boob-lover like myself, anyway.

Former boob-lover, I reminded myself.

But even so, I let my eyes linger for just a second longer before moving on. The dress clung just tightly enough to tell me that it hid voluptuous, luscious curves that my hands might have been itching to get on in a previous life.

As things were, I stuffed them in the front pockets of my jeans just in case.

Her lips, while as full as any of the fake pairs I'd seen recently, looked soft and perfectly natural. There was only a coat of clear gloss swiped across them, making the pink of them appear shiny.

My tongue darted out to wet my own lips, my mouth suddenly going dry. With a twist in my stomach I hadn't felt in years, I realized I wasn't just looking at her anymore.

I was checking her out, wondering what her moans sounded like when they spilled from those lips and whether those gorgeous breasts were sensitive to the touch. The thoughts alone nearly made a groan rip out of my chest, prompting me to tear my gaze away.

"All right, Mr. Grimes," Ms. Austin said, drawing my attention back to her. "Would you like me to get you the paperwork?"

"Sure." I cleared my throat when my voice came out husky. "Please, yeah. We'd love that."

She smiled and nodded, pivoting on one heel without acknowledging the woman in the waiting room a few yards away. I supposed she wanted to get one thing done before launching into the next.

While I waited for her to get the enrollment forms and whatever paperwork we'd need, my gaze drifted back to the woman. Winter had gotten distracted by a toy a few rooms back, so I didn't have to worry about her for the moment.

"So," I said, surprising even myself by talking to her. "Do you have any children here?"

There. See? Harmless conversation. Research even, speaking to other parents about their experience with the center.

Those dark blue eyes, so deep that looking into them was like looking into the deepest part of the Pacific Ocean, flared when she realized I had spoken to her. An awkward laugh rang out from her beautiful lips as she shook her head and pointed at her ample chest.

"Me? No. No, I don't have any kids."

Her cheeks flushed a rosy red hue and she blinked fast multiple times.

It was obvious she was embarrassed by her answer, but before I could ask why, Ms. Austin reappeared and handed over the paperwork. Sighing internally, I decided to just let it go.

She was embarrassed and I was done here. *Best leave it at that.*

"Thanks," I said to the manager, then inclined my head at both of them before I left. All I had to do now was retrace my steps to find my main and only girl. Then we could get out of there and I could put the beautiful woman behind me.

Later, I'd deal with why she'd affected me the way she had when I hadn't felt any sort of physical attraction to anyone for a long-ass fucking time. After that, I'd have to get down to business figuring out if I was really even allowed to feel that kind of attraction to someone else just yet.

A year and a half wasn't that long of a time, even if it felt like forever most days. It looked like Myrtle Beach was making me feel alive in more ways than one.

I just didn't know if that was a good thing yet.

CHAPTER 6

TIFFENY

"Ms. Hurst?" the day-care manager asked, a frown crossing her brow as she glanced down at her watch after handing over the papers to the Hot Dad. "I'm so sorry to have kept you waiting. I wasn't expecting you for another ten minutes. When I saw you sitting there earlier, I assumed you must be here for someone else. I didn't realize how long that tour had taken."

"That's okay, I'm early," I managed to say, but I was mortified over how I'd just answered Hot Dad's question. The way I said it made it sound like I thought having kids was the worst thing in the world when in reality, it had only come out that way because I'd felt like I'd been caught gawking at him.

"Do you mind waiting just two more minutes?" the woman asked. "There's a conference call I need to take with two of our board members. I've told them I have an appointment and they've said they'll make it quick."

"It's really fine," I said, already pushing to my feet. "I'm not in a rush. I can wait."

"Thank you," she said, pivoting and darting into her office.

At the same time, I took off down the corridor Hot Dad had disappeared down. I needed to apologize if I could catch him. I was so damn embarrassed.

Obviously, he was a dad. He'd been given the paperwork for enrollment at a day-care center, and when he'd just been trying to be friendly, I'd gone and offended him over something he should have been proud of.

Being a parent was something to be proud of, not embarrassed about. Yet that was exactly the way I'd made it sound.

God, I am such an idiot.

I didn't usually make such an ass of myself in front of men, even good-looking ones, but this one was next-level good looking and he'd caught me off guard. *Like way off guard.*

There I was, sitting and waiting for my big meeting, when suddenly the hottest guy I'd ever seen just casually starts strolling right up to me. Seriously, I'd thought I was hallucinating for a second there.

Guys who looked like that didn't just walk up to girls. Girls flocked to them, dropped to their knees for them, and tossed their panties at their heads. Those guys definitely didn't need to go up to anybody, but he had been. He'd been walking straight to me.

My ears had gone hot and my heart began pounding way too hard.

But then I realized I was in a day-care center and I was sitting right outside the manager's office. He wasn't coming up to me. He'd just been walking to the office.

Real smooth, Tiff.

Just when I'd thought at least I didn't have to be embarrassed because he didn't know what I'd been thinking, he spoke to me and I blurted out the first thing that came to mind.

Because really, no red-blooded woman who hadn't gotten laid in months would have been able to speak articulately when surprised by a guy who looked like that. The man was sex on a stick as far as I was concerned. To my sex-deprived body anyway.

When I'd looked up to find the most gorgeous eyes ever boring into mine, I'd completely lost any chance of saying something not entirely mortifying. *But those eyes...*

Light green but rimmed by a ring of the richest emerald color and flecked with bright golden flecks. They were brought out and made to shine by messy, pitch-black hair on top of his head and even blacker lashes.

Guys weren't meant to have lashes like that, I was sure of it. But of course, this one did. Physically, he had to just go and be my very definition of perfect. Light eyes, dark hair, tanned skin, tall with ripped muscles, and a whole bunch of tattoos wrapping around his muscled forearms, disappearing beneath his T-shirt's sleeves. *Yum. Where do I sign up for some of that?*

Regardless of all that, there was an actual person inside that delicious wrapping. A person who had a kid and had just been offended by an idiot because he was hot.

It wasn't right.

Unfortunately, in my haste to chase after him, I didn't have any time to consider what I actually wanted to say when I apologized. And so the blurting out continued as I pushed through the outer doors of the center and saw him waiting patiently behind a little girl who was inspecting a flower planted beside the path leading to the parking lot.

"It's not that I don't want kids—" I clapped my hand over my mouth to stop myself. "Fuck."

His little girl was standing right there and I'd just cursed. Not mention that I'd made things so much more awkward by giving him that little tidbit of information. Why the hell would he care if I wanted kids or not?

Amusement danced in his eyes as he watched me scramble for words, his lips twitching as if he was trying his damn best not to smile. Obviously, he hadn't been as mortally offended by my outburst as I'd thought.

Seeing that made me relax enough that I finally found words, despite once again feeling disarmed by those fucking eyes of his. "I'm sorry. I didn't mean to tell you that. I wanted to apologize for what I said inside and for the way I said it. I just... my head was in a different place."

Like in bed. With you. Licking along the colorful, rippling muscles of your arms and—

Stop it!

Hot Dad's lips curved into a beautiful, annoyingly perfect smile. "It's fine. It's nothing to stress about."

"It's nothing to stress about," the little girl standing next to him said.

She was the spitting image of her father with the black hair and the smooth, slightly tanned skin. But her eyes were a sparkling shade of ocean blue.

Also gorgeous.

Obviously, this family came from some superior-eyed gene pool.

Suddenly, completely out of nowhere, the little girl strode forward and gave me a hug around my leg, patting the side of it. "You shouldn't feel bad. Hugs make me feel better."

Surprised but totally charmed by her, I hugged her back. "Thank you. Hugs make me feel better too."

She let me go, walking back to her father's side. He had watched the interaction between us with a slight crease between his brows, but it smoothed out the second he realized I was looking at him. I wondered about the frown, but there was no way I was making things even more awkward by asking him about it.

Instead, I reached into my satchel until my fingers found the sharp edges of the business cards I'd brought along for the meeting. I pulled one out and handed it over to him. "I'm Tiffeny and I own an ice-cream shop a few miles from here. Come in and get some free ice cream whenever you guys want, okay?"

"Thanks," Hot Dad said, pocketing my card before reaching out to shake my hand. "I'm Callen, and this is Winter."

Winter waved at me, and I waved back, but I was terrified of saying anything for fear of making the situation worse again.

Because holy moly.

There were sparks of electricity running up my skin from where he gently squeezed my hand. The sparks became lightning bolts that exploded in my core and left me wondering exactly how inappropriate it would be to ask him to touch me somewhere else. Anywhere else.

If the guy could turn me on by shaking my hand, I had to imagine what it might feel like if he really touched me. But again, his daughter was right there and I was a complete stranger.

Apparently a very strange one at that, as of today.

He actually seemed like a pretty friendly, polite guy. He definitely did not deserve to be treated like a piece of meat or asked to touch random strangers.

"It's nice to meet you," he said, his deep, smooth voice ripping me back to reality where I was still holding his hand. It must have been my imagination, but just before I released it, I could have sworn I saw a flicker of heat deep within the green depths of his eyes.

But no, I had to be wrong. Guys who were dripping in tattoos and were hot as fuck dated and were interested in women who were conventionally hot as fuck.

While I didn't mind the few extra pounds I carried around—I did own an ice-cream shop, for heaven's sake—I definitely didn't fit the conventionally hot as fuck bill. *Snap the hell out it. It doesn't matter. He's a total stranger.*

"Nice to meet you, too," I said. "I'd better get back inside for my meeting, but I hope you'll come by for that ice cream sometime."

"We will," Winter promised.

Callen nodded and lifted his hand in a casual wave before taking Winter's and leading her farther down the path to the parking lot. Clearly, our entire encounter hadn't shaken him at all. He seemed cool as a cucumber while I was all hot and bothered and rehashing every one of the few words I'd said to him.

Of course, considering how much of a non-event the encounter had really been, I wasn't surprised he hadn't been shaken by it. I shouldn't have been either.

That's it. Temporary insanity break over. Get to work.

I inhaled a deep breath through my nose, squared my shoulders, and got my ass back to the manager's office. She was just finishing up with her call when I knocked on her door.

She signed off and motioned me into a seat, an apologetic smile on her lips. "I'm so sorry, Ms. Hurst. It's one of those days around here."

"Call me Tiffeny, please. You don't need to apologize. I understand all about those kinds of days." I didn't have them very often, considering I was never really that busy, but I was hopeful this meeting would change all of that.

"Only if you call me Shelly," she said, moving her hand to the phone on her desk. "Would you like something to drink? I can ring one of the girls and ask them to bring us some tea or water perhaps?"

"I'm fine, thank you." I pulled a sheaf of papers I'd prepared for this meeting out of my satchel, ready to put the horrifying encounter with Callen the Hot Dad and Winter the Cute Kid out of my head and focus on my future.

Shelly must have seen I was ready to get down to business because she held out her hand for the papers. "Well, let's jump in then. You said you had a proposition for me?"

"Yes, I do. Like I started explaining to you over the phone, I'm thinking about branching out my business and, if it's within your budget, doing something special for the kids on Fridays. Every Friday, I could come up with a new flavor of ice cream or bring new toppings and deliver them to you at lunchtime."

Her eyes dropped to the proposal I'd drafted containing the exact details, flying to the bottom of the page where I'd printed the price. My heart nearly stopped beating as I waited but then raced when I saw her lips inching up into a smile.

"That's well within our budget and I love the idea of ice-cream Fridays. It'll give the children something to look forward to, and like I said, we're always looking for things that set us apart from other centers. Supplying the children with homemade, handcrafted ice-cream flavors and toppings made especially for them certainly makes us sound snazzy."

My eyes widened in surprise, a laugh making its way out of my mouth. "It certainly does."

"Well, that's settled then." She held out her hand to shake mine, and this time, I didn't practically seize up from something as simple as a handshake. "Shall we start next Friday?"

"Yes, I'll be here," I said, slightly dazed by how fast and relatively easy it had been to make my first big sale.

I was still in a state of shock when I reached my car and realized my phone was ringing.

I pulled it out, saw it was my mother calling, and stuffed it right back into my satchel. I didn't know what she wanted from me, but I didn't want to speak to her right then. I didn't want her to ruin this for me. I just wanted to enjoy this win and bask in it for a little while longer.

If this worked out, the shop really would be okay. It was a huge moment for me. The kind of moment that my romance-loving heart wished I had someone to share it with, but hey, at least Julia would be happy for me.

CHAPTER 7

CALLEN

Our living room was finally properly unpacked. It had taken me a couple of days, but it had been worth it.

There were pictures of us, friends, and family on the walls. The TV had been connected and there were even scatter cushions on the couches.

I still didn't quite understand the point of those, but Alice had always loved them, and keeping them around made me feel closer to her. Even if she would never see these, I still liked to buy new ones from time to time.

The new ones were black, as opposed to the brightly colored ones Alice had chosen for us, but at least they were shimmery. Winter and I had reached a compromise in the shop earlier. I wanted black. She wanted shiny. These were perfect for us.

Our gray couches were comfortable, packed out to form an L-shape to fit into the living room. Winter and I had gotten ourselves a new rug too, a bright red one that now sat underneath our coffee table.

Winter was picked up earlier from day-care and was now sitting cross-legged on the new rug, a coloring book opened on the table and a tub of crayons next to it. I sat on the couch with my guitar in my hands, my legs spread wide and my head bowed as I let the music wash over me.

"I like this song, Daddy," Winter said, looking up from her coloring for the first time in almost an hour. "It's nice."

"Thanks, sweetheart." I smiled and strummed once more before I set the guitar down on the couch next to me. "Hey, do you feel like going out somewhere this afternoon? It's a Friday afternoon, after all. I think we should celebrate the coming weekend by going to the park."

Her face lit up with a bright smile. "Yes. I love parks. We haven't been to the park here yet."

"No, we haven't." I got up, then held out my hand to help her to her feet. "But we've driven past it, so I know where to go."

"You know everything, Daddy," she said, looking up at me with that adoration she sometimes got in her eyes. It made me feel like a superhero and a failure all at once.

A superhero because that adoration was enough to make me feel like I could fly. A failure because, at the end of the day, I hadn't managed to save the one person who had really mattered to us.

But I shook the feeling off, something I had become way too good at to protect her, and shrugged. "Not everything, but I do know a lot."

She smiled and shook her head in disagreement. "Everything."

Chuckling as I ran my hand through her soft hair, loose today, I accepted that there were worse fates in the world than having a daughter who thought you knew everything. Besides, it broke my heart to think that someday she wouldn't think I knew anything, never mind everything. "Okay, baby. Sure, but remember that, okay?"

She frowned but nodded. "Okay, Daddy. I'll remember."

"I hope so," I said, but I knew it was a lost cause. Eventually, she'd become a teenager and it didn't matter what she thought now. She wouldn't look at me like I was a superhero anymore.

It was another reason why I was determined to spend as much time with her as possible while she was little. She was only going to be little for so long. I could always go back to recording later in life, even if it wasn't on the same scale as the band had been. I could write songs until the day I died, but this time with Winter was fleeting.

Spending it while traveling all around the country and eventually the world would have been something I'd have regretted later. I just knew it.

Since it was a Friday afternoon and a nice one at that, the park was packed when we got there. There were families everywhere and kids all over. Winter brightened up instantly, pointing at the monkey bars. "That girl is in my class. Can I go play with her, Daddy?"

"Sure, baby girl. Just stay where I can see you, okay?" I looked around until I found a spot I thought would be nice to settle in, then jerked my thumb at it. "I'll be right over there if you need me."

She nodded and turned to race off toward her friend. I made my way over to the old tree I'd pointed out to her, sinking down until I was sitting with my ass on the grass and my spine against its trunk.

As I watched Winter join up with a little blonde girl, I saw a woman who had to be the girl's mother hovering near the play area. I knew the day was coming when Winter would ask me where her mother was, but I was glad we weren't there yet.

Luckily, she was too young to remember any of what happened to Alice. It was a real blessing that she wouldn't remember her mom like that. I had made her a box filled with some of Alice's old things, letters she'd written to Winter after being diagnosed and pictures of her in various phases of her life.

When the time was right, I'd give her the box. I'd answer all of her questions and tell her about her mommy. I was just glad I didn't have to do it today because that day was going to fucking suck furry donkey balls.

My phone ringing yanked me out of the rabbit hole my thoughts had been rushing down. I glanced at the screen, grinning when I saw it was Clark calling.

"Hey, man. What's up?" I said when I answered, leaning with my head against the tree to talk to my best friend. He always seemed to know exactly when to call, when my thoughts were taking a turn toward the dark side and I needed to be distracted.

"Nothing much. Just thought I'd check in with you. How's it going in South Carolina?"

"It's nice," I said, then looked up at the thick canopy of bright green above me. "It's different, but it's nice. Winter loves it."

"That's great news," he replied. "So I'm guessing you guys are going to stay down there for a bit?"

"Yeah, I think so. I think it's going to be good for us to be here."

He sighed. "Don't get me wrong. I'm happy if you're both happy, but I was hoping you hated it and wanted to move back."

"No such luck." I laughed, shaking my head. "Why'd you want us to move back? Do you miss us that much?"

"I don't miss *you*," he retorted. "I do miss the fuck out of my goddaughter, though. Now you? I was only hoping you would move back so we could work together again."

Still chuckling, I flipped him off mentally before getting serious. "What are you talking about? We're on sabbatical, remember?"

"Yeah, but I've been thinking about something. You and I should do an album together. Just the two of us. We'll record the stuff we've always wanted to, have the kind of fun we couldn't while being under contract and just get back to basics."

I stilled, tracking Winter moving from the monkey bars over to the slide with my eyes. "It sounds like fun but not right now."

"You sure?" he asked.

"Yeah. Thanks for letting me know, but I'm still okay with taking some time off for now." This last week with Winter had solidified the decision for me. The slower pace of life, us being able to spend more quality time together, and the lack of stress were good for us.

It was what I needed to find my feet again and it was good for Winter, too. Plus, having a father that had his shit together would ultimately also benefit her. And I needed time to track all my shit down before I could get it all together.

"Maybe I'll give you a call in a couple of months and we can talk about it, but for now, I think I just need to breathe."

"I get it." He sighed. "But look, even if you just want to write a few songs, I'd be willing to split the profits from the album with you. You might need to breathe, but I need to record. It's only been a week and I'm going out of my damn mind."

"Yeah, you weren't built for taking time off." Writing didn't sound too bad to me. It had always been my way of clearing my mind. "I'll think about writing for you. In the meantime, there are those songs we wrote during the tour for the band we never got around to recording. You can always start with those."

I knew Clark, and I knew he'd want to get started on something right away. Writing would take me some time, if I even decided to do it for profit again eventually. I didn't want to leave Clark high and dry in the meantime.

"Yeah, I'd forgotten about those," he said, his voice an octave higher with excitement. Hearing it made me smile. "I think I'll do that. Thanks for reminding me. You wouldn't mind if I used them solo? I'll credit you for the writing, of course."

"Sure, bro. No problem." I spoke to him for a few more minutes, promising to let him know once I'd made up my mind about writing new material for him before we hung up.

Winter was walking toward me now, her friend and her mom leaving on the other side of the park. She was still smiling though, even if her friend was obviously done there for the day.

"Hey, sweetheart. You ready to leave or do you still want to play a while?" I pushed up off the ground and dusted off my butt. "It hasn't been that long."

As I ran my hands over my ass, I felt something in my back pocket. I stuck my fingers in and took out a business card, instantly recognizing it as belonging to Tiffeny. My blood heated for a second as I thought about her.

Damn, she was hot. What I'd imagined her curves to be like while she'd been sitting down hadn't done them justice.

When she'd been standing only a few feet away from me after chasing me down outside, I saw I'd underestimated her body. The dress hadn't exactly clung to her, but it had been cinched at the waist and gave me a much better idea about what lay beneath it.

And I'd liked what I'd seen.

I'd tried to fight it, but as soon as I'd touched her hand, it was like that one simple casual touch broke through to parts inside me I'd thought were dead and buried. I'd wanted her so much in that moment, it was like all the pent-up need that had been building for the past two years just slammed right into my crotch.

I'd thought about it later that night in the shower, trying to dissect why I had been so attracted to her and trying to work through the guilt I felt about it. Just like I'd told myself I would.

My mind hadn't stayed on that, though. While I'd been standing there, trying to work it all out, it strayed again to what it might feel like to really touch her.

Before I could yank myself out of my fantasies, I'd gotten hard. *Over thoughts about another woman.*

Wrecked by guilt, I hadn't touched my goddamn throbbing erection. But I hadn't forgotten about it either.

Sex wasn't something that had been on my mind a lot for the last two years. After Alice had fallen pregnant and the symptoms started, we'd still done it occasionally, when she felt up to it.

Then Winter was born, and she was diagnosed, and treatment started, and we had a newborn to care for, and everything was just so busy and confusing and new. Sex fell by the wayside.

Just before one of her last rounds of chemo started, we'd gone away together for the weekend. Alice had insisted.

Clark had taken care of Winter and she'd whisked me off on one last romantic weekend away. Although I hadn't wanted to believe it would be the last one, I was pretty sure Alice had known.

That weekend had been just about two years ago, and it had been the last time I'd had sex. There was nothing physically wrong with me, so every once in a while, in between the hectic craziness that was my life, I made a minute or two for myself. Took care of business.

I was only thirty-one years old, after all. But I'd never fantasized about a specific other woman. When it hadn't been Alice I was thinking about, it was some nameless, faceless girl with luscious curves and a great rack.

Now that girl with the luscious curves and the great rack had both a name and a face. I'd freaked the fuck out at first, berated myself to within an inch of my life before I left that damn bathroom.

But then I'd realized that something Clark had been saying to me was true. Alice was gone and she wasn't coming back. Sure, I didn't think she'd want me to be whoring around, but she wouldn't want me holing up and isolating myself like I had been either.

I'd even done some reading on it, dating after losing a spouse. It seemed like the norm for feeling an interest in starting to see someone new was anything from a month to five years. A month seemed ludicrous to me, but five years?

I'd never really thought about it before, but five years was a long fucking time. Even if I'd previously thought I'd be alone for the rest of my life, I was coming around to the idea that maybe I didn't need to be.

While it didn't mean that I was ready to get serious about anyone, it did mean that I'd come to the conclusion over the last few days that I'd stop actively taking myself out of action. Winter would always come first to me, but that didn't mean I couldn't have *anyone* else in my life.

With all that in mind, I waved the card at Winter. "Do you want to go get some ice cream from that lady we met at the day-care the other day?"

She smiled wide, letting me know her answer before she'd even said it. Then again, she was three and I was asking if she wanted ice cream. It was kind of a no-brainer. "Yes, Daddy. Let's go. I love ice cream."

CHAPTER 8

TIFFENY

"How did it go with your first delivery?" Julia asked a few hours after I'd gotten back from the day-care center. She'd just finished up with a client and didn't have any more appointments for the afternoon, but she wanted to be around in case she got a walk-in.

She sat at one of the small, round tables in my shop, a cup of salted caramel ice cream in hand. It was her favorite, so I always made sure to have some in stock.

"It was really good," I said, taking a bite of my own scoop. I usually made a point of not eating the merchandise too often, since I'd bankrupt myself and end up looking like a beach ball, but I was celebrating today. "You should have seen how excited the kids were. Their faces lit up like Christmas trees when they saw how much ice cream there was."

"I can imagine." She dipped her spoon into her cup and had another bite. "I'm pretty sure I light up like a Christmas tree every time we indulge like this."

"You do, but you're not nearly as cute," I teased. "There's something about seeing toddlers and kids so happy that makes my heart warm."

"It's called being a good person," she said. The corners of her eyes crinkled as she smiled. "It only makes my heart warm when the kids leave."

"That's not true. I know you secretly love kids. You can't hide the truth from me."

She mimed zipping her lips and throwing away the key. "Maybe not, but that doesn't mean I'll ever tell. Back to the point, you were telling me about the delivery."

"The manager was really happy. As were all the other staff members. It was definitely a success."

"How much did you get for it?" she asked, her brown eyes worried on mine. "Was it worth having to close up shop while you went to the center?"

A gigantic grin spread on my lips. "With this contract, I'll be able to cover just a bit more than half of the new rent price. I think I'm going to be okay."

"That's great," she exclaimed, getting up and coming over to throw her arms around my neck. She pulled me into a huge hug, coaxing me into jumping with her.

I laughed but did it. I was just so unbelievably happy, I didn't even care about how unprofessional it was that we were hugging and jumping in the middle of my business.

Unfortunately, I only didn't care until we separated and the bell above the door rang, signaling the arrival of a customer who would have seen us through the windows.

My cheeks flushed. I turned to face the customer, ready to apologize when I saw who it was. "Winter, Callen. Hi."

Winter's eyes widened as I said her name, almost like she was surprised I remembered her. "Hi, Tiffeny."

Callen smiled, his big hand on Winter's shoulder. "Hi, Tiffeny. How are you?"

"I'm fine," I managed to say without stuttering or embarrassing myself this time. On the other hand, they'd only been in the shop for a few seconds, so there was still plenty of time for it to happen. "How are you?"

"We're good," Callen said. When he looked into my eyes, I nearly fainted. *Why does he have to have the prettiest eyes known to man?*

"I went to school for half a day," Winter added, thankfully distracting me from the intensity of her father's gaze. "I saw you there today, but you were leaving when my class came out."

"Sorry I missed you," I said genuinely. She was a cute kid. And she liked hugs, so we had that in common. We had to be destined to be great friends. "I'll look for you next time so I can say hi before I go, but I can't stay too long. It's more of a drop-off, unpack, and go situation."

"Did you get some good news?" Callen asked, eyes traveling from mine to Julia's and back again. "I couldn't help but notice the jumping thing you were doing when we came in."

"Yeah, erm…" I swallowed and glanced at Julia, who simply raised an eyebrow. "This is Julia, by the way. She's my neighbor here. If you ever want to get your nails done, she's your girl. Julia, Callen and Winter."

Crap. Why did I have to be so awkward around these two?

"Hi," Julia said, her voice squeaky. It was weird, but I had my own weirdness to deal with right then.

"Hi, Julia," Winter said in her sweet voice. She curled her fingers in and looked down at her nails before turning her head up to her dad. "Can I get my nails done?"

"Sometime," he said, then shot a pained smile at Julia. "How old are girls supposed to be before they start getting their nails done? Also, hi. It's nice to meet you."

For some reason, my usually confident friend looked slightly starstruck. Although that was probably what I looked like whenever I saw Hot Dad too. "Anytime. It doesn't need to be more than a coat of paint. Nothing fancy or stuck on. Nice to meet you too."

He breathed out a sigh of relief. "Just paint doesn't sound too bad. I'll bring her by sometime."

It occurred to me then that a mother usually did things like painting her little daughter's nails. I'd briefly checked for a wedding ring when I'd met Callen the other day, and he didn't wear one, which wasn't to say he wasn't married or involved with someone, but it did make me wonder about Winter's mom.

Look at you, going all inappropriate on him again. I shoved the curiosity out of my mind and pointed a finger behind me. "I'm guessing you've come to claim the free ice cream I promised you?"

"You don't need to give it to us for free," he said, moving closer. Logically, I knew he was only coming closer to me to be able to read the signs saying what flavors I had in stock, but my heart still kicked up a notch.

"Nope, you're getting it for free," I said. "A promise is a promise, and I owe you for acting like such a nutcase the other day."

"You don't owe us anything," he said. I could tell he was trying to sound firm, but there was a definite hint of laughter in his tone. "Besides, Winter and I like nutcases. We're nutty too. We're paying for our ice cream."

He liked nutcases? Why did he say that? Did he like me?

Jeez, girl. Get a grip. He does not like you. He doesn't even know you. "Well, sorry. But fellow nutcases don't pay here. What's it going to be?"

"Insisting on giving away your product for free doesn't seem to be a great business plan," he said. Then his lips pulled into a sexy smirk and he pointed at one of the machines. "But I'm not going to complain. We'll have two buttered pecans please."

"Coming right up." I smiled and grabbed two large sugar cones, filling one and then the other before whirling around to hand them over.

Callen's eyes were on mine again. It seemed like every time I looked at him, he was already looking at me. Then again, I was about to give him an ice cream. It was perfectly reasonable that he'd be looking at me.

"There you go," I said. "I hope you like them."

"We will," Winter said, then took her first lick and immediately smiled, taking a few steps back to take a seat. "This is so yummy."

"Yeah, it is." Callen's tongue came out and he gave the ice cream a long, slow lick that made my body nearly seize up. He smirked at me as he swallowed. "So, you still haven't told us about the jumping, hugging thing. Is it just something you two do? Because you've made me curious about it now."

"Tiffeny got a contract with the day-care center," Julia said, finally finding her voice. "We were celebrating."

"Ah." He tapped his chin once. "That was what you were doing there the other day then. Meeting with the manager about the contract?"

"Yeah, I was. Contrary to what you might believe about me, I don't generally go around to day-care centers to tell parents I don't have any kids."

"Really?" he asked. "I thought it was a pretty cool hobby."

And he has a sense of humor too. Well, that's just great.

I laughed. "Well, maybe it will turn into one. You never know. I'm between hobbies right now."

"So am I. I wonder if it will be as much fun to go around to places where single people hang out and tell them I have a kid. I might give that a try."

"Do." I tried to keep a straight face, but a smile broke through anyway. "Let me know how that goes for you."

"I will." He took another bite of his ice cream. And once again, it made me want to bite him. Lick him. Do all sorts of things to him I'd never get to do, but he turned to look at Winter and beckoned to her with his finger. "Come on, sweetheart. We'd better get going."

He lifted his half-eaten ice-cream cone and inclined his head. "Thanks for this. We'll definitely be back, but next time, I'm paying."

Winter waved goodbye after thanking me as well. Then the two of them left the shop. Julia and I both stared at the door in silence for a minute after they were gone.

When I looked at her to ask why she was so quiet, I found her eyes had grown so wide, they looked like they were about to bug out of her head. "Do you know who that was?"

"Uh, yeah." I frowned. "I just introduced you, remember? Callen and Winter."

"No, no." She shook her head fast. "What I mean is, do you know who Callen Grimes is?"

"How do you know his last name?" My mind whirred as I tried to remember if he'd mentioned it.

"Because he's Callen fucking Grimes," she just about shrieked, excitement burning bright in her eyes. "Do you remember I told you about my new favorite band, the one called Kraken?"

"Yeah," I said, my brows pinching.

"Well, he's their lead guitarist. He's a legend in the making, Tiff. Seriously. He's that good. I wonder what the heck he's doing here, though? Do you know?"

"I don't have the faintest idea." It made sense that he was rich and famous, though. Everything about him screamed *I'm cool and awesome and I know it.* "Here's a quick question for you. Is it okay to fantasize about random strangers during a dry spell if the random stranger in question is a celebrity?"

"Yes," Julia said without hesitating, a knowing smile on her lips as she bumped her shoulder against mine. "If that's who you're fantasizing about though, then it's no wonder you're single and in a dry spell."

I groaned. "I know, right? But don't worry. I'm not holding out for someone like him in real life. If I did, I'd be single forever."

"I wouldn't be so sure about that if I was you." The knowing smile was still on her lips, making me wonder what the hell she was insinuating.

CHAPTER 9

CALLEN

"Have a good day, honey." I hugged Winter tight, then watched as she skipped up the path and into the day-care center. She turned once she reached the door, waved, and disappeared inside without even waiting for me to wave back.

She loved it there. I felt how happy she was and how excited she was to get to the center every day. It was a totally different ballgame in the mornings now, compared to what it had been in California.

She'd dragged her feet getting dressed when we'd been there. Every morning on the way to the day-care, she'd looked sad.

The same could not be said for the way she acted now.

Seeing her thriving was fucking incredible. It gave me a sense of rightness I hadn't felt in a long time. This was where we were meant to be, for now anyway.

It also made me feel like maybe, just maybe, everything would be okay. Like the sun was starting to rise after the longest night ever.

Ever since Alice's death, I'd felt like I'd just been slogging through to make it to the next day. The only bright spots in the last eighteen months were times I'd spent with Winter, and now I was getting to spend quality time with her every day.

And every day, I felt like I could breathe a little easier. Every day, it felt a little more like I might just be able to carry on.

Exhaling a deep, relieved breath, I climbed into my car and set the GPS on my phone to a park Alice had always told me about. She'd spoken about the cherry blossoms and how there was a bench in the shade of a big old ash tree that used to be her thinking spot back when she'd lived here.

There were lyrics rattling around inside my head and I couldn't think of a better place to try get them all out. With all these new, more positive things going on in my life, I felt like going to her spot was a way to feel connected to her to help me figure it all out.

When the GPS said I was only a few minutes away from the park, I stopped to grab a coffee before going the rest of the way. Once I found a parking spot, I walked up a dirt path that led to a small, but well-kept park.

There was a pond in the middle, just like Alice had described. Wildflowers grew around the edges of the park and there were plenty of trees.

I knew what I was looking for, though. It was a wooden bench with a dedication to someone on it. There was a wooden bench right next to the pond, nestled behind some rocks that gave it privacy, but it wasn't the right one.

I kept walking across the green grass and found another bench set farther back. It was near another path, but there weren't many other people around.

A smile curved on my lips as I sat down and pulled my notebook out of my pocket. Alice had been right. It was peaceful there, the perfect place to get some thinking done.

So I did.

I thought about Alice and how I cherished the memories I had with her, but thinking about her didn't make me feel like I wanted to rip my heart out to try to stop the pain anymore. Tears no longer burned my throat, and rage at the universe itself no longer consumed me.

It wasn't because I didn't love Alice anymore. I did and I always would. It was because it felt like my heart had grown a few sizes, like it was big enough now to accommodate the grief along with other emotions now. It hadn't happened overnight, nor had it happened only in the weeks since we'd gotten to Myrtle Beach.

It had been a long time coming. I just hadn't had the time to process what was happening. Even if I hadn't been the most popular guy in the band, I'd still had a lot of responsibilities. I was expected to appear on every talk show, do every interview, and visit every charity foundation for good PR. And all that was outside the responsibilities of actually being part of the band, like practice, performing, working out, and attending all the planning meetings.

Between all that and trying to take care of Winter to the best of my abilities, I hadn't had much time to pay attention to myself. There just hadn't been many opportunities for me to sit somewhere out in nature like I was now and just think, feel, and let the changes to what I felt wash over me.

That was the thing I was learning about grief, though. It changed as time went on. *I* had changed because of it as time had gone on.

I wasn't *getting over it* or *moving on*. I was learning to make space for it and to keep living anyway. As I realized all these things, my hands automatically reached for my notebook and pen.

Before I knew it, two songs had come flowing out of me, and another was on its way. My coffee had gone cold, but I sipped it anyway as I tried to organize my thoughts around the next song.

"Hey, aren't you that guy?" an unfamiliar voice asked from the direction of the path.

I lifted my head, my eyes landing on a guy around my age walking a shaggy brown dog. He snapped his fingers a few times, his head cocked as he tried to remember something. "Callum, right? From Kraken, the band? What are you doing here, man?"

He came up to me and excitedly shook my hand. I didn't want to be rude to a fan, but I also didn't really want it getting out that I was here. If it did, even people who'd never heard of me before would look me up, and things would snowball from there.

All I wanted was to carry on with this new life Winter and I had started here, and in it, no one knew who I was. I just got to be me.

"No, sorry. I've been mistaken for Callen before, but I'm not him."

Skepticism darkened the guy's eyes as he cocked his head again. "Are you sure? I've watched all their music videos like a thousand times and you sure do look a lot like him. You're right, though. It's Callen, not Callum."

"I'm sure Callen wouldn't mind," I said with an easy smile. "The two are pretty close together. Anyway. Yes, I am sure that I'm nobody special."

That much was true.

He let out a disappointed sounding huff but took a step away from me. "Yeah. Okay. Sure. Sorry to have bothered you. I just love that band and it would have been awesome to meet one of the members. I can't believe they've broken up. I mean, the media are reporting that they're just taking a break, but every true fan knows what that means."

I made a sympathetic but noncommittal noise in the back of my throat. "Maybe they *are* just taking a break. Sorry to have disappointed you."

He let out a dry laugh. "It's not your fault you're not the best guitarist of our generation, man. I'm not it either. But that Callen guy? He just might be."

The guy took off after that, leaving me to really think about our fans for the first time since we'd told Craig to shove it. It wasn't that I didn't care enough about them to have considered them before. It was just that I felt like I was emerging from a thick fog and could think clearly again.

Before, I'd only been thinking about myself and Winter. I'd listened to Clark wonder about the fans, but it hadn't really sunk in.

It was sure sinking in now, though.

Thousands upon thousands of people had bought our records, had come to our concerts, and had supported us. Without any warning to them, Clark and I had essentially ripped the band we'd built apart.

Sure, we'd been backed into a corner with the whole Axe thing, but maybe I should have considered Clark's offer more carefully. Not to go right back to recording, but to write for him.

That way, I could still be doing something for the fans. And for Clark.

I'd been leaning toward saying yes to him anyway, but my mind was made up now.

Picking my pen back up with renewed determination, I pored over the first two songs and got the lyrics as perfect as I could before the third was back from the vortex it had gotten sucked into when I had been recognized and it came spilling out too.

By the time I left Alice's spot in the park, I had four new songs for Clark and I was feeling pretty damn good about myself.

The good feeling ended when I decided to see if I could find my way back from the park to our house without my GPS. My internal navigation system never had been great, and I ended up miles away from where I'd been intending on going—and in the very last place I'd have wanted to come today.

Looming in front of me was the Myrtle Beach Oncology Center. It was the same sprawling white building it had been the first time I'd come here. It was where Alice had been diagnosed for the first time.

We'd been in Myrtle Beach to introduce Winter to Alice's mother, who had also been ill at the time, when one of the doctors we'd consulted had sent us to a specialist here.

The appointment had been made without either of us seriously believing she had cancer. She'd just been tired and stuff. We thought she'd be fine.

Then we'd sat in this same parking lot an hour after leaving it, both of us devastated and in total shock because it turned out that she really did have cancer.

As I sat in that parking lot again, just sitting there without going in, I hung my head and my mouth opened in a silent scream. That was the funny thing about grief, wasn't it?

It was always one step forward, two steps back.

Just when I started thinking I had a handle on it, *boom*. Something would happen and it would punch me in the heart, stomach, and balls so hard the pain was crippling. And then I'd have to start all over again.

But this time, I was determined not to drown. Even if the onslaught of pain and longing and unfairness tried their best to drag me under.

CHAPTER 10

TIFFENY

The bell above the door in my shop chimed just as I put a new mixture into the churner. Wiping my hands on my apron, I headed to the front with a smile on my face.

It dropped right off when I saw my mother standing in the front of the shop, her blue eyes narrowed as they darted this way and that. They snapped to mine when she heard the door from the back room opening, exasperation filling them instantly when she saw the expression I was wearing.

My mother was dressed the same as always, a sharp charcoal power suit with a crisp, pressed white linen shirt beneath it. Shiny black stilettos adorned her feet, her nails perfectly manicured with a nude polish and her dark brown hair pulled back into a slick bun.

She was as intimidating standing in my shop as I imagined she was in boardrooms all over the city. As the second in command at our family's company, she had been raised to be a ruthless businesswoman and it showed.

"Tiffeny," she said curtly, her fists flying to her hips. "Is there a reason you haven't been answering my phone calls? Really. Why you insist on making me chase you down like a rabid dog is beyond me."

And there it was, the reason I didn't take her phone calls if I could

63

help it. She was mean. I'd never lived up to their expectations and she wouldn't let me forget it.

I cleared my throat, lifting my chin. As intimidating as she was, I'd lived with her all my life. I wouldn't back down because even though I hadn't lived up to their expectations, I'd been raised the same way she had. I just didn't choose to live that way. "I've been busy."

"Too busy to speak to the woman who gave you life?" She arched a perfectly tweezed brow.

I braced my hands on the counter and forced a nonchalant shrug. "The last few weeks have been challenging. You know how it goes when you're running a business. Sometimes, it requires your sole focus."

She rolled her eyes, her left hand flicking in the air dismissively. "Are you really comparing running this place to running Hurst Enterprises? We're the premier baby product manufacturer and supplier in several states, darling. You sell ice-cream cones to kids."

My jaw clenched. I hated how condescending she was toward my business, but it wouldn't help to get into a fight with her about it. Lord knew we'd fought that particular fight too many times to count and it hadn't changed anything.

She looked around the shop before walking up to the counter and meeting my eyes. "How much longer are you still going to try to make this place work? It's never going to do well enough to allow you to live the life you deserve. If you'd just stop being so stubborn and go back to law school, you know your spot as our corporate counsel is waiting for you."

"I'm not being stubborn, Mother." I drew in a deep breath through my nose and sighed. "You know I don't want that life, so why are you really here? Surely, you didn't think coming in to have the same argument we've been having for years would change my mind, did you?"

"No." She held my eyes, an imploring expression in hers. "I didn't come here to argue. I came here to find out why you don't want to speak to your own mother and to try to reason with you."

Translation: she'd come to make me feel bad about not taking her calls and to make sure I remembered they didn't approve of my career choice.

While I'd never really been good at standing up to her despite my upbringing, it didn't stop me from trying once again. "I'm sorry I haven't been taking your calls. I really have been busy, but I'll make more of an effort in the future. As for trying to reason with me, I'm not going back to law school. I have a successful business, and even though it's not a glamorous life, it suits me just fine. I don't want to be a fancy corporate counsel."

She pursed her lips before giving me a nod. "Very well then. I see you're not ready to make the mature, responsible decision yet. Since we've reached an impasse on what you've chosen to do professionally, tell me about your personal life."

"What about it?"

Her gaze dropped to my hands. The left hand, more specifically. "You're never going to get married if you refuse to date anyone. You're a pretty girl, you're smart, and you have good breeding, so why don't you have a boyfriend yet?"

Jeez. She made me sound like a puppy she was trying to sell. "I—"

The arrival of another customer cut me off. My heart jumped to my throat when I saw Callen walking in. His lips curved into a friendly smile when his bright beautiful eyes landed on mine, but his gaze quickly darkened in concern when he realized he'd walked in on something.

"I do have a boyfriend, Mom," I blurted out without thinking at all. "This is him. My boyfriend."

It was like a foreign force took control of my mouth and my feet. I had no control of the words I said, and I walked over to him, slipping my arm around his trim waist and tipping my head up to his.

I widened my eyes, silently begging him to play along.

Callen didn't miss a beat. His arm came up and slung around my shoulders, holding me tightly against his side. He even dropped a kiss on top of my head. "Hey, sweetheart. Everything okay?"

"Yes," I breathed, blood hammering in my ears from how hard my heart was throbbing.

Despite the absurdity of the situation, it was impossible not to notice how solid his frame was beside mine, how hard and yet comforting the muscles in his arm were around my shoulders.

And oh my Heaven-Scent did he smell good. A sexy, masculine scent that was not only crisp and subtle but refined and sophisticated.

If my mother hadn't been there and if it wouldn't have made things even weirder between us, I would have leaned in to get a better sniff of him. As things were though, I stood rigidly still and hoped my mother would buy our act.

Callen cocked his head and held out his hand. "Mrs. Hurst, I presume? I'm Callen Grimes. It's a pleasure to meet you."

My mother shook his hand, but her eyes performed one of her quick, brutal assessments. I knew exactly which parts of him she was taking note of. The shaggy, styled to look like he'd simply rolled out of bed that way hair. The tattoos that peeked out above the neckline of his V-neck T-shirt and wound their way down his bare arms. Probably also the casual cargo shorts and shirt he wore.

There wasn't a hint of preppy sophistication in sight, so the disapproving twist of her lips didn't surprise me. "Angela Hurst. I wouldn't know if it's a pleasure to meet you because I don't know anything about you. My daughter hasn't told us a thing about having a man in her life."

"It's..." I trailed off, scrambling for a reasonable explanation that just wouldn't come.

Callen stepped in smoothly, the lies rolling off his tongue with ease. Combined with the cool confidence that always radiated from him, even I almost believed what he was saying was true.

"We've been keeping our relationship private. It's still quite new and we didn't want any pressures from the outside to disrupt getting to know each other. Too many relationships these days fail because of the opinions of people not even in them. We didn't want to fall victim to that. We've just been letting things evolve and it's going really well. Wouldn't you say, babe?"

"Yes, um, yup, absolutely," I stammered before I felt his fingers tightening ever so slightly on my shoulder, a reassuring squeeze that seemed to transfer some of his confidence to me. "We wanted to see where things went before we announced our relationship to everyone."

My mother surveyed us in that razor-sharp way she had, and my breath caught. She was trying to get a read on our body language. I just knew it. Whatever she saw must have satisfied any suspicions she had about the timing of my "boyfriend" appearing at just the right moment because she released a quiet breath and nodded.

"Yes, well I suppose it's better to get to know one another in private so as not to make a public spectacle of things when they don't work out." She gave me a pointed look. "Less chance of humiliation that way. Now that I know though, you simply must come to dinner on Saturday night. We'd love the chance to get to know the man who has stolen our daughter's heart."

I was surprised by the sincerity of her last sentence, but it didn't really matter. I had to backtrack somehow. Callen playing along for a quick meeting was one thing, but expecting him to keep up this ridiculous charade over a family dinner was too much.

My mother didn't give me the chance to say no, though. She simply waved and marched herself out of the shop, only pausing for a moment at the door to look over her shoulder. "We'll be expecting you at six."

The door clicked shut behind her and I stood there, blinking in shock for a good minute. Callen gave my shoulder another squeeze before releasing me and taking a step back. Amusement mingled with curiosity in his eyes when he bent slightly to look into mine.

"Well, that was interesting," he said with a smile. "If you wanted to date me, you could have just asked. Maybe even taken me out for dinner or something."

I buried my flaming cheeks in my hands, separating my fingers to peek at him through the cracks. "I'm so sorry. I promise you I'm not usually such an awkward person. I know it probably won't make up for it, but I can offer you an ice cream?"

"Yeah." He nodded, tapping his chin with his finger as that sexy smirk appeared on his lips. "I'd like an ice cream and an explanation."

"Okay, yeah." I closed my eyes and massaged my temples, suddenly feeling like I couldn't breathe in there. "You deserve an explanation, but can we not do this here? I need to get out. I feel like I'm about to have a panic attack. God, Callen. You have no idea how humiliated I am. I shouldn't have done that. I'm so sorry."

Big, warm hands were suddenly on mine. When I opened my eyes, Callen was gently pulling them away from my face. "We don't have to talk in here. Just breathe, okay? Is there someplace nearby we can go?"

I gulped in breath after breath, eventually feeling my heartrate calming down. "Yeah, there's a ramen place on the corner. It should be pretty quiet at this time of day. We can talk there."

CHAPTER 11

CALLEN

What in the ever-loving fuck just happened? I was still reeling a bit, but I'd be lying to say I'd minded playing along with her little ruse back there.

Having her soft body pressed against mine, feeling how well she fit under my arm, and catching the sweet smell drifting off of her hadn't been much of a hardship. It had felt good knowing I was helping her in some way too.

The past twenty-four hours had been tough after I left the treatment center, but I'd kept reminding myself of all the realizations I'd come to recently, and eventually, the tsunami of grief threatening to drown me yet again started receding.

As I came up for air, I decided to take another positive step forward. Tiffeny intrigued me, and I was obviously attracted to her physically, so I figured dropping by to support her business and getting to know her a little couldn't hurt.

I sure as shit hadn't expected to leave the shop with a fake girlfriend on my arm, but I hadn't been able to resist playing along when she looked at me with such hope in those deep blue eyes. I'd seen it was important to her, and though I didn't know why it was so important, I hadn't wanted to let her down.

The press might have labeled me as intimidating and the strong and silent type, but in reality, I was a fixer, a protector. Come at anyone I cared about—or wouldn't mind fucking apparently—and I was willing to go to the ends of the fucking earth to make things okay again.

Tiffeny and I walked in silence to the restaurant on the other side of the strip mall, grabbed a table near the back, and ordered coffee. Once we were seated, I leaned back in my chair and raised my eyebrows at the beautiful, mortified girl sitting across from me.

"Mind filling me in on what happened back there?" I asked, keeping my voice low despite the fact that there were only two other tables taken in the restaurant.

Tiffeny's eyes filled with remorse. "I panicked. That's what happened. Again, I'm so sorry to have involved you in this. It was like the idea popped into my head and I had no choice but to go with it."

"Do you regularly tell your mother you're dating a virtual stranger?" I asked, amusement setting in.

She shook her head, a small smile ghosting across her lips when she noticed the humor in my expression. "No, I promise I've never done anything like this before. My mom was just questioning all my life choices, and when you walked in, I couldn't help myself. Like I said, the idea took over from all reason and logic."

I chuckled. "I'm taking it you don't have the greatest relationship with your parents?"

"That's putting it mildly." She sighed, thanked the waiter when he brought over our coffees, and wrapped her hands around her mug. "Look, thank you for playing along, but you don't have to come to dinner. I'll tell her we broke up. No harm, no foul."

"Why on earth would you tell her that?" I leaned forward, capturing her gaze and holding it intently. "I like the idea of helping you with this. I wouldn't mind some context, but we don't have to pull the plug on the whole thing right now."

Her eyes rounded in surprise, her lips parted as she blinked rapidly, and her eyebrows climbed up on her forehead. "Are you really offering to fake a relationship with me?"

"Sure." I shrugged like it didn't mean a thing to me, but it did. I just wasn't ready to get into the why with her after only having had a few conversations. "It doesn't have to be a big deal. We can get to know each other a little, I'll come to dinner, and we'll take it from there."

"You're serious?" She blinked a few more times, but I didn't the miss the flash of hope entering her eyes again. "I mean, you're not shitting me right now? You're really willing to do this for someone you don't even know?"

"I'll get to know you." Besides, it would be a fun distraction. "So no, I'm not shitting you, and yes, I'm being completely serious. I meant what I said about needing some context, though. We're probably also going to have to actually get to know each other some before Saturday if we have any hope of pulling it off."

Tension melted out of her tightened muscles, and she relaxed, a relieved, curious kind of grin tugging at the corners of her lips. "You're my kind of weird for agreeing to do this. Do you know that?"

I barked out a laugh. "Thanks. I'm taking that as a compliment."

"You should." She inclined her head and set her coffee down, spreading her arms open wide before resting them on the armrests of her chair. "Okay, so you want to get to know each other? Ask me anything. I'm an open book."

I cocked my head. So many questions about her mother and their situation flew through my brain. It was better to work up to it, though. There were a lot of things I was curious about, and since I didn't know much about her, this was an opportunity to learn some of those things.

"Are you from here, or are you a transplant too?"

"Myrtle Beach born and bred, though I have spent a lot of time away from here." She took a sip of her coffee and swallowed quickly as though she needed it to fortify herself. "My parents sent me to boarding schools all over the place. I ended up at Harvard Law, and once I finally decided I didn't want to be a lawyer, I dropped out and moved back home."

"Wow." Okay, so it seemed she didn't need to work up to the serious stuff. She'd said she was an open book and it looked like she'd meant it. She was a straight shooter. I liked that. No bullshit. "I'm assuming your parents weren't happy with that decision."

She blew out a breath, her head shaking and her eyes wide. "Not at all. In fact, that was among the things my mother and I were talking about earlier. I've never been what I was supposed to have been, and they haven't forgiven me for it. I'm just an eternal disappointment."

"Ouch." My own parents hadn't exactly been supportive of me pursuing a career in music, so I had some idea of what she was talking about. "I know the feeling, but doing what you love is ultimately what counts. Life is too short to do anything else."

"Yeah, I agree. My mother is the one who needs to be told that." She leaned forward, folding her hands on the table and taking a deep breath. "Speaking of doing what you love, I heard you were in a band. What are you doing here?"

My head jerked and a jolt of lightning straightened my spine.

I was legit taken aback by her question. I hadn't thought she was a fan. She'd given no indication of recognizing me before. "You know who I am?"

She nodded. "I didn't at first, but Julia recognized you. Apparently, your band is one of her favorites."

Unease tied my stomach in knots. I'd wanted a fresh start here, a new life. It seemed it wouldn't be that easy, though. "I'm not going to lie to you. I'm surprised you know about me and didn't say anything before."

"She only told me after you left the other day, and I haven't seen you since, so I haven't been able to tell you," she said, which was reasonable. "You should know it doesn't matter to me that you're supposedly famous. That's not why I told my mother you were my boyfriend."

The sincerity in her tone made me believe her, which made some of the knots undo themselves. "Fair enough. So you're not a fan?"

"I've never even heard of your band, aside from Julia mentioning the name." She crossed her heart, smiling as she did. "It's pretty cool that you're a musician. She tells me you're a guitarist?"

"Yeah, I picked up my first guitar in music class when I was seven and never wanted to put it down again." I ran the backs of my fingers across the scruff on my jaw and grinned, fond memories playing in my mind. "I wasn't very good at it at first, but I refused to give up. All that hard work paid off eventually."

"I'd say." She cocked her head, curiosity burning in her eyes. "Which brings us back to the obvious question. What are you doing here when you're so passionate about your music and your band is doing so well?"

"Things changed." I dragged both palms over my face. "I still love the music, but I needed a break from recording and performing. Winter needed a break, too. We'd just finished a tour and it felt like the time was right."

She nodded slowly. "I'd love to hear you play sometime."

"Well, now that we're dating, I'm sure you'll get the opportunity at some point," I teased, surprised by how easily I was adapting to the idea of pretending to date her. Somehow, it didn't scare the shit out of me or make me feel like I was moving on too soon. It didn't even really make me feel guilty, especially considering how we weren't really dating.

Tiffeny laughed, the melodic sound worming its way into my chest until I was laughing too.

"I'll be looking forward to hearing my talented boyfriend playing his instrument," she said.

A hundred retorts about how my fingers weren't only talented with my instrument and puns about the instrument thing itself crossed my mind, but that felt too much like flirting. So I kept it simple.

"Let me know when you can pencil me in and we'll arrange a private viewing for you." I smirked. "You're just going to have to work out a way not to jump me when you realize how talented I am."

Damn it. I definitely hadn't been planning on saying that last part.

Tiffeny's eyes widened in surprise, but then she laughed again. "Yeah, well, I can see why you feel like you have to warn me about that. I have been pretty impulsive around you, haven't I?"

As easily as that, she'd diffused a moment which had had every chance of being awkward as fuck. Although there had been a spark of heat in her eyes before she'd started laughing.

Suddenly, despite the fact that she'd kept the moment light, it felt like there was a sexual tension brewing in the open space between us. Before, I had only been attracted to her physically, but this felt different.

It felt like the slightest spark of that same heat from before could ignite this tension. It wasn't enough to have me backing out of our agreement, but I was going to have to be careful from here on out.

Until I figured out how I felt about having sexual tension with someone else.

Needing to change the topic, I took a sip of my coffee and circled back to an earlier point in our conversation. "Would you say you're an impulsive person in general? You mentioned earlier that you've never been what you were supposed to be, but somehow, I get the feeling your decision to do what makes you happy wasn't an impulsive one."

"No, it wasn't impulsive." She took the seriousness of the question in stride, not seeming to mind skipping back to heavier topics. "It took me years to gather the courage to tell my parents I didn't want the same things they wanted for me. I planned what I was going to say to them for months, and when I did, the conversation went exactly as I'd known it would. Which was horribly. I was prepared for it, though."

"I'm sorry," I said, really meaning it. "It sucks when family can't support something they know makes you happy."

"You said you knew the feeling," she said, obviously remembering my own comment earlier. "I take it your family wasn't supportive, either."

"No, they definitely were not supportive. They thought I was a fool for chasing this dream. Out of the thousands of talented people out there trying to make it, they didn't think I stood even the slightest chance of being one of the lucky few."

Empathy softened her eyes, and her voice became gentler as well. "I get where you're coming from. My parents think I'm a fool for trying to make the shop work too. Since you're speaking about your family in the past tense though, I'm assuming they're not around anymore."

"They were in an accident," I said, not offering an explanation. Tiffeny didn't push me for one either, which I appreciated. "Okay, enough of the deep stuff. Let's get back to basics. The stuff we'd know about each other if we were dating. You said you hadn't even heard of our band other than being one of Julia's favorites. What music do you like then?"

Her eyes brightened and she smiled. I admired her ability to see when things needed to be let go of and then actually doing it. I hadn't come across a lot of people who could do that. Not outside of myself. "I mostly like country music, but there's some pop I don't mind and some rock I can listen to."

"Some rock you can listen to." I scoffed, clutching my heart in mock injury. "But you couldn't listen to Kraken? You wound me. Besides, we had a lot of songs with a definite country influence in them."

"Really?" Excitement crept into her tone. "Maybe I'll give you a try then. How bad can it be?"

"It's not bad. We were great." But we were also getting too close to another heavy topic, so I steered the conversation away from it. "Next question, what's your favorite color?"

She hesitated for a beat. "Right now, it's green. Yours?"

"Blue." The exact blue of her eyes actually. But I wasn't going there. "If you had to choose between reading or watching TV and you could only do one for the rest of your life, what do you choose?"

"Reading." No hesitation this time. "You? Also, it's my turn for a question. Do you like board games?"

"Reading and love them. Feelings about puzzles?"

"Love them." She smiled. "We have a lot in common, surprisingly."

"Why is that a surprise?"

She lifted her shoulders in a shrug, a playful smile pulling on the corners of her lips. "Because who would've thought that celebrities were real people, too? You know, people who like the simple things in life like reading and puzzles."

75

I scoffed, but I couldn't help chuckling. "I'll have you know I have a real taste for the simple things in life."

"I can see that." She grinned. "You did give up fame and fortune to play boyfriend to a local gal. That's quite the demotion."

My gaze snagged on hers and stayed there. I dropped the guard I kept up at all times to let her see how honest I was being when I said, "I'm not so sure about that."

Silence passed between us for a beat. I picked up my coffee to give my hands something to do other than reaching for hers. When I did, I caught a glimpse of the time and my stomach jumped. "Shit. I have to get going soon. I didn't realize how late it had gotten."

"Yeah, of course." She cleared her throat. "Thanks for this and for agreeing to come to dinner."

"I'm actually kind of looking forward to it now." I winked as I got to my feet, pulling my wallet out of my back pocket. "I am going to have to find a reliable babysitter for Winter, though."

"I'll take care of that," she replied immediately. "It's the least I can do."

I paused, but then I realized that I knew literally no one else in the city, and she'd lived there, albeit not permanently, all her life. "Yeah, okay. Thanks."

Just as I started to say goodbye, another thought occurred to me. "Is your number on that business card you gave me? We're probably going to need to exchange numbers to make arrangements for Saturday."

"Yeah, it's the number on the card."

"Well, okay then." I briefly debated how to say goodbye, but then she stood up, and the decision was made for me. Without giving her any warning, I caught her hand and tugged her into me for a hug.

God, she felt good.

Both of us lingered for a second, then stepped back at the same time. "I'll be seeing you around, girlfriend."

She smiled, wiggling her fingers in a wave. "See you around, boyfriend."

CHAPTER 12

TIFFENY

"You're not going to believe what just happened to me," I said as I walked into Julia's salon.

There was a client with her, but she'd never minded talking in front of them before. Most of her clients ended up being something like friends to her, and they knew not to be offended when she ignored them to speak to me.

"What happened?" She paused, the nail file in her hand stilling. "I saw your mother's car, so I was expecting a visit from you an hour or so ago after I saw her leaving."

"Yeah, well." I shrugged, smirking as I drew out the moment. "I had a fake date to go on first."

"What?" Her focus on me sharpened. "Explain."

I grabbed one of her free chairs and wheeled it up to the table, turning it around and sitting down with my front to its backrest. "I had another one of my favorite conversations with my mother."

"And she made you go on a date?" Julia gaped at me, but her hands had started moving again. "That's terrible. I hope the guy knows you're not going to be agreeing to an arranged marriage with him anytime soon."

Julia's client, a petite, older blonde lady, snorted. "Please. People don't arrange marriages anymore."

"Her parents would." Julia pointed the nail file at me. "You should hear how her mother talks about her being single. It's like she's committing a crime."

"But a well-bred young lady should narrow down her prospects early so she doesn't get stuck with the dregs at the bottom," I said, doing a poor imitation of my mother's voice.

The client let out an incredulous laugh, shaking her head. "Well, that's just terrible. You poor thing."

"Yeah," Julia agreed. "But let's get back to the story. You were saying."

"Right." I couldn't fight the smile begging to be set free, and since I didn't know why I even had to try, I just let it happen. "It wasn't my mother setting me up on a date. I kind of accidentally set myself up on a fake date."

"Oh." Julia's eyes went wide with understanding. "So you told her you had a date and went out for an early lunch by yourself?"

"Nope." I popped my lips, wagging my brows at her. "I had coffee with a real, flesh and blood man. A really hot one, at that."

Her eyes blew all the way open. "No way. You can't mean Callen?"

"Yep." I grinned. "I've just come back from my first fake date with the legend-in-the-making himself."

"No way," Julia breathed, the surprised gleam in her eyes making her seem almost dazed. "How the hell did that happen?"

"Who's Callen?" the customer asked. "And do you have a picture of him? You called him really hot and she immediately knew who you were talking about, so I'm assuming really hot means *really hot.*"

She dragged out the last two words and I nodded my agreement. "That's exactly what I mean, but I don't have a picture."

"We can just—"

I cut off Julia's suggestion, which I knew was going to be looking him up on the Internet, with a warning look. He hadn't said it point-blank, but I'd seen his reaction when I'd told him I knew who he was.

For whatever reason, he was trying to keep a low profile. He hadn't looked happy about me knowing, and for a second, I'd thought I'd doomed our brand new but very much fake relationship by letting him know that I knew.

His relief when I'd told him how I knew and that I wasn't a fan had been palpable. I didn't think he wanted the news of his being here spread around town too much just yet, even if it was inevitable that it would spread eventually.

Since I owed him about a thousand favors for the one he was doing me, I wanted to help him in any way I could.

Julia heeded my warning thankfully. Picking up a bottle of blood-red polish, she shrugged. "I was going to say you could just ask him to send one, but I guess that would be a little weird. Anyway, how did you end up on a fake date with him, and why do you keep calling it fake?"

"What even is a fake date?" the client asked.

"It's when you're enduring yet another inquisition from your very judgmental, very pushy mother, and just when she starts grilling you about not having a boyfriend, a hot guy walks into your shop."

Understanding dawned in Julia's chocolate eyes. A wide smile hooked up the corners of her mouth. "Oh my God. Tell me you really did it. You told your mom he was your boyfriend, didn't you?"

I nodded. "I was so damn embarrassed about it afterward, but I just couldn't stop myself. She was coming down on me like a ton of bricks again, and then, in walked the answer to my problems."

"That's hilarious." She laughed. "Oh my fuck, I am so damn proud of you."

"What did he say?" the client asked, leaning forward. It seemed she was as invested in hearing the details as Julia was. "I'm assuming he played along?"

"He sure did." I smiled as I thought back to our time together. "He asked for an explanation after, though. We went to have coffee, and when I offered to tell my mother we'd broken up, he told me not to."

Julia paused with the polish brush just above her client's nail. "Wait, what does that even mean? Are you two, like, dating now? Just like that?"

"Nah, we're not really dating. He's just going to pretend to be dating me for dinner with my parents on Saturday night. My mother insisted on us coming over."

Julia rolled her eyes. "She would. She probably can't wait to grill him. Did she see his tattoos?"

"Yep." I was going to have to remember to warn Callen about the grilling because Julia was right. It was definitely going to happen. "Anyway, I'm going to need you to help me on Saturday."

"Sure. You want me to come help you get ready for your hot date?" She glanced down at the chipped nail polish on my fingers, her lips pursing. "I'm going to need to take care of those for you before then, too."

"Thanks, but that wasn't what I was talking about." I wheeled a few inches closer to her, letting my eyes widen into my best puppy-dog expression. "I need you to babysit Winter while we're at dinner."

She sputtered, her head shaking so fast I was worried it might fall off. "Hire a babysitter. I'm not thirteen. There's no way I'm babysitting."

"Please, Jules? I really need your help. I owe the guy. I can't leave him to have to find a good babysitter in a brand new city just so he can do me a favor. I don't know any babysitters I can call, either. Plus, I'm sure he'll be more comfortable leaving his little girl with someone we know."

Her head kept shaking. "She doesn't know me, though. I don't even like kids."

I rolled my eyes. "You and I both know that's not true. Please, Jules. Please help me. This is important."

Her gaze slid to her client's. "Help a girl out. Please tell me you know a babysitter?"

"My kids are in college, so no, I don't know babysitters anymore. Sorry." To her credit, she really did look it.

Julia sighed as I stuck out my lower lip, not above getting down on my knees and begging her to do it if I had to. Thankfully, it didn't have to go that far. "Fine. Okay. I'll do it, but only if I get paid at least thirteen dollars an hour and you leave me food and a bottle of wine."

My eyes rolled again. "I can do the food and wine I will get you later, but I'm not paying you in anything but ice cream."

She released a long-suffering sigh but then smiled triumphantly. "Then it looks like we're both getting what we wanted."

"Thank you." I threw my arms around her and hugged her tightly. "I really, really appreciate it."

She waved me off, careful not to swipe the red polish brush through my hair. "I know. Now, get back to your shop so you can make some money and let me get back to doing poor Lucy's nails."

"Sure thing." I grinned and waved goodbye to them as I headed out of her shop. As soon I was back in the familiar comfort of my own, I pulled out my phone.

I hadn't really been expecting to have heard anything from Callen yet, but there was a message waiting for me when I unlocked my screen.

Unknown number: Thought my girlfriend should have my number ;-) See you on Saturday, gorgeous.

My heartbeat morphed into an irregular rhythm. Gorgeous? Surely, that had to have been a joke.

It made me smile anyway, though. Two could play this game, and it was going to be considerably easier for me since I did actually think he was hot.

Tiffeny: Thanks for the number, sexy beast. I've got the babysitter covered for Saturday. Can't wait. X

I deleted the kiss before I sent the message, then replaced it with a smiley face before I hit enter.

As crazy and impulsive as the whole thing had started off, I was starting to have a feeling that it might also just end up being really fun.

CHAPTER 13

CALLEN

"Julia is going to stay with you tonight," I told Winter as I rolled up the cuffs of my sleeves. "Do you remember Julia? We met her in Tiffeny's shop a few weeks ago."

Winter's head dipped where she sat cross-legged on my bed, watching as I smoothed out my button-up shirt and gave myself a last once-over.

"I think so. She has red hair."

"Yeah, she does." Red hair and love for my former band. Enough love that she'd recognized me and told Tiffeny Kraken was one of her favorites.

I was a little uneasy leaving Winter with her for that reason. Having a fan in my house, alone, looking after my little girl was unsettling.

But she wasn't just any fan. She was Tiffeny's best friend. Plus, she was the only person around here Winter had at least met before. I wasn't about to leave her with someone neither of us knew at all.

It was also only going to be for a few hours. Even if she did go digging through my stuff once Winter went to bed, there wasn't all that much for her to find or to take so she could sell it to other fans online.

She's not just a random fan, I reminded myself for the umpteenth time. *She's not gonna steal a spoon or my toothbrush as a souvenir.*

I'd seen and heard of fans doing some crazy shit before, though. I'd never personally been a target of anything really weird or disconcerting, but I'd also never left a fan alone in my home before.

Logically, I knew the probabilities were highly stacked in favor of nothing weird happening, considering who she was, but I'd have been naive if I hadn't at least thought about it.

With all that in mind, I'd decided I'd see how she interacted with Winter when she arrived, and if I got any uncomfortable vibes off her, I'd ask Tiffeny if Winter could come to dinner with us.

A knock at the front door told me my time for all the back and forth over the date, leaving Winter with Julia, and wondering if I should feel guilty was over. They were here, and I was going on a first date again.

A fake date, but it was still a date.

Blowing out a breath, I turned and motioned to Winter to walk with me. "Let's go say hi to Tiffeny and Julia."

"I like Tiffeny." She smiled as she hopped off the bed and slipped her little hand in mine.

Thankfully, she was still too young to question me much about what I was going to do with Tiffeny tonight. She didn't understand we were going on a date or any of the possible implications of that.

"I know, sweetheart. So do I."

When I opened the door, Winter let go of my hand and went to stand behind my legs. She was always a little shy at first when people came over.

My next breath got stuck in my lungs as my gaze landed on Tiffeny, wearing a black dress that was much tighter than anything I'd seen her in before, black heels, and with her hair loose and tumbling over her shoulders.

Dark liner around her eyes emphasized them and made them seem bigger, while the hemline of her dress hit just below mid-thigh and made her legs look like they went on for miles. *Damn, this girl really does have curves like a goddamn scenic railway pass.*

"Hi," she said when her eyes had raked down every inch of my body in a perusal every bit as intense as mine had been of her. She swallowed, then cleared her throat and lifted her gaze to mine. "You remember Julia, right?"

"Right." Still feeling the aftereffects of her eyes taking me in so intently, I tried to ignore my stiffening dick and looked at Julia instead. She was, after all, the one I had to be focused on right now. "It's nice to see you again. Thanks for agreeing to watch Winter for me."

Julia's brown eyes slid to Tiffeny's for a moment. Then she smiled and nodded at me. "Of course. We're going to have some fun tonight, us two girls."

To my surprise, she dropped down to her haunches and dug around in her bag. When she extracted her hand, she had three bottles of nail polish in it. She held them out to Winter and tilted her head.

"Hey, Winter, you wanna come out from behind Daddy's legs real quick?" she asked. "I brought these with me. I thought we could start our girls' night in with a manicure. What color would you like?"

I glanced down in time to see Winter release the hold she'd had on my jeans, stepping around my legs to pluck a bright pink bottle out of Julia's hand. "I like pink."

Julia nodded decisively and stuck the other options back into her bag before straightening up and offering Winter her hand. "Pink, it is. I've also brought along DVDs of my favorite princess movies. Want to come check them out and choose what to watch while you're getting your manicure?"

"Yes," Winter said, a hum of excitement in her voice. She took Julia's hand without hesitating. "Do you know the songs in the movies?"

"Every word," Julia promised solemnly, following Winter deeper into the house. When they reached the arch leading into the living room from the entrance hall, she stopped briefly to glance at us over her shoulder. "Well, what are you waiting for? Go. We have stuff to do."

Tiffeny laughed and mouthed "thank you" while I took a deep

breath and accepted that there wasn't even a small part of me that was still uncomfortable with this arrangement. Julia clearly had a way with Winter, and my little girl only gave me a wave, too excited to get on with the night Julia had planned for them to bother sticking around to give me a hug.

"Yeah, okay," I said. "Thanks again. Her bedtime's at eight and there's dinner for both of you in the fridge. Don't let her con you into staying up until nine because that's her very latest to be asleep. Not to only get into bed then."

Winter mumbled a protest, but Julia nodded and winked at us. "We'll both be asleep by nine. Girls need their beauty sleep, you know? Us smart girls also need to give our brains time to rest, so we won't stay up too late."

Winter nodded along, gazing up at Julia as if she was now the one who knew everything. I gave her a grateful smile, knowing she'd just given me a line to use again and a foundation to work on from here. Then I closed the distance between us and kissed the top of Winter's head. "You be a good girl for Julia now, okay?"

"I will, Daddy." She waved at us again before grabbing Julia's hand and leading her away. Julia tossed her hand up in a wave too, not turning to look at us again.

"You ready to go?" Tiffeny asked from the door. "They'll be fine. Julia has a real way with kids, even if she won't admit it."

"I can see that," I said quietly, taking another deep breath before turning to face my gorgeous date. "I was a little nervous about leaving her with Julia, but I think they're going to get along just fine."

"They will." She gave me a tentative smile, almost shy. "You know it's not too late to back out of going to dinner with my parents, right? You could just take the night off and go see a movie or something."

"Nope. I made a promise. I'm not bailing on it." I patted my pockets to make sure I had my wallet, phone, and keys. Then I pulled the keys out and inclined my head toward the garage. "I'll drive if you'll be my co-pilot and tell me where we're going."

"Co-pilot." The shyness melted out of her smile. "I like that. It makes me feel like less of a damsel in distress and more like I'm actually part of a team."

"Guys make you feel like a damsel in distress when they drive you on a date?" I asked as I opened the door to the garage, letting it swing open and flicking on the light.

Tiffeny walked in behind me as I rounded the hood of my car to open the passenger door for her.

"What about opening doors?" I asked. "Is that acceptable?"

A laugh bubbled out of her as she climbed into the car. She waited until I was in the driver's seat to answer. "Maybe damsel in distress wasn't exactly the correct term to use, but I guess I prefer to feel like I'm part of a team when I'm dating someone and not like they just have to do or plan everything while I go along for the ride."

"That's an interesting way of looking at it," I said as I backed out of the garage, one of my arms on her seat as I twisted to get a look behind me. "I've never thought about it that way before. What about the door thing, then?"

"Opening doors is perfectly acceptable, so long as you don't do it with that arrogant air that says 'look at me being a gentleman even though it's totally fake.'"

I let out a surprised laugh as we waited for the garage door to close. "Guys really do that?"

"All the time." She sighed, but there was a soft smile playing on her lips. "There's a big difference between performing gentlemanly acts because you are an actual gentleman or because you feel like you have to, in which case, eww. Just leave it. I can open the damn door myself."

"I think I get where you're coming from. I have similar thoughts about the way women act sometimes, and men too, for that matter. Whatever you do, just be real about it and we'll have no problem. Faking things to elicit a particular reaction from another person makes me sick."

"Ironic that you'd be saying that while we're headed to my parents' house for dinner to introduce you as my boyfriend when you're not."

I chuckled, shrugging. "Fair enough. Maybe I'm a hypocrite, but our situation feels different to me."

"Yeah, same here." She turned in her seat to look at me, then spent the rest of the drive alternating between giving me directions and warning me about her mother and the inquisition I was about to face from her.

When we arrived in front of a sprawling manor type house with about a thousand windows, fountains lining the driveway, and a person who appeared to be an actual valet waiting in front of the wide double doors, I turned to her with my eyebrows at my hairline.

"You didn't tell me you were rich."

"I'm not," she said grimly. "My parents are. Is that going to be a problem?"

"Nope." I grinned and pointed a finger at my jeans. "But you could have told me to wear a suit."

Motioning for her to look down might have been a bad idea, considering that her eyes had fallen to my crotch and were lingering there. My dick stirred immediately, but I clenched my jaw and shut the fucker down. *This is so not the right time, but fuck me, I like it when she looks at me like that.*

"Shall we go inside?" I asked finally, my voice slightly hoarse from the truckload of lust that had just been dumped all over me.

"Yeah, sure. Don't worry about the jeans. She'd have told me if she expected a certain dress code for this dinner."

My eyebrows lifted again. "Your mother has dress codes for a family dinner sometimes?"

She shrugged, her lips pressing into a tight smile before she climbed out of the car when the valet opened the door for her. I followed, sliding my hand into hers as we ascended a short staircase to get to the front doors.

Bolts of electricity shot up my arm from where our palms were connected. They flew down my spine and hit me in the crotch, making me want her all over again.

Jesus. The chemistry I felt with this girl whenever I touched her was off the fucking charts. I didn't have much time to think about it, though.

Mrs. Hurst was waiting for us in the entrance hall with one arm raised as she checked the time and her foot tapping against the marble floor.

"You're late," she snapped as soon as we walked in. Her lithe body was wrapped in a blood-red dress that seemed far too extravagant for a dinner at home.

Tiffeny didn't react to her mother's harsh tone, other than the slight tightening of her fingers on mine. "Only by seven minutes. Where's Dad?"

"At the office," she said. "He's not going to make it."

"Surprise, surprise," Tiffeny muttered under her breath, then offered her mother a polite smile. "Since we're late, I'm guessing we're behind schedule."

"Yes. The appetizers are being served in three minutes." She spun on her heel and, obviously expecting us to follow, didn't check to see if we actually were.

"She was only going to give us ten minutes between arriving and appetizers?" I whispered as we walked down a wide corridor with expensive-looking paintings on the walls and a thick carpet beneath our feet.

Tiffeny rolled her eyes as she smiled up at me. "But of course. Time is money and no one pays her for small talk with her daughter."

I chuckled, but my heart hurt for her at the same time. My parents hadn't been supportive of my dream, but at least they hadn't been made of ice.

Mrs. Hurst sat down at the end of a long dining table that seated at least sixteen people. It looked a little sad with only three places set.

Heavy silver candlesticks had been placed between a plethora of cutlery and crockery, but at least I knew what to do with it all. Tiffeny took the seat across from mine, her feet almost immediately hooking around my ankles when I sat down.

I arched a brow at her in surprise, but she simply gave her head an almost imperceptible shake in return. *Right. Ask her about this later.*

"So, you're dating my daughter," Mrs. Hurst began as a server filled our glasses with red wine. I was starting to realize Tiffeny really had a point with the not wasting time thing. "How long has that been going on for?"

"Not very long," I said, trying to be honest while also omitting to telling her the whole truth. "We met, had an instant connection, and decided to see where things went."

Surprisingly, even that wasn't a flat-out lie.

Mrs. Hurst's eyes narrowed, but eventually, she nodded and her expression smoothed out again. "I see, and where are you from? I don't recall having seen you around before."

I didn't bother pointing out how many people lived in this city and how she couldn't possibly have seen them all before. I was aiming for charming here. "I actually just moved here a while ago from Los Angeles."

"LA, huh?" Curiosity crept into her gaze. "What were you doing for a living there?"

"I'm a singer and a songwriter," I said, seeing the disgust curl the corners of her lips down. "I'm on a break right now, so I decided to move over here to see how things went."

"You're not much of a planner, are you?" She pursed her lips and pressed the tips of her fingers together in front of her mouth. "Everything seems to be a 'see how it goes' situation."

I didn't argue with her. I couldn't. All my plans had gone to shit and I honestly hadn't had it in me to make too many new ones yet. "Yes, ma'am. My life has been pretty well planned to this point. I've been on a hectic schedule and now I'm just trying to take things as they come."

She cocked her head, bringing her fingers to her lips in thought. "A singer/songwriter from LA who's been on a hectic schedule. Have you done well for yourself?"

I shrugged. "It depends on what you define as having done well."

"Have you made any money?" she asked, not a hint of shame in asking directly.

"Some," I replied. I wasn't the type to brag, and the amount of dollars in my bank account didn't have anything to do with anyone but me.

Mrs. Hurst pressed her lips together tightly, obviously assuming that my answer meant I was a struggling musician. *Good. Let her think that.*

"I'm not going to beat around the bush here, Callen," she said, which was when it clicked into place that Tiffeny had obviously gotten her trait as a straight shooter from the woman sitting in front of me. I had to respect that.

"No, ma'am, let's not beat around the bush," I said because I appreciated not being bullshitted or pandered to. Lord knew I'd had enough of that these last few years since we'd started making it big.

She leveled her gaze at me. "You're not much of a planner, you're between jobs, and you've just moved here. That doesn't sit well with me. My daughter is twenty-seven and she isn't getting any younger. All that being said, have you two discussed the future at all? Marriage, having children? Do you even know if you're on the same page concerning all that?"

The very thought of marrying again used to make my balls shrivel up, but while it wasn't anything I was near ready for right then, I couldn't deny the possibility of it *ever* happening again anymore.

As for having more children, I loved Winter, and if I ever found someone I felt as deeply about again as I had with Alice, I wouldn't be opposed to discussing the possibility of more of those either.

Both of those things were hypothetical for me at this point, something that might be considered in the very far off future, but I could answer Mrs. Hurst at least partially honestly.

"We've talked about it, but we're taking things slow. Just because we're not making any concrete plans yet doesn't mean they won't be made." Also true. Tiffeny and I might not end up making them together, but eventually, both of us were going to make some kind of plans.

"I—" She was interrupted by the insistent buzzing of her phone on the table. It struck me as strange that a woman like her would have it lying right there on the dinner table, but Tiffeny didn't seem surprised at all.

Mrs. Hurst grabbed for the device, unlocked it, and quickly began scowling at whatever was still coming through on her screen as her phone kept buzzing. Abruptly pushing her chair back and straightening to her full height, she gave us an apologetic smile.

"I have to go back to the office. Darling, why don't you show Callen around a little bit? I'll ask the chef to hold our dinner until I return." Her gaze softened slightly on Tiffeny and then turned to mine. "As I said, Callen, I'm not completely sold on the idea of you yet, but you seem honest and you're charming enough. I'd appreciate if you could stay for dinner tonight, but if it gets too late, I'd like to have you over again."

"Of course, Mrs. Hurst." I untangled my ankles from Tiffeny's and rose, waiting until her mother had given us a curt nod before hurrying out of the room to sit again.

Before I could do it, Tiffeny stood up too. She looked significantly more relaxed now that her mother was gone. "Come on. Let me show you around. Since she asked me to, she's sure to bring it up if you see her again."

"Right." I didn't miss that she'd used *if* instead of *when* when referring to me seeing her mother again, even though I'd literally just been invited to another dinner. "I am going to see her again, you know. She said she'd like to have me over again."

"You'd actually come back after the grilling you just faced?" She walked around the table and put her hands lightly on my chest, tipping her head back for her deep blue eyes to meet mine. "If you are, I'm not the only one between the two of us who's interesting. Unless you're some kind of masochist."

"I believe masochism refers to deriving sexual gratification from one's own pain or humiliation." I made my eyes go wide. "I definitely don't want to receive any sexual gratification from your mother, so let's just call me a sucker for punishment and be done with it. Because I'll definitely be back if you want me to come back."

Surprise flared in her eyes. Then she let her head tip back even farther and laughed. "Score one for the away team. Okay then, sucker. Let me show you around if you're so determined to come back for another round of that."

She led me through the expansive, opulently furnished and taste-fully decorated home. It had a somewhat museum-like quality to it, but there were touches of homeliness too that made me suspect Mrs. Hurst did have a softer side.

"Tell me about your mother," I said.

Tiffeny stiffened beside me momentarily as we walked up a flight of stairs with various family pictures mounted on the wall. "She's always chasing more power. She practically runs the company my grandfather built now. She married a man on the brink of death, my grandfather's business associate, and got a ton of money and her spot on the board with it. Her brother got her family's spot once my grandfather passed away, which means it's fully a family company now."

"What about your father?" I asked.

Tiffeny chuckled, but there was no humor in the sound. "He's always working. My mother met him after her ex-husband passed and she inherited everything. She gave him a spot in senior management and I don't think he's ever felt like he's earned it. So he works for it. Every day of his life."

I blew out a soft whistle, my hand reaching for hers almost on instinct. She wrapped her fingers around mine, sending that same current from before through me, and then opened another door.

This one led into a bedroom. A guest room, by the looks of things. But there was a bed in it.

All it took was the sound of the door clicking shut behind us for me to forget what we'd been talking about and even where we were.

Tiffeny and I were alone in a mostly dark bedroom, only ambient light spilling in through the large windows from the rest of the house. I heard her breathing hitch and felt the atmosphere between us change, charge.

Fuck.

It suddenly felt like I had a choice to make. Did I give in to my body's demands to make a move, or did I get the hell out before the chemistry between us made the choice for me?

CHAPTER 14

TIFFENY

C allen went completely still as the heavy door swung shut behind us. I hadn't intended for it to happen. I'd just forgotten how heavy my mother's mahogany doors were and I'd let it go to reach for the light switch.

Now we were standing there in the near dark, Callen completely immobile while I fumbled for an explanation that didn't sound like I'd led him up there to ravish him in one of Mom's guest rooms.

The confusing thing was that although he was standing stock still, he'd tightened his hold on my hand, and when I looked up at him, I could practically see the gears turning in his brain. *God, what he has to be thinking about me right now.*

"I'm sorry. I didn't mean to—"

"I know," he said, but his voice sounded tighter than before. There was a roughness to it that was super sexy, though.

Not that my own mind hadn't jumped straight to sex as soon as I'd heard that definitive click. I was alone in a dark room with a man I found extremely attractive and had been fantasizing about practically since I'd met him.

Of course, I'd immediately, briefly, imagined both being ravished by him and ravishing him on the very large bed in front of us. It was why I was trying to come up with an explanation about me not bringing him up here for ravishing purposes in the first place.

Callen's broad shoulders shifted, pulling back. Those eyes of his came down and his head turned slightly so he was looking right into mine, a smirk appearing on his full lips. "You don't need to apologize. I know you didn't bring me in here to fuck me."

Oh my. Should it do things to me to hear him say the words "fuck me"? Because it does. It really, really does.

My blood rushed south, but then he released my hand.

Stupid, Tiff. He wasn't actually asking you to.

I'd known that, but I couldn't deny there had been a spark of hope between my legs that my dry spell was about to end in the most spectacular way possible. Well, with the most spectacular man anyway.

"Why are you walking to the bed then?" I asked, my voice barely above a whisper as I watched him move across the room.

A shadow appeared on either side of him as the mattress dipped when he sat down. Then he kicked off his shoes and lay back. He folded his arms behind his head on a stack of pillows, biceps bulging against the constraints of his black button-up shirt.

His eyes stayed on mine the whole time. It was too dark to see the expression in them from this distance, but it was almost like I could feel the heat in them on my body. Maybe it was because his voice still had that same sexy quality to it.

"It's a bed," he said simply. "I'm lying down. It's what these were made for, right?"

"Right." As if some unseen force was pulling me to him, I found myself slowly moving to the bed. "It is, in fact, among other things, what beds are made for. This particular bed, however, is in my *mother's* guest room."

"I'm a guest of hers, aren't I?" He unfolded one arm to use his hand to pat the space beside him. "So are you. Therefore, I think we're allowed to lie down in her guest room."

"No." I shook my head, trying not to let my mind wander to what it might feel like to take him up on his offer and crawl in next to him. Maybe make use of the bed for one of those other things it had been made for. "We should go. Come on, Callen. Let's get on with the tour."

"I like this room. I think we should hit pause on the tour and hide out here for a little bit longer. When will your mom be back?"

"Not for hours," I answered automatically, reaching down for the hand still resting on the mattress beside him and tugging on it. "Why aren't you budging? These beds aren't even comfortable. They're too hard and the bedding is too starched."

"Doesn't bother me," he said, dislodging my hand on his to move it to mine, then sharply tugging me toward him instead.

I was caught off guard and fell to the bed, the upper half of my body suddenly covering his. "What the hell was that?"

He shifted beneath me, acting so fast that before I could comprehend what was happening, we were lying side by side, our chests touching and my head cradled by one of those biceps I'd been admiring earlier. There was no mistaking the heat in his eyes now, not when my face was only inches away from his.

"I want you to know that you can stop me any time, but there's something I want to try," he said, his voice even raspier than before. "Hold still, okay?"

"Okay—" His lips slammed into mine before I could finish murmuring my agreement, his hand coming up to cup my face as he kissed me.

My mind spun out in confusion for a second before I realized this was really happening. Callen freaking Grimes was making out with me, and he was good at it too.

A low moan sounded from the back of my throat as my body came alive against his. It made my lips part, and Callen took advantage of the opening, his tongue sliding inside when I met the tip of his with mine.

A groan rumbled out of him, and the way he angled his body forward so his head and shoulders were on top of me, pressing me deeper into the pillows while he kept kissing me, flooded me with need.

My panties grew damp fast and my fingers wound their way into his black hair, tangling into the soft strands while my fingertips trailed over his scalp. Another pleasurable sound escaped him and I briefly remembered where we were.

But then I also remembered that my parents' staff didn't come to the upper levels of the house at night unless they were summoned. This was where the bedrooms were, and God forbid anyone outside of myself or my father ever see my mother without her being perfectly groomed and dressed.

My parents themselves wouldn't be back for hours, as I'd told Callen earlier. That was *if* they even made it home tonight. She might have told us to hang around and that we'd eat later, but that was only because she knew she couldn't just throw us out minutes after we'd arrived when she'd invited us over.

Whatever crisis they were facing at the office had to be bad for her to leave so abruptly just as the appetizers were being served. So no, she wouldn't be back soon.

There was no doubt in my mind that once we made it back downstairs, the chef would have packed us our dinners to go and there would be apologies from my mother.

Which meant Callen and I were alone, not to be disturbed, and he was kissing me like he'd been craving it for months. I responded to every kiss, every touch with a fervor of my own.

My dress had ridden up almost to my waist and Callen's hand was on my thigh, his kisses urgent and his cock hardening against my leg. If I hadn't known any better, I'd have thought he was almost starved for this.

Then again, I didn't know any better.

I certainly wasn't reacting any differently to our make-out session, but I actually was starved for this. I hadn't been touched by anyone but myself in months, and I'd never been touched by someone who made me feel the way he did.

When he'd mentioned to my mother that we'd had an instant connection, my eyes had popped wide open. I thought I'd been the only one who'd felt that tingle the first time we'd seen each other, the first time we'd touched.

Lust at first sight still counted as an instant connection, though, even if it wasn't one I'd ever explain to my mom. Either way, it seemed like he hadn't been lying to her or saying what he thought I wanted to hear.

When his hips rocked into mine, it felt involuntary, like he just couldn't help himself. A hiss tore out of him, breaking off the kiss.

"Do you want to stop?" I asked, bringing my eyes up from his slightly swollen lips to look into his half-lidded ones.

"Fuck no," he bit out. "You?"

"Not even a little."

Another emotion broke through the heat in his gaze. Vulnerability, I thought, though I couldn't imagine why. Some of the lust receded to make space for whatever this new emotion really was just before he screwed his eyes shut.

"Are you sure?" he asked, his voice breathy and rough. "Because I know I said you could stop me anytime, and I will stop, but I want you so fucking bad that I don't want to have to."

"I want you too," I breathed and put my hands on his cheeks, feeling the stubble of his five o'clock shadow on my palms. For some reason, even that turned me on about him. "So no, I don't want to have to stop either."

He licked his lips as his eyes opened, landing on mine with whatever else he had been feeling erased. Only need remained. "Thank God."

His lips crashed into mine again, his kisses more passionate and hungry than before. Lifting his shoulders off mine, he rolled us so I was on top of him, and he reached around my waist. Long, deft fingers found my zipper and pulled it all the way down in one go. Then he was sitting up to help peel it off.

Leaving me in lacy black underwear that I might have chosen especially for him in what I'd thought was a moment of unrealistic optimism at the time, I stayed still as his gaze explored every inch of my skin he could see.

His chest hitched on a breath and a much louder groan ripped out of him. Then he was back on me. He devoured my lips and touched my bare hip, my stomach, the sensitive parts of my ribs just underneath my breasts.

The places he was touching weren't necessarily where I wanted to be touched, but every brush of his fingers over my skin left a trail of heated bumps in their wake. I was so wet, I felt my panties clinging to me, drenched and transferring my juices to the insides of my thighs.

Callen's hardness ground into me as we kissed, his body pressing mine into the hard mattress once again as he flipped us over. He deftly got rid of my underwear while I writhed and squirmed underneath him, bucking my hips and chasing my release even though he was still fully clothed.

Spurred on by my own blind need, I reached for his shirt. It had already come out of his jeans from all the making out like teenagers. Callen's hand left my ribs to yank at his collar, pulling the shirt clean off.

His pants came next, both of us clawing and kicking to get them and his briefs off as fast as we could. All that yummy, inky skin finally pressed up against me, and I couldn't even appreciate it. I needed him too badly to stop him now to explore and adore his body the way I wanted to.

Next time, I promised myself. With as explosive as things were between us, I was pretty sure there would be a next time. I would make sure of it.

Running my hands down finely toned muscles in his back, I settled for touching instead of looking. Not that it felt much like I was settling. The guy was damn fine to touch.

As he came back to the position he'd been in before, I felt his hot, heavy cock sliding between my slick folds and whimpered. When his tip ran over my clit, I didn't even try to hold back a cry.

"Callen. Fuck. I need you. Inside me. Now."

He moaned too, his muscles quivering with restraint as he drew back. "Do you have a condom?"

Everything inside me screamed, but I forced my body to quiet down so I could hear myself think. "I think there's one in my wallet.

It's pretty old, though. It was given to me as a joke once by a friend when we went out."

His jaw clenched. "Think it'll work?"

"It should, but maybe pull out too. To be safe."

Nodding before planting another lingering kiss on my mouth, he lifted himself off me and grabbed my small purse. He handed it over, and I rifled through it, my fingers eventually sliding over the jagged edge of the foil packet jammed in between old receipts.

I pulled it out and presented it to Callen between two fingers, my legs spreading farther open as I lay back and tossed the wallet on the floor without taking my eyes off him. Since it was still dark, I couldn't make out the exact shapes of his tattoos. They were nothing more than whorls of ink on his skin, but what I could see was way better.

His leanly toned muscles rippled as he moved, his stomach dipping as he gripped the base of a very impressive erection to sheathe himself. There was a tremble in his hands, though I wouldn't have noticed it if I hadn't been looking at him so intently.

"You sure you're okay?" I asked. "You're shaking."

He lifted his head and spread his big body out over mine again, his broad, latex-covered tip pushing at my entrance. Looking into my eyes, he brought his hands to my hips. "I'm shaking because I want you so goddamn much and it's been a really long time since I've wanted anyone the way I want you right now."

Surprised by the sincerity in his words as much as I was by the words themselves, I looped my arms around his neck. There would be a time to ask why, but this wasn't it.

Hooking my legs around his hips, I clung to him like a spider monkey as I angled my pelvis up. "I want you just as much, so take me, Callen. I'm all yours."

"Hardly," he groaned, taking me in one fast, powerful thrust. His cock split me open in the best way, touching every part of me inside. He hissed again, dropping his forehead to my shoulder. "Jesus. Fucking. Fuck. Oh God. You feel so good. Too good."

Threading my fingers through his hair, I held him to me until I felt him relax again. Then I brought his lips to mine and kissed him as I urged him to start moving with small thrusts of my own hips. It was obvious from his reaction he'd been telling the truth about how long it'd been since he'd wanted anyone the way he wanted me. I didn't understand it, but I didn't really need to.

What I *did* need was exactly what he was just starting to give me. His thrusts were hard, determined, punishing in the strength behind his hips.

Callen transformed before my very eyes. The friendly, easygoing guy morphed into a man who wanted to fuck and knew how to do it well. It was like he'd given over to some raw, carnal thing inside of him, and to my sex-addled brain, it was beautiful and sexy as all hell.

There wasn't a single spark of humor in his darkened eyes. His jaw was set and his body worked like a well-oiled machine. Every touch had a purpose, every single thrust driving me toward an impossible edge.

His mouth worked with his hands and his extremely talented dick, licking and sucking and flicking until I was a trembling mess. With one last thrust, I went flying to that place where only exquisite bliss existed and lost myself to a mind-blowing, toe-curling rollercoaster of pleasure.

I heard his moans in my ears, felt his hips twitch and his stomach dip, then something else deep inside. Next thing I knew, ropes of his come were covering my stomach and he wore his own contorted mask of pleasure as his fist glided up and down his dick, pulling the very last drops of his orgasm from him.

"What happened to the condom?" I asked when I eventually caught my breath and Callen had collapsed beside me, one of his arms draped over my waist.

He turned his head on the pillow to look at me, his delectable body covered in a light sheen of sweat. "It broke right at the end, but I pulled out fast enough."

"You're sure?" I frowned, panic flooding my previously blissed-out brain. "And clean? Because if not, you need to tell me right now. I am. Had a physical just the other day."

"I'm clean too," he said, bringing one hand to my cheek and

stroking it as he held my gaze. "The band used to get checked out once a month and I haven't been with anyone since I got my last test results. You?"

"No, I haven't either." I let out a relieved breath, but I had to ask again. "You're sure you pulled out soon enough?"

His forehead furrowed as if my question required deep thought, but his eyes stayed on mine. "Yeah, I'm pretty sure I pulled out the moment I felt the tear."

"Okay." I breathed out again. "Good. That's good."

He placed a gentle kiss on my lips, his mouth opening to say something when we both heard a car in the driveway. My eyes went wide. "Shit. She's never come back that fast before."

"I think she's been gone longer than you realize." He smirked at me, then sat up and swung his legs over the bed. He bent over, grabbing his pants and tossing my dress to me. "God, first we made out like teenagers. Then we hooked up in your parents' house and now we're hurrying to get dressed before they come inside. It makes me feel like we've gone back in time fifteen years."

"Yeah," I agreed, a grin curling my lips as I thought about what he had said. "I kind of like the excitement, though. Don't you?"

"Call me crazy, but yes, I do," he said as he pulled on his shirt. "Now get dressed before we get caught, gorgeous, partner-in-crazy, fake girlfriend. I'd prefer to keep that invite for coming back. Especially now that I know what these beds feel like."

I laughed and didn't stop until I heard my mother walking in through the front door.

CHAPTER 15

CALLEN

The last of our things unpacked, I stood in the center of the living room with my hands on my hips and smiled. I might look crazy to anyone who got a peek at me through a window, but I couldn't *not* smile.

The house was finally feeling like a real home, and this was the first time I was feeling that way in a very, very long time. My date with Tiffeny had gone surprisingly well, and the sex? Fuck, the sex had been incredible.

So yeah, I had to smile. Every lucky son of a bitch in my position would.

I hadn't planned what had happened between us in that guest bedroom, but I couldn't say I regretted that it had happened. All I'd done was whatever had felt right in the moment and it had led to explosive sex that had woken my body up in ways I'd forgotten it could be woken up.

There had been a few bumpy bits. Jumping into bed with another woman for the first time was never going to be all easy, but fuck, had it felt good when I'd finally gotten out of my head.

I wasn't even only talking about how fucking awesome it had felt physically. It had felt amazing on every level. Like I had been given back parts of myself I had lost ages ago, parts that had helped shape me into the man I was today. Maybe because I actually felt like a human being again and not just a shell of one. I was feeling a sense of possibility again and actually wanting to find out what those possibilities might be.

Waking up the next morning, I felt more like myself than I had in years. After I'd dropped Winter off at school, I raced back home and started on the rest of the boxes.

I had that feeling of getting life on some kind of track again and I couldn't do that if I was constantly surrounded by boxes. It had taken me a couple of days, but with all the boxes now flattened and every last thing of ours unpacked, I was feeling pretty good.

The feeling got even better when my phone rang and Tiffeny's name appeared on the screen. "Hey, you. What's up?"

"Hi," she said, her voice warm but hesitant. "I was wondering if you wanted to come over to the shop for a bit."

"Sure. I finally finished unpacking, so I could use some celebratory ice cream. I'm paying for this one, though."

"We'll see," she replied. "So I'll see you soon?"

"See you soon." I hung up and went to grab a quick shower so I wouldn't smell like someone who had just finished moving in. Then I headed out.

Tiffeny looked as good as ever when I got there, a bright smile on her face as she handed over a cone to a teenage customer. Her blue eyes shone with happiness and her hair was pulled up into a messy bun on top of her head.

She had on a pair of jeans and a black T-shirt, but it might as well have been lingerie for the way my blood heated at the sight of her. She said something to the customer just before I opened the door and walked in, the beautiful sound of her laughter meeting my ears along with the jingling of the bell.

"I could never do that," the teenager said, sounded horrified and intrigued all at the same time. "Girls don't ask boys out. It's supposed to be the other way around. I don't even know if he likes me. What if he says no?"

Tiffeny shook her head at the girl, her smile now aimed at me as the door swung shut after I'd stepped inside. "Back me up here, Callen. Teenage boys can be blind as bats when it comes to girls. They need a little push sometimes, right?"

"Right," I agreed, walking up to the counter instead of joining her behind it and pulling her into my arms like I wanted to. "Take it from me. Boys can be very, very stupid. Noticing subtle hints isn't a specialty many teenagers have. If that's what you've been doing, Tiffeny's right. Just ask him out."

"You really think so?" she asked, clearly doubting the advice. "What if he turns me down?"

"He won't," Tiffeny said firmly. "From what you've told me, he's definitely into you too. I wouldn't have told you to ask him out if I didn't think he'd say yes."

"Even if he says no, at least then you'll know you tried instead of wondering what might have happened if you'd just gone for it," I said.

Tiffeny nodded and the teenager mulled it over before doing the same. "You're right. It's got to be better to know than be stuck wondering forever. Thanks, guys."

She spun on her heel and had her phone in her hand before she was even out of the shop. Tiffeny lifted her hand and presented me with her palm. "High five, partner-in-crazy. Thanks for backing me up again."

"No problem." I slapped my hand against hers, grinning as I watched the girl walk away. "You really think he likes her?"

"I do. I just hope he's man enough to admit it and say yes when she asks him. Otherwise, I might have just lost a customer that I genuinely like."

"We wouldn't want that. I meant what I said though. It's always better to know you went for it than to wonder, right?"

Tiffeny's teeth sank into her lower lip, the lightness in her eyes disappearing as she suddenly frowned. "Speaking about just going for things, I asked you here because we haven't spoken in a couple of days and I wanted to make sure I didn't screw up the other night."

"You didn't screw up," I assured her, my lips curving into a smirk as I walked around the counter and put one of my hands on her hip. "You screwed *me*, but you didn't screw *up*."

She held my gaze for another beat before the frown faded and she gave me a shy smile instead. "I sure did, didn't I? I still can't believe we did that in my mother's house."

"Neither can I, but no regrets, right?" I took a step closer to her.

"No regrets," she repeated, taking a step of her own to close the distance between us.

I broke eye contact to glance down at her lips, and when I looked back up at her, hers were on mine as well. My heartbeat kicked up a notch and I brought my hand up to touch her cheek.

It was that electrifying moment just before a kiss, and I couldn't wait for it, but as I lowered my head, the bell jingled again, and Tiffeny jumped away from me. She turned in the same movement, her eyes wide in panic over having been caught in a moment by a customer, but when she saw whoever had walked in, her face fell and her hands balled into fists by her sides.

With my lips still tingling from the almost kiss, I frowned when I noticed her response to whoever she had seen and twisted to get a look at them. The customer was a man who had on an expensive suit, but it wore him more than he wore it. His hair was slicked back and his eyes narrowed on a glare at us.

"Mr. Nicolson," Tiffeny said. "What can I do for you?"

His gaze flicked toward me, but his words were obviously for her. "It's that time of the month, Ms. Hurst. What do you think you can do for me? I want my money."

"Oh." Her jaw was tight and her nod curt. "Yes, of course. I have it right here."

She bent over and drew her purse out from under the counter, keeping it low as she extracted a wad of bills from an inner pocket. The man reached for it as she handed it over, then thumbed the notes as he counted.

"You know," he said, a smirk forming on his lips as he gave her a look I really didn't fucking like. "I can always give some of this back to you in exchange for some one-on-one time like you're obviously giving him."

Tiffeny opened her mouth, but no sound came out. Her discomfort around this guy and her dislike of him were clear as day, but he didn't seem to fucking get it. The insinuation he'd made that I was somehow paying her for the time I spent with her made red spots dance in my vision, and rage over the situation simmered in my stomach.

Without needing to think about what I was doing, I rounded the counter and grabbed his arm to lead him firmly to the door. "You got what you came for. It's time for you to leave."

The much smaller man shrank away from me. The intimidating glare I gave him must have worked because he didn't argue. He simply left.

"That's your landlord?" I asked her when the door had shut behind him.

She nodded, letting out a heavy sigh. "Unfortunately. I'd have paid double the rent I am now just to keep him out of my shop, though. I don't know why he comes to collect the cash when I've offered to wire it to him, but it's like he enjoys coming in here and making us feel like shit. Thank you for getting him out so fast."

"No problem." I dragged my hands over my face and let the prick of my stubble into my palms distract me from the need to chase him down and make sure he never came back to her shop again. "Is he always like that?"

"Pretty much." She lowered herself onto the metal stool behind the counter and shook her head. "He doesn't seem to take a hint very well, or even a flat-out denial."

"If you ever need me for anything, but especially to be here when he comes around, all you need to do is call me, okay? I can be here anytime you need me."

A part of me wanted to demand she call me at the first trace of the guy, or that she let me use her backroom to do all my stuff in just so I could be at the store all the time, but I knew I had no right to make any demands of her. Tiffeny could take care of herself, but strangely, I found myself not wanting it to be necessary for her to have to do it.

CHAPTER 16

TIFFENY

"Hey, guys and girls," I said to the kids as I walked into the day-care on Friday morning. I was getting used to making these deliveries and had bought a cart especially for them so I could bring in all the ice cream in one go. "You ready for today's surprise flavor?"

The kids swarmed around me, clapping and calling out guesses. A smile I couldn't contain spread across my lips. These kids were so damn cute. "I guess that's a yes, huh?"

More cheering and shouting followed. It was madness whenever I came here, since they all knew by now I was the one who brought them treats once a week, but I loved it.

As I rolled the cart to a stop in front of a table the center had already gotten ready for me under a big oak tree outside, I lifted one of the tubs and tapped the side of my mouth, pretending to have to think. "You know, I think I'm going to need help remembering what's in here. Anyone want to volunteer to come have the first taste so we can try to work it out?"

Little hands shot into the air, but then I noticed Winter in the crowd. Her hair was pulled up into pigtails and her hand was waving around as she stood on her tiptoes.

Smiling as I engaged shamelessly in a nepotistic act that didn't even make me feel bad for the grin it got me, I pointed at her. She rushed to the front of the group and bounced on the balls of her feet.

"Hi, Tiffeny. I can help you remember."

"I know you can. You're an ice-cream expert." I reached out to touch her shoulder, guiding her the last few steps to the table. After popping the lid off the first tub, I scooped out a large ball of ice cream and placed it in one of the little cones I'd brought with me. "Here you go. I'm looking forward to hearing if you like it."

She took it from me and gave it a tentative lick. Recognition flashed in her eyes and she smiled proudly. "It's butter pecan. Daddy's favorite."

"You're right." I lifted her arm into the air to celebrate her victory, and the other kids cheered again, then surged forward while the teachers tried getting them into a line.

I winked at one of the teachers I'd spoken to during the deliveries once or twice. "Good luck with that."

"They really like to test our organizational skills every time you come here, but we love it." She gave me a small smile before returning to the kids.

Winter stayed at my side, patiently waiting for my attention to come back to her. I frowned, bending my knees a little to talk to her. "Are you okay, sweetheart? Why haven't you run back to your friends?"

"I want to give you a tour of my classroom. Would you like to see it?"

Surprised, I nodded and swept my arm out ahead of us to let her lead the way. "I have to get back to the shop soon, but I'd definitely like to see your class first."

"Okay." She beamed at me, grabbed my hand without any hesitation, and pulled me toward the building. I made sure to let one of the teachers know where we were going, adding that I knew Winter and her father. She smiled and waved me on.

A short walk down an open-sided corridor led us to her classroom. She kept her hold on my hand as she pointed things out to me. "I sit there. Nathan sits next to me. He's my friend."

"That's nice. You're so close to the front of the room *and* you're already making friends."

She looked up at me and smiled as she nodded. "I didn't have any friends in California. I didn't like my old school."

"Well then I'm glad you like this one and that you've made friends." I paused beside the small plastic desk she'd said was hers, admiring the bold, bright colors of a picture she must have been busy coloring before they'd been called outside. "This is beautiful, Winter. I love the colors."

"Thank you. So do I." A line appeared between her eyebrows as she frowned. "Nathan said I used too many."

I traced a finger along the page, shaking my head. "I don't think so. The more colors, the merrier. Which ones are your favorites? Mine are purple and yellow."

"Mine too, but I also like pink and orange." She walked around the desk and reached into a space underneath it to extract some beads strung together on a skinny shoelace. "I made this yesterday. Do you like it?"

"I love it." It was multicolored and the ends of the shoelace had been tied together. "Is it a necklace?"

She nodded, placing it in both palms and holding it up to me. "My teacher said we could keep them or give them away. Do you want mine?"

My heart melted, my limbs turning to jelly. This girl was just too damn sweet. "I'd love to have it, but are you sure there's no one else you'd rather give it to?"

"No. I want you to have it." She looked almost scared, like she was afraid I was going to reject her. It confused me, but I didn't want to ask about it.

Instead, I dipped down to my haunches and looked her right in the eyes. "In that case, I definitely want it. I'll treasure it every day."

Her smile turned radiant as she handed it over, then helped me get it over my head when I bent it forward. I touched the wooden beads resting over my heart, not able to resist drawing her in for a hug. "Thank you, Winter. It's beautiful."

"You're welcome." She hugged me back, her thin arms winding around my neck and holding me close. "Thank you for wearing it."

"Of course." After I released her, I straightened up and hooked a finger beneath the necklace, pulling it away from my body to look down at it. "I'm going to wear it so much, I might need a new one soon."

"I'll make you a new one." She turned and reached into the space underneath her desk again, coming back with a smallish box containing more beads. "You can choose which ones you want next time."

"I think I'll leave that up to you. You did so well with this one." She nodded again, put the box away, and showed me around the room some more.

We talked about the pictures on the puzzles they'd built, how they'd made Play-Doh, and about the small class garden they watered together every afternoon. When I heard some of the other kids moving into the hallway, I inclined my head toward the door and held out my hand.

"Come on. We'd better go get you some more ice cream before it's all gone and you have to come back to class."

We walked outside together, got Winter a scoop of the butter pecan, and then she left me to go eat with some of her friends who were still outside. I was packing up my things when I overheard her bragging to her friends. "Tiffeny gives me free ice cream when we go to her shop. She's so nice."

Another smile touched my lips, but I ducked my head so my hair would hide it. I guessed any three-year-old would brag about getting free ice cream, but it was cool that I got to be the one to give it to her.

My shop might make a lot of kids happy, but I liked being directly responsible for putting a smile on Winter's face. Before I left, she came up to me and gave me another hug.

"Thank you for the necklace," I said. "I'll see you next week, okay?"

"Can I see you before then?" she asked, uncertainty clouding her eyes as her teeth sank into her lip.

"Sure, you can see me whenever you want. You know where to find me."

That earned me another smile and I returned it easily, reaching out to tug gently on one of her pigtails before saying goodbye. "I'll see you soon, okay?"

"Okay." She hugged my leg, squeezing it tightly before letting me go and running off after the remaining members of her class.

When I got back to the shop, Julia was waiting outside. She pushed away from the railing she had been leaning on, coming over to help me with the few bags I was carrying.

"How did it go?" she asked as she hoisted a material bag filled with scoops I'd left behind at the center last week onto her shoulder. "Do the kids still treat you like their fairy sweet-mother?"

"Yeah, it's awesome. I love it. I got to spend some time with Winter today, which was cool too. She showed me around her classroom and gave me this."

I touched my chin to the beads around my neck. Julia leaned in to examine it while I unlocked the shop. She followed after me and we set the bags down on the counter.

Once we offloaded the bags, she turned to me with a thoughtful expression in her eyes. She drummed her fingers on her cheek as she sat down at one of the booths.

"Don't get me wrong. I think it's great that you spent some time with her and all, but isn't something like that a gift she should be making for her mother?"

"Probably." The thought had crossed my mind when she'd presented it to me. "I don't think her mom is around, though. Callen's never mentioned her and neither has Winter. I mean, if she was around, I'm sure Winter would have kept the necklace for her."

"If she's not around, then where is she?" Julia frowned, concern etched into the tightened corners of her eyes. "I don't want you getting attached to them if she could just swoop in at any moment."

"Whoa, whoa, whoa." I lifted my hands and turned my palms out. "I'm not getting attached to anyone, so you don't need to worry about that. Besides, if there was a chance she could just swoop in at any moment, I'm sure one of them would have mentioned her by now."

"Okay," she said but didn't look convinced by my denial at all. Then again, I wasn't either, so I couldn't exactly blame her. "You have no idea what happened with her mother?"

"No clue." I really didn't have an answer for her, but I realized she was right.

Before anything went any further with these two, I should probably find out where Winter's mother was. I might not have gotten attached to them yet, but I had a feeling I was in the process of doing just that, and as much as I didn't want to push Callen, it felt like it was time to find out a little bit more about what I was getting into.

CHAPTER 17

CALLEN

"Can we have spaghetti tonight?" Winter asked late on Saturday afternoon. She looked up from the paper doll she was dressing and tilted her head. "We played with cold spaghetti at school this week, but we weren't allowed to eat it."

We were out in the backyard, both of us sitting on loungers next to the covered pool. I had opened our large umbrella to shield us from the sun and a breeze from the ocean kept us cool.

It was the perfect day to relax outside and I was glad we got to do it together. The corners of my mouth lifted in a lazy grin. "Sure, baby. I should be able to handle making that."

"I'll help you," she offered excitedly. "My teacher told us that you cook spaghetti in a pot."

"That's an excellent place for us to start then." While I knew my cooking skills were severely lacking, I was confident that even I couldn't fuck spaghetti up.

Winter sat up straighter, her eyes widening in that way that let me know she'd just had another idea. "We should invite Tiffeny over."

I nearly choked on my own breath, my eyebrows lifting. "What? Why would we do that?"

"I saw her yesterday at school when she brought us ice cream. She said I could see her whenever I wanted."

"She did, huh?" I mulled the idea over in my head. While I was hesitant to dive right into a relationship with anyone and especially to let a new woman into Winter's life, inviting Tiffeny over for dinner didn't seem like it could do much harm.

"Well, if she said you could see her whenever you wanted and you want to see her, I think it's a great idea to invite her. It's a Saturday though, so she might already have plans. Let's give her a call and find out." *Damn it, and now I sound like a game show host.*

If I was being honest with myself though, I wanted to see her as well. It had been a few days since I'd gone to hang out with her at the shop, and this was as good a time as any to see her again. With that in mind, I picked up my phone from the table beside me and fired off a quick text to her.

She replied a minute later, saying she'd see us at seven. I grinned at Winter, trying my best not to let her see how excited I was about Tiffeny coming over.

"She said yes."

Winter cheered and her lips spread into a smile that lit up her whole face. Clearly, she didn't have any similar concerns about tamping down her excitement. It made my own feel more acceptable, so I decided to stop fighting so hard not to let Winter see that Tiffeny coming over made me happy too.

She was my friend, which Winter already knew. I'd been happy at times when Clark came over, so it wouldn't look that much different to her.

Both of us kept smiling for the rest of the afternoon, then rushed through getting cleaned up and ready before she arrived. At seven on the dot, our doorbell rang.

Winter dashed to the door, reaching up to open it and let Tiffeny in. I stood behind her, impatiently waiting to get my next first look at the woman who never seemed to fail at making breathing—and other things—a little harder for me.

When the door swung open to reveal her standing there wearing a deep purple sundress and her hair cascading past her shoulders, I wasn't disappointed in my reaction. The next breath I inhaled staggered and caught before it came out again. *Hot damn, she's beautiful.*

"Hey, guys," she said, lifting her hand in a wave as she stepped inside. She slung an arm around Winter's shoulders and pulled her in for a tight but casual side hug. "How are you, sweetie?"

"I'm good." Winter gazed up at Tiffeny with adoration shining in her eyes. "You're wearing your necklace."

"Of course I am," she said, bringing her hand to her chest to lift a string of beads. Even though I knew full well it hadn't been her intention, it made my eyes drop to her cleavage and linger there as I remembered the sounds she made when I toyed with her nipples.

"I told you I was going to treasure it every day, didn't I?" She ruffled Winter's hair when she finally let her go.

Realizing that the time for staring at her rack and fantasizing about what had happened between us was *not* now, I shoved the thoughts to the back of my mind and took a step forward to greet her. "Hey, you. Glad you could make it."

"Yeah, me too." She shut the door behind her. "So what can I do to help?"

"Nothing," I said, tilting my head toward the kitchen and motioning for them to follow me. "We're having spaghetti. Hope you don't mind that we're keeping it simple."

"I like simple." She laughed as Winter grabbed her hand and dragged her past me to enter the kitchen first. "Whoa, where's the fire?"

"Hopefully not in there later," I muttered.

Tiffeny must have caught my comment because she turned to wink at me over her shoulder. Before she could say anything though, Winter explained. "Daddy said I could cook. Do you want to help me?"

"Daddy said you could help," I reminded her, arching a brow at my daughter as we entered the kitchen. "Not cook. There's a hot stove and boiling water involved."

Winter shrugged her shoulders, her eyes sparkling as she slid them to Tiffeny. "Yes, but Tiffeny will help me."

"Yeah, I won't let anyone get burned," she assured me, looking around the kitchen as if she was getting her bearings.

I walked toward the fridge, shaking my head. I pulled out a bottle of soda and filled three glasses I'd set out earlier. "I'm sure you wouldn't, but you're also our guest. You're not cooking for us. We'll do the cooking. You sit. Relax and keep us company."

"Okay," she said, but she noticed the pot standing on the stove already and cocked her head. "Are you sure that's not too small for enough pasta for all three of us?"

I waved my hand, smirking as I walked around the island and got myself situated behind the stove. "It's the only pot we use. It will be fine."

It wasn't fine.

Ten minutes later, we were all sitting around the island talking when I smelled something burning. I'd just dropped the noodles into the pot, so I figured it couldn't be those. Not sure what else it could be, I frowned and sniffed the air.

At the same time, Tiffeny stopped telling Winter about something that had happened to her in kindergarten. A confused frown marred her beautiful forehead for just a moment before she looked at something behind me and burst out laughing.

"What?" I asked, twisting around with a jerk to see what she was laughing about. Thin streams of smoke were rising from the uncooked noodles resting on the side of the pot. My eyes widened before I jumped to my feet and grabbed a mitt to remove the pot from the heat.

"What the fu—" I cut myself off just in time, my eyes darting from Winter's to Tiffeny's and then down to the pot in front of me. Tiffeny's shoulders were shaking with laughter and Winter had her head tilted, a deep confused V between her brows.

"What happened, Daddy?"

I had no clue what the fuck I was doing in the kitchen apparently.

That was what was going on. "The spaghetti got burnt, baby. It's fine, though. We have more. We'll just try again."

Tiffeny stood up from her stool, coming over to reach around my waist. For a moment, with her body so close to mine I could feel the heat coming off her, my gaze snagged on her lips and the urge to kiss her nearly overtook me.

Thankfully, those lips were quirked into a grin and mischief shone from her eyes. I felt a tug at my back. Then she stepped away and beckoned to me with her index finger. "Come on. Hand it over. Winter and I are taking over from here."

It took me longer than I was proud of to snap myself out of the haze she'd plummeted me into when she got so close to me. Eventually, I realized she was waiting for me to take off the apron. That was why she'd gotten so close and what the tug had been at my back: her undoing the tie.

Such an innocent move on her part and I'd been halfway ready to maul her. This woman seriously did things to me, but I couldn't say I minded it too much.

"Fine, but just so you know, my second attempt would have been perfect." I lifted the apron over my head, gave it to her, picked up my glass, and took a seat. "I have no idea what went wrong, but I would have figured it out and corrected it."

Tiffeny's brows lifted and amusement danced behind her blue eyes as she settled the apron in place. "What happened is that you just managed to burn raw spaghetti. I don't think I know anyone else who's been able to get that right. I mean, older kids and drunk people alike are able to toss some spaghetti into a pot and cook it without it burning."

She's teasing me, I realized. *And I like it.*

Like so many other things with her, it felt natural, like she was already so comfortable around us that we'd reached the stage where she didn't feel like she needed to hold anything back with us.

"Yeah, I'm talented like that," I retorted, giving her a smirk. "If you think that's impressive, you should see what I can do with instant pancakes."

"You mean the type where they've already premixed all the dry ingredients and you only have to add eggs and milk?" she asked, disbelief in her tone.

I nodded, puffing my chest out with faux pride. "I might have forgotten to add the eggs and I might have thought it was a good idea to add oil to the mixture."

"That couldn't have ended well." She chuckled, shaking her head. She pushed herself up on her toes to grab a bigger pot from the rack hanging above the stove. "I can't wait to hear that story, but let me get some water on to boil while you tell it."

"What can I do?" Winter asked.

Tiffeny pursed her lips, then snapped her fingers and smiled. "You can get us some more pasta. Once the water boils, I'll set a timer and you can watch it for us."

"Okay," she agreed, sliding off her stool to hurry to the cupboard.

"What can I do?" I asked.

Tiffeny smirked at me and nodded at the fridge. "You can get us more soda and tell me what you wanted to have with the spaghetti."

"There's a jar there next to the kettle. It's a tomato and basil sauce. There's also some parmesan we could sprinkle over the top."

"An instant sauce?" Her nose wrinkled. "I'm sure I can do better than that. Let me see what I have to work with."

I motioned for her to go ahead. "You're welcome to use anything you can find, but there might not be much. I do my best, but I'm obviously not great in the kitchen."

"Obviously." She winked and shot me a grin. "But that's okay. We'll work on it."

Tiffeny and Winter rummaged through the kitchen and came back to the island with tins and bottles of some of the stuff that the realtor must have arranged to have brought in before we moved.

They got to work, with Tiffeny letting Winter help where she could, talking nonstop while they did.

"I'm glad you're wearing the necklace," Winter said. She'd told me this afternoon that she'd made one in class and had given it to Tiffeny. Now that I wasn't staring at her cleavage, I took a moment to notice the necklace instead. "I've started with a new one for you. It's purple and yellow, like your favorite colors."

"That's great." Tiffeny's smile was warm and genuine. "I can't wait to see it, but I'll keep wearing this one as well. I'm attached to it now."

Winter looked as proud as if Tiffeny had just told her she was going to be in the Beading Olympics. Watching them interact with one another, I liked how Tiffeny was with Winter and how Winter reacted to her.

I was glad she'd asked if we could invite Tiffeny over. This was fun, and it looked like it was good for my little girl. Between the two of them, there wasn't silence for a second.

"Okay," Tiffeny said about forty minutes later. "Grub's up, guys."

A silky looking tomato-based sauce was transferred to a serving dish, and Winter carried the tub of parmesan shavings to the dining-room table. I'd set it while they cooked and waited for both girls to be seated before taking my own.

"All right, dig in," Tiffeny said. "If you hate the sauce, I'll go heat up your instant one. No offense taken."

"Yours smells delicious. Those other ones always have a distinctly plastic-ness to them that I'm sure I'm not going to miss." I served Winter before letting Tiffeny help herself. Once she was done, I grabbed my own food and dug in.

Fresh basil and rich tangy tomato exploded in my mouth when I took the first bite, and I nearly fucking groaned out loud because of it. I chewed, swallowed, and blinked at Tiffeny. "Turns out ice cream isn't the only thing you know how to flavor. This is great."

"I can get by." Her cheeks flushed. "I'm glad you like it. I'm not an excellent cook, but I wouldn't mind showing you some basics sometime."

"Sounds good." Winter and I couldn't live off instant or fast food for the rest of our lives, nor could we go out for every meal. As much as the internet had helped in my pursuits of becoming better in the kitchen, it obviously wasn't going very well for me.

Plus, it gave us an excuse to spend more time with her.

Winter cleared her bowl in record time, then told us all about her teacher's pet rabbit and her friend, Nathan. By the time we'd finished our own meals, her eyelids were drooping.

"That's it, kiddo," I said. "Time for bed."

Winter gave me a crestfallen look. "Do I have to? I'm talking to Tiffeny."

"Yeah, but you're going to have to talk to her again some other time," I said. "I'll give you five more minutes. Then it's off to bed for little girls."

"Fine." She stuck her lower lip out, her eyes drifting over to Tiffeny. "But will you come tuck me in and lay down with me tonight?"

Tiffeny blinked back her surprise, darting a glance at me. "I can if it's okay with you."

A range of emotions passed through me, but I pushed them all back. One look at the big, round pools of hope Winter's eyes had become wiped any hesitation from my mind. "Sure, I'm fine with it."

The truth was that I just didn't know if I was or if I wasn't. Maybe having Tiffeny over hadn't been such a good idea after all.

CHAPTER 18

TIFFENY

Winter's warm body was curled up next to mine on her double bed. She was lying on her back while I was on my side and running my fingers through her hair.

"Thank you for coming to lie down with me," she said quietly in the near darkness. A nightlight was on, depicting shapes of animals and stars in pastel shades on the ceiling, but there was no other light.

"It's my pleasure, sweetheart." I kept my voice soft, too.

A few beats passed where the only sound was our gentle breathing. Then Winter turned to face me and put her hands under her head. "I can't fall asleep when I'm alone. That's why I like my Daddy to lie down with me."

"I'm sure he doesn't mind." I kept stroking my fingers through her hair, my mind flashing to the conversation I'd had with Julia after I'd gotten back from the day-care center.

"I like it when you lie down with me, too," she said. "When we stayed in hotels, I had to lie by myself. The ladies who stayed with me didn't always tuck me in. Daddy lay with me sometimes, when he wasn't with Uncle Clark." She yawned. "I don't have a mommy, so when Daddy wasn't there, I was alone."

My heart gave a painful clench. I couldn't imagine what it must be

121

like to have to say those words at three. The innocence in her eyes and her voice as she said it almost broke me because she really thought she didn't have a mother.

There was no undercurrent of pain or confusion in her tone, though. She'd simply stated a fact.

Tears burned in my eyes, but I didn't let them fall. "Luckily, Daddy is with you almost every night now."

I didn't know what else to say. Asking her questions about her mother or why she didn't have one seemed like a recipe for disaster.

Callen and I would have that conversation. I couldn't try to have it with Winter, so I just let the mommy thing go, even if it hurt my heart to do it. Later tonight, I planned on telling him what she'd said because I felt like it was something he needed to know about anyway, and then I would ask him where her mother was.

My heart reached out to hers. Wanting to give her whatever comfort I could, I started humming "You are my Sunshine" under my breath. My mother had never sung it to me, but one of my nannies had. I always felt soothed when I heard it. To this day, I played it when I felt bad or was sick.

Winter smiled, burrowing into my side as she finally closed her eyes. I kept humming and stroking her hair until however long later, I felt her breathing even out and knew she'd fallen asleep. As gently as I could, I moved away from her and pressed a quick kiss to her temple before I lifted her comforter to her hips and left the room.

Faint sounds of a guitar being strummed filled the house when I opened the door. I didn't know the song, but it was slow and steady, an almost melancholic melody that I suddenly felt like I wanted to know.

Following the sound, I found Callen sitting on the deck in their backyard. He had his guitar in his lap, his hands moving along the fretboard seamlessly while he stared off into the distance.

Fingers plucking at the strings, he seemed completely lost in thought. Light from the inside streamed out, but he hadn't turned on any outside.

He stopped and reached for one of two beers sitting on the plastic table next to his chair, letting out a sigh before taking a long sip. I didn't think he knew I was there and I didn't want to startle him by just appearing suddenly, so I put my hands together and clapped softly.

"Bravo. That was beautiful. You might not be particularly talented in the kitchen, but you sure seem to know your way around the guitar."

The somber expression slipped from his face and he chuckled. "Yeah, I guess you could say both of those things are sort of an occupational hazard. I hardly ever had to cook for myself, and if I sucked at guitar, well, I'd have to have changed said occupation."

"Good point." I moved farther out onto the deck and he patted the spot next to him on the lounger. I sat down, trying not to get distracted by his muscular thighs spread out and hanging over the sides of the chair.

My knee brushed against his as I sat down, but he didn't move it out of the way. Those familiar tingles I got from touching him sparked between us and raced through me, but I ignored them. I could *not* be horny for the conversation we had to have.

Leaning back with my palms on the thick pillow covering the lounger, I contemplated how best to bring it up.

Callen broke the comfortable silence first. "Thanks for going with her. I've been trying to get her to go to bed by herself, but it's just not taking."

"That's fine. I liked it to be honest. She's such a sweetheart, and cuddling with her was nice."

A soft smile touched his full lips. "Yeah, it is nice. She's the best cuddler in the world."

My head bounced up and down in agreement, my eyes focused on branches swaying in the breeze as I chewed the inside of my cheek. There was no easy way to ask what I wanted to.

"She mentioned that she doesn't have a mommy," I said, deciding to just rip off the band-aid. "I don't mean to pry, so you can tell me to fuck right off if you want, but where is Winter's mother?"

I heard him sucking in a breath, then released a deep one of my own and finally gathered the courage to look at him again. He wasn't looking at me, his gaze on the dark expanse of the ocean as he answered.

"I'm not going to tell you to fuck off." He lifted one of his hands from the guitar and dragged it over his cheek. "It's a valid question and one you deserve the answer to. It's just not easy for me to talk about it."

Taking a sip of his beer, he lapsed into silence. It felt heavy this time, though. I kept quiet, too. This was obviously a sensitive subject for him, so if he needed time to think before he said anything, I could wait.

About a minute passed before he squeezed his eyes shut, dropping his head back against the chair. "Her mother's name was Alice. She passed away about a year and a half ago. She's in some of the pictures inside."

He opened his eyes again but still didn't look at me and kept his gaze on the sky instead. Pain lanced through me on their behalf. I couldn't even begin to imagine everything they, but especially him, had gone through.

Although I didn't know the circumstances and he didn't seem to be willing to go into any greater detail, losing someone he had a child with must have been really tough. To face the prospect of having a little girl and raising her without her mother had to be daunting as hell, and that was without even beginning to unpack his own loss.

I reached out and put my hand on his thigh. There was nothing sexual about it. It was meant to be a comforting gesture, and since he didn't shake me off, I assumed he took it for what it was. "I'm so sorry, Callen. For your loss and for Winter's, but also for bringing it up."

He slid his hand underneath mine, turned his palm up, and laced our fingers together. "Thanks, but you don't have to be sorry for bringing it up. It's only natural for you to have wondered where she was."

I tightened my grip on his fingers and ran my thumb along the length of his. "If you ever want to talk more about her or about what happened, I'm more than willing to listen."

"I might take you up on that someday." He didn't sound convinced, but that didn't matter. We'd only known each for a short amount of time, and I had no right to expect him to open up to me, especially about another woman.

"Just keep it in mind, okay? I won't be weird or awkward about it."

A small smile curled on his lips and his eyes finally flickered to mine. "You? Not be weird or awkward about something? I doubt it, but I like that about you."

I laughed quietly, shaking my head. "Hey, I haven't done anything really weird or awkward in a while."

"Also true." He released his grip on my hand and picked up the guitar again. "Want to hear a new song I'm working on?"

"I'd love to." I watched intently as he started strumming again, a different melody than before. It was a little more upbeat, but it still had a soulful sound to it.

Callen didn't sing, but even though I wasn't usually a fan of instrumental stuff, I liked just listening to him play. At times, he would close his eyes, his head slightly tilted, and his lips would part. Other times, he either looked at me or out at the water glittering under the stars.

In between songs, we talked about his music. He told me a bit about his time in the band and his friend Clark. Mostly though, he played and I listened.

I was absolutely captivated by him, by the sounds he could coax from his instrument without even looking at it. When he set the guitar down again, I scooted closer to him. "That was beautiful, Callen. Thank you for letting me hear you play."

"Anytime." He reached for my hips and hauled me even closer to him so that I was nestled in the crook his legs. "If you're interested, you can really hear me play anytime. There's a lot of me playing on this little thing called the internet."

I chuckled and leaned my head against his chest, angling it so I could look up at him. "For someone with so many muscles, you're surprisingly comfortable to lie on."

His lips formed a smirk. "You think I've got a lot of muscles?"

"You know you do." I rolled my eyes at him. "But if you're fishing for compliments, I'm happy to give them."

"Yeah?" He cocked his head.

"Yeah." I twisted around, still sitting in my spot but with my upper body now facing more toward him. I cupped his face in my hands and stroked my thumbs across his defined cheekbones. "Aside from the muscles, you're a pretty decent person, too."

"You only think that because you don't know me very well," he teased. "But I think you're a pretty damn decent person too."

I smiled and brought my head closer to his. "Okay, if you don't want to take that one, here's another for you. You're a really good kisser."

"So are you," he whispered, one of his hands sliding into my hair.

A sliver of pleasure raced down my spine. I brought my lips to his slowly, only brushing them over his before I pulled away.

When he didn't try to bring me back or kiss me again, disappointment stabbed through my gut like a spear. But then he released a shuddering breath, and there was so much want in his eyes when he looked into mine again that it was hard to hang onto my disappointment.

"It's not that I don't want to," he said, his voice husky. "It's that I can't do anything with Winter here."

His hand was still in my hair, his long fingers playing with the soft strands. I leaned into his touch, my lips aching to kiss him again and my body eager to go, but I didn't act on any of it. "I understand."

"I'll make time for just you and me soon. I promise." He took my hand with his free one, bringing it up to place a soft kiss on the back of it. "Very soon."

"There's no rush," I said. Our gazes were locked together and it felt like I could tumble into the soulful green depths of his. "I should probably get going anyway. Thanks for inviting me and thanks for dinner."

"No, thank you for dinner." He stood up after me, walking me out. When the front door shut behind us, he grabbed my hand and pulled me to him. "Just to say goodbye."

The next thing I knew, his mouth came crashing down on mine and he kissed me in a way that left no doubt in my mind that he'd been honest about why he'd put a stop to things earlier. It wasn't because he didn't want me or had already gotten what he'd really wanted from me.

He was just dedicated to being a good father and I respected that. In fact, it was one of the things I liked most about him. A goodhearted, nice, sexy man who was a great father? Now that was a man I wanted to get to know better.

CHAPTER 19

CALLEN

"**G**ood job, sweetheart." I added the flower Winter ran over with to the growing collection of treasure-hunt items she'd found in our backyard so far.

With my guitar still resting on my lap, I picked up the list I'd made earlier. "Next up is a feather."

Winter nodded and took off again, leaving me alone with my guitar on the deck while she carried on with her nature hunt. It was an overcast day, but it was good weather for running around outside without getting burned to a crisp.

Smiling to myself as I watched her foraging, I absently strummed my guitar and went back to the thoughts I'd been having before she'd brought me the flower. Tiffeny had been on my mind all morning, and no matter what I did, I couldn't seem to shake her.

Telling her about Alice hadn't been easy, but I was glad I had. I also appreciated that she hadn't tried to push me for more information and had simply offered her quiet support.

Blowing out a heavy breath, I tried not to think about how it had felt to have her body so close to mine while talking about my late wife. I'd expected to feel guilty, like I was doing something wrong, but those feelings never came.

It had felt right instead, to let her in that little bit further, to reveal our loss to her. It wasn't like Alice and her death were a big secret or anything, but it meant a lot to me that she hadn't simply looked me up on the internet to determine who and where Winter's mother was.

For the most part, I'd managed to keep Winter and Alice out of the press, but I knew the truth was out there. It wasn't something I could hide and I hadn't wanted to.

A part of me had wondered when Tiffeny hadn't asked earlier if she already knew, if perhaps Julia knew and had told her. When I saw her reaction last night, I knew that hadn't been the case.

She genuinely hadn't known and had waited to hear about it from me. Sure, I hadn't told her everything just yet, but I would.

All in good time.

I hadn't wanted to overwhelm her with everything when things between us were still so new. I didn't want to take the chance of scaring her off with all my damage. It shouldn't have surprised me that Tiffeny hadn't reacted like I'd expected her to react either.

There hadn't been an outpouring of sympathy or that rearing-back thing some people did when confronted by someone else's grief or loss. She hadn't tried to sweep it under the table and she hadn't tried to cheer me up somehow.

All of those things had made it feel that much more right to have told her about Alice. Even when that wave of want had hit me when we kissed, I still hadn't felt guilty. I supposed this was what it felt like to accept Alice was gone and that it was okay for me to have a life after her.

Honestly? It felt good to have reached this point.

Without Tiffeny, I wasn't sure how much longer it would have taken me to get here, and I wanted to thank her for that. I also had to keep my promise to make up for last night.

I had a plan, though. All I had to do was set it in motion.

I picked up my phone again and scrolled to Julia's number. Tiffeny had sent us Julia's number before she'd watched Winter the first time, but I'd never used it before.

It explained why Julia sounded surprised when she answered. "Callen? Hi. Is everything okay?"

"Everything's fine," I assured her. "I was actually calling to ask you a favor."

"Okay," she said slowly, confusion in her voice. "What's the favor?"

"Will you be able to watch Winter for me tonight? I want to take Tiffeny out to dinner, just the two of us."

She paused for a beat, then cleared her throat. "Sure, okay. I'll watch her, but then you'll owe me one, right?"

"Right." I frowned, my eyes narrowing as I wondered what I was getting myself into. "Do you have something in mind, or would I just owe you?"

"Don't sound so suspicious." She laughed. "It's my birthday on Friday and I've rented out a bar. If I watch Winter for you tonight, I'd like you to play a song at my birthday party."

A relieved breath I hadn't realized I'd been holding left my lungs. "That's it? I play one song at your party and you'll stay with Winter tonight?"

"That's it."

I grinned. "In that case, you got yourself a deal."

"Great." There was a definite undercurrent of excitement in her tone now. "What time do you need me to be there?"

We worked out the logistics, then hung up. Winter brought over a feather she'd found, then went in search of a worm while I got back to my guitar.

Julia arrived at precisely six, the time we'd arranged for her to get there. I'd told Winter Julia was coming, and she was excited, zooming to the door the second she heard the knock.

"Thanks for agreeing to do this," I said when she walked in.

She tossed her red hair over her shoulder and shot me a grin. "No problem, but just so you know, I'd have done it anyway. It's no big deal. I like Winter."

"Yeah, well, having to play one song at your party isn't going to be much of a big deal to me either, so I guess we both got off easy."

A sparkle shot into her eye that let me know she wanted to make some kind of joke about getting off easy, but then her gaze drifted to Winter, and she let it go. "Hey, honey. You ready to have some fun?"

Twenty minutes later, I pulled up outside Tiffeny's house. Julia had given me her address and I was ridiculously excited about surprising her. Even if it was on a Sunday night.

When she opened her door, she just blinked at me for a few seconds, as if she was trying to make sure I wasn't about to disappear and that I really was here.

I smirked. "Told you I'd make it up to you soon."

She gaped at me, but then her full lips spread into a slow smile. "You did. I wasn't expecting it to be quite so soon, though."

"Yeah, well." I shrugged. "I figured I'd strike while the iron was hot. So are you coming?"

"Coming where?" She looked down and motioned to her torso. "I'm not exactly dressed to go anywhere."

She was wearing black yoga pants and an oversized black T-shirt. Her hair was pulled up into a high, messy ponytail, and she didn't have any makeup on. She also wasn't wearing any shoes, and her toenails were painted bubblegum pink.

"You're perfect just the way you are. We're not going anywhere fancy."

It took another minute to get her to agree not to change, but then she went inside to grab shoes and her purse, and we were off. She turned in the passenger seat of my car to look at me. "Where are we going?"

"You'll see." I grinned and shifted gears, driving out to a picnic spot I'd looked up online.

It wasn't far from her house and overlooked the ocean and a park. Moonlight broke through the clouds occasionally, and the orange glow of the streetlights nearby provided the only other light as we made our way to a grassy patch on top of a small hill.

I spread out the blanket I was carrying and set down the basket of picnic stuff I'd picked up on the way to her house on top of it. Tiffeny arched a brow at me, a smile playing at the corners of her lips.

"I don't know if I took Mr. Tattooed Rock Star as a romantic picnic under the stars kind of guy." She sat down with her legs crossed and watched as I did the same. "I have to say, though, I'm impressed. I've always wanted to do this."

"You've never had a picnic before?" I reached for the basket and unpacked the contents while she leaned back on her hands.

"I have, but not like this. I've always wondered why people insist on going to restaurants for dates when they could be doing something like this. It's more personal, you know?"

"Agreed." Spreading out the containers with the food, I pointed at each one as I went. "So we've got Asian chicken lettuce wraps, mini crab cakes with horseradish sauce, and lemon garlic orzo with roasted vegetables." I smiled as I pulled out the last container. "Also cheesecake and berries for dessert."

Tiffeny rubbed her hands together, reaching for one of the small cheesecakes first. "Why save the best for last?"

"Apparently, you don't." I laughed, shaking my head as I uncorked the bottle of champagne I'd brought along. Unfortunately, I hadn't thought of everything. "I just realized I don't have any glasses. We'll have to drink out of the bottle."

"I don't mind." It sounded like she meant it, which was just another example of why this woman was different from so many others I'd met in the last few years.

She didn't put on any airs and graces, despite her privileged upbringing. She was genuine, real, easygoing, and was perfectly happy to eat out of cardboard containers and drink from a bottle. *My kind of girl.*

"What made you decide you had to make up for last night as soon as tonight?" she asked, her head cocked as she took small bites of her dessert. "I meant it when I said there was no rush."

"I know, but I didn't want to wait," I said. "I felt bad about last night. I didn't want you to think I wasn't interested or that I was just trying to use Winter as an excuse."

"I knew you weren't using her." She lowered her head and looked at me through thick, dark eyelashes, humor lighting her eyes. "Was that your way of telling me that you're interested, though? Because that's kind of smooth, saying it without really saying it."

"Guess I'm just a smooth guy then," I joked. "But yeah, I am interested. I thought I'd made that clear by now."

"You have, but it's still nice to hear it." She tucked an escaped tendril of hair behind her ear and pointed at me with a crab cake. "In case *you* didn't already know, I'm interested too."

"Good. Glad we got that out of the way." The truth was that I was more than interested in her. I was starting to have feelings for her. But luckily, I was good at hiding those because it was way too soon to tell her how I felt.

"How was your day?" I asked instead. "Do anything interesting?"

She shook her head and swallowed the bite in her mouth before answering. "It was Sunday. Sundays were not designed to do interesting things. They were designed to be lazy and not feel bad about it."

"True story, but only until you have kids. Once you do, you've got to figure out interesting things to do every day. Sundays included."

"Isn't it good for them to be bored sometimes?" she asked, narrowing her eyes in thought. "I read somewhere that it is."

I nodded. "Sure, it's supposed to be good for them because it forces them to think of creative ways to keep busy, but it still doesn't mean you've got the day off."

"It doesn't seem like parents ever get the day off," she said, her teeth tugging at her bottom lip. "I think I'm still too selfish for all that. I love my days off. Sometimes, it feels like my shop is my child, but at least I get to lock the doors whenever I want and walk away."

"Maybe, but the constancy of parenthood is totally worth it." I popped another bite into my mouth, chewing as I thought. "You do want kids though, don't you? I know we touched on it the other night at your mom's, but we never actually had the conversation with each other."

Her eyes widened, but her tone was teasing. "Isn't it a little early in our relationship to be talking about this?"

"We were on the topic." I shrugged. "But fine. Let's talk about something else then. How do you feel about the state of global politics?"

"I'd rather talk about kids." She laughed. "Like I said, Sundays are for being lazy. Debating global politics is not something one does while being lazy. I will tell you this, though. Overall, global politics is becoming increasingly dysfunctional and there's so much at stake that I really feel like a lot of leaders need to get their shit together."

"Sometimes, I forget that you're actually really smart," I said with a smile.

She rolled her eyes. "What? Because I own an ice-cream shop and never finished law school?"

"No, because you don't feel the need to show off your intellect by rubbing it in people's faces or walking around with an overly inflated ego because of it." Another thing I liked about her.

"You're one to talk," she threw back at me. "You're smart, rich, and literally famous, but you're not a cocky dick. Why is that?"

"Hey, I can be as much of a cocky dick as the next guy. I just choose to focus on what's actually important rather than superficial material stuff."

She paused for a beat, her head dropping to one side and her eyes on mine. "What do you consider as being really important then?"

"Who a person is over what they have," I said. "Staying true to myself and being around people who do the same. Winter, obviously. Keeping my feet on the ground and my head on my shoulders for her. What about you? What's important to you?"

"The same stuff, but also friendship, following my heart, and seizing every day."

"Even the lazy ones?"

"Even the lazy ones," she confirmed with a smile. "Speaking of friendship, I'm assuming Julia is watching Winter?"

"Yes, she is. Those two get along like a house on fire. I just hope they don't literally set mine on fire with whatever it is they get up to together."

"They won't." She laughed. "I'm kind of jealous of her for getting to spend the time with Winter, but I'm also really happy to be here with you."

"So am I." We changed the topic to lighter things for the rest of our dinner, then packed up after lingering for a while once we were done.

It was a Sunday night, after all. Tiffeny had to open up her shop early in the morning, and although I wasn't ready to end our night and take her home, that was exactly what I did.

I walked her in, holding her hand as we entered her dark entrance hall. Expecting her to tell me goodnight, I could only stare when she suddenly released my hand to put both of hers on my chest. She pressed her body flush against mine and looked up at me with an entirely different look in her eyes than had been there earlier.

There was only desire there now. Pure, raw lust that slammed into me and turned my brain to its most carnal setting.

"So are you going to make up for what we missed out on last night now?" she asked, her voice low and husky and a sexy smile lifting the corners of her mouth.

"Yes." I needed to fuck her. Hard. My brain was repeating that sentence as if it had adopted it as its new mantra. We'd had a good night together, talking and getting to know each other, but we'd changed gears now.

The time for talking was done.

I reached behind me and pulled off my shirt, dropping it on the floor before hauling her against me and crashing my mouth down onto hers.

CHAPTER 20

TIFFENY

Callen kissed me like he was on fire and I was the only one capable of dousing it. Or maybe the analogy had just come to mind because I felt like I had flames licking under my skin and I knew he could put them out.

I ached for him, needed him more than I'd previously have thought it was possible to need another person. My hands slid across his broad shoulders, my fingers meeting at the nape of his neck. I toyed with the short hair I found there, tugging and holding him to me at the same time.

He kicked my front door shut behind him, then turned us around and walked us backward until my back was pressed to that same door. He didn't stop kissing me, his tongue twisting and stroking mine with expert-level technique. *God, he's good at this.*

I moaned into his mouth, arching my back to bring my body even closer to his. One of his hands was on the wall slightly above us, caging me in like I used to see boys do to girls back in high school. I'd never been one of those girls, though. This was a first for me and I liked it. *A lot.*

Then again, I liked everything he did. Especially when it came to more intimate activities.

His other hand had been on my hip, but it slid underneath my shirt now, and his fingers splayed across my rib cage. His thumb brushed the underside of my breast, and I gasped, another moan escaping right after.

He did it again, the corners of his mouth curving up against mine. "You like that, huh?"

"Yes," I practically hissed.

When I ran my fingers into his hair to bring his lips back to mine, he resisted and lowered his head instead. He nipped and sucked at the skin on my jaw, my neck, his hand staying maddeningly still and not moving to touch me in any of the places I wanted to be touched—except for little brushes he kept giving me.

"Callen, please." I knew it wasn't exactly sexy that I was this desperate already, but I was. *Really desperate.*

My clit throbbed painfully, and since my yoga pants didn't have much of a seam, there wasn't any relief to be found in friction there. I squeezed my thighs together, and Callen noticed.

"Callen, please *what?*" he growled against my collarbone, sliding his strong, thick thigh between my legs and making me cry out when he pressed it firmly against me. "You want to come?"

I nodded, my eyes shut against the pleasure of having his leg where it was. If I wasn't careful, I was going to grind myself to orgasm right there. *Now* that *would be embarrassing.*

But I was so ready for him that it was a real possibility if I didn't watch out. Biting my lip, I felt him sliding his hand out from under my shirt and touching his fingers to my chin.

My eyes flew open to protest against his hand now being even farther away from anywhere I so desperately needed to be touched, but then I saw the look in his eyes. They were half-lidded and pools of molten, liquid heat, his pupils dilated, and his breathing labored.

It seemed he had been waiting for me to look at him. "If you want to come, all you have to do is say so."

Say so? As in, say it out loud? Okay then. I could talk dirty if I actually gave it a try. I was sure of it. Forcing my mouth to form the words turned out to be rather easy, considering what the prize for doing it was going to be. "I want to come, Callen. Please."

That was shockingly easy. Unfortunately, the empowerment that flowed through me for having told him in so many words what I wanted got me even hotter and more desperate. *Note to self: practice dirty talk so as not to get turned on by the power of your own words.*

As I bucked my hips against his leg, he pulled it away. A groan tore out of my chest. "I thought all I had to do was ask."

"It is, but I'm not letting you come by getting yourself off on my leg. We can do better than that."

"We can? Because that felt pretty damn good to me."

"But this will feel better. I promise." Callen smirked and dropped to his knees. My heart started pounding when he hooked his thumbs into the waistband of my yoga pants and panties. He rolled both off at the same time, removing my sandals when he reached my feet.

I kicked the clothes free, extremely self-conscious of the fact that there was a very hot, very talented man kneeling in front of me, face to face with my pussy. *And I've been in yoga pants all day.*

Before I could cringe or even try to warn him, he let out a sharp groan, followed by an unsteady breath. "Jesus, Tiffeny. I want to live down here. Do you know how fucking beautiful this pussy is?"

Stunned that he could just say stuff like that so naturally and casually, I was still trying to process when he suddenly licked me. His tongue was soft when I needed it to be and speared when I needed that.

It didn't take long before he reduced me to a shaking, moaning mess as he sent me skyrocketing into the abyss. Exquisite pleasure spread from my pulsing core to the very tips of my damn hair, curling my toes and making me feel like my knees were no longer strong enough to support me.

Callen's strong hands held me up, his mouth staying on me until he'd seen me through to the other side of my spectacular orgasm. Then he stood up. Without a word, he slid one hand behind my back and the other behind my useless knees, then lifted me up like I weighed nothing.

"Which way is your bedroom?" he asked, his voice rough.

I pointed a shaky finger down the hall. "Second door on the left."

As he carried me, he looked down and raised an eyebrow. "What's the verdict? That was better than just grinding against me, right?"

"Definitely. You know you don't have to carry me, though, right? I can walk."

"I don't have to, but I want to. Also, I prefer to think that I just rocked your world so hard that you can't." Effortlessly moving us into my room, he laid me down on my bed and stood at the end of it.

The way he looked at me lying there, half-naked and probably embarrassingly soaked down there, made me feel like some kind of Queen of Seduction. Like I was so damn irresistible that a man like him had to clench his hands into fists and bite his bottom lip to keep from attacking me.

"What?" I asked, feeling his eyes on every inch of my exposed skin. Emboldened by the way he was looking at me, I decided to expose more. I sat up slightly, tugged my T-shirt off over my head, and quickly unhooked my bra.

Callen was still frozen, the ripped muscles on his stomach dipping as he watched me. There was a massive bulge in his pants, but he didn't seem to be in any hurry to get to it. He swallowed, then gave his head a little shake. "Nothing. I was just taking a very detailed mental picture because I don't think I have seen a sight this sexy for a long-ass fucking time."

I got up on my knees and moved over to him, looking into his eyes as I reached for his belt. "Really? How about now?"

"Holy shit." He swallowed, his Adam's apple rising and falling as he did. "Yep. Getting even sexier. Fuck."

Fingers on the buckle of his belt, I undid it as fast as trying to be at least a little sultry would allow and unzipped him. He stepped out of his pants once I pushed them past his hips and stood in front of me in nothing but black boxer briefs.

I rolled them off next, careful when I freed his raging erection. The tip of it was already wet. Without even having to think about it, I leaned forward to take him into my mouth.

The sound he let out was borderline animalistic. His hips thrust forward, and his hands wound into my hair, holding it so tightly that it was right at the edge between pleasure and pain.

Encouraged by his reaction, I took him deeper. My hand came up to wrap around his thick shaft, covering what I couldn't fit in my mouth.

"Fuck, Tiffeny. I—" Breath left his lungs in a hiss and his head tipped back as he sent a piercing glare to the ceiling. Watching him made me ache all over again, my sensitive skin humming to be touched.

Before I could second-guess myself, my free hand was between my legs while my tongue swirled around his tip. His head fell forward, his eyes raking over me.

As he noticed the ministrations of the hand not on him, he moaned so loudly, I was afraid my neighbors might have heard him. "As much as I want to see that, your pleasure belongs to me tonight."

He pulled out of me the next second, pushing my back to the mattress more gently than I'd have thought following a statement like that. He had his wallet in his hand faster than I knew a person could move, extracting a foil packet.

"I hope it wasn't too presumptuous, but I bought these after our first time. Figured it was better to be prepared."

"Preparation trumps presumptuousness." I took the condom from between his fingers and ripped it open with my teeth. Letting the foil fall, I unrolled the latex onto him and smiled when I met his eyes. "Well, what are you waiting for?"

His eyelids flared. Then he covered me with his big body and thrust into me without any further ado. *Thank God.*

"Apparently, I was waiting for you to make all my dirty daydreams come true," he whispered against my ear.

"Glad I could be of service." I gave up trying to hold back my moans and proceeded to throw caution to the wind as far as my neighbors were concerned.

Let them hear me because Callen sure as hell deserves to know how good he is making me feel.

After making me see heaven and hear angels sing two more times, he finally followed me over the edge. His muscles quivered and he kissed me deeply as he came buried deep inside me.

Collapsing next to my side after taking care of the condom, he held me close for what felt like hours. I snuggled into his side, my hand on his chest feeling his heartbeat returning to normal.

"I would stay," Callen murmured as he ran his fingers through my hair, "but there's this other woman I need to get back to."

Despite my sleepy, sated state, I let out a laugh and gently smacked his chest. "You know, this is the only kind of circumstance I'm okay with you saying something like that."

"It's the only circumstance in which I would say something like that," he promised, his voice barely above a whisper and still oh-so-damn sexy. "I'd better get going. If I lie here any longer, I'm going to give in to the cellular wiring to go to sleep after having sex like that."

"Sex like what?" I asked, my lips curling into a smile as I sat up when he did.

He shot me a pointed look and lifted a brow before bending over to grab his underwear and pants from the floor. "You know exactly what, but I'll say it anyway. That was incredible, and I can't wait to do it again."

"Who says you're going to do it again?" I teased, bringing my knees up to my chest under the sheet and draping my arms around them.

He pulled on his pants, then his shirt, unfortunately hiding that glorious body from my view while also rolling his eyes at me. "I say we're going to do it again. A lot, as often as we can."

"Fine." I blew out a breath in mock exasperation when in truth, there were all these bright, happy bubbles of joy floating through my insides. "If you insist. I suppose I could pencil you in. How'd you get Julia to watch Winter to give us this opportunity, though?"

"I have to do something for her Friday night." He leaned over and kissed my forehead, clearly just about ready to leave. "I'll see you then, yeah?"

"Yeah, I'll be there." Before he lifted his head away from mine, I grabbed it and kissed him again, a long, slow kiss full of passion and promise. I hated that he had to leave, but I understood why. So I stopped mauling his lips with mine eventually and gave him a pat on the butt. "Okay, you can go now."

"Thanks." He chuckled, pressing his forehead to mine for a full minute as we just breathed each other in, all traces of humor disappearing. "I really am sorry I have to go, beautiful. Maybe, hopefully, one day, I won't have to."

CHAPTER 21

CALLEN

"We're going to Julia's party," Winter sing-songed from her car seat in the back, the serene smile she'd been wearing all week still fixed to her face. I couldn't say I didn't like it, though.

Winter was happier than I'd seen her in a long time, thanks in no small part to knowing Tiffeny was coming with us tonight. She'd also had a blast with Julia on Sunday night and had insisted that I take her to the mall with me to pick up a present for Julia, even when I told her I already had it handled.

"Yeah, but remember what I said, okay?" Usually, I wouldn't be taking Winter to a party at a bar with me. Especially if I had to perform. For however brief a period I was obligated to do it.

I'd called ahead, though. There was no smoking area anywhere near where we'd be and the manager had assured me that although the place wasn't labeled to be family-friendly, it wasn't rowdy or rough either.

Plus, Tiffeny and I had discussed it and she'd offered to help me take care of Winter. She also said she wouldn't let her out of her sight while I was up onstage.

While I knew it was frowned upon to take your baby to a bar, I was pretty excited to have her with us tonight. So was Tiffeny. No one was more excited than Winter, though.

"Yes, Daddy. I remember. Stay close to you or Tiffeny and I'm not allowed to talk to strangers."

"Good girl." I grinned at her in the rearview mirror as we pulled up outside of Tiffeny's house.

She was waiting for us on her front porch. When she saw my car, she waved and walked up to meet us.

As always, she took my breath away when I first saw her. She wasn't wearing anything fancy, just jeans and a frilly purple top with sandals, but she was fucking stunning. Her hair was loose, framing her face and tumbling past her shoulders in shiny dark waves.

She had on a little more makeup than I was used to seeing her in, her eyes lined with charcoal and her lids covered in shimmery, dark gray. It made her eyes stand out, and the overall effect was dazzling.

"Hey," she said when I climbed out of the car to greet her. "Thanks for picking me up."

"Anytime." I drew her into a hug that ended far too soon. "Winter's really excited to see you."

"I'm excited to see her, too." Tiffeny got into the passenger seat, buckled up, and immediately turned to start chatting to my daughter while I took my place behind the wheel again.

The girls talked all the way to the bar, where Julia had reserved space for us and her other guests in a small lot nearby. The weather was nice, the sun starting to set as we walked down the sidewalk. Winter held my hand in one of hers and Tiffeny's in the other.

"It always smells like the sea here," she said. "Are we close to the beach?"

"It's just a couple of blocks that way." Tiffeny jerked her head to the left, smiling as she looked down at Winter. "Do you like the smell of the sea?"

"I love it." Winter beamed. "I love Murple Beach."

"Myrtle, honey," I corrected as gently as I could. "It's Myrtle Beach with a T."

"Oh." She giggled and nudged Tiffeny with her shoulder. "Do you like the smell?"

"I do. It's one of my favorites." She met my eyes over Winter's head and whispered, "Your smell, too."

Well, fuck if I could stop smiling after that. I'd used the same body spray since shortly after high school and rarely wore cologne. I preferred crisp and clean, and apparently so did Tiffeny.

We pushed through the double glass doors into the bar Julia had rented out, and I laughed when I heard Clark's voice coming through the speakers. I smirked at Tiffeny and nodded at the one closest to us. "This is one of our songs. Kraken, I mean."

Her eyes widened, but then she smiled and shook her head. "Go figure. I told you Julia was a huge fan of yours. I wouldn't be surprised if she's cued your music up to play all night."

"You made it," Julia squealed with a huge grin. She threw her arms around Tiffeny first, then hugged Winter next. She just nodded at me, though. "Thanks for coming."

"Of course." Tiffeny dug a small, gift-wrapped package out of her purse. "Happy birthday."

"Thanks." Her eyes swept across the three of us, her lips curling into a knowing smile. "You know, you guys look good together."

Tiffeny's cheeks flushed, but she didn't reply. Winter had been carrying our gift in her fluffy backpack and was too preoccupied trying to find it in between all the coloring books and toys that we'd brought to be paying much attention.

Before I could even begin to formulate how to reply to that, Winter found the gift and presented it proudly to Julia. "This is from Daddy and me."

"Thanks, sweetheart. Thanks Callen. You want me to open it now?"

Winter nodded enthusiastically, practically bouncing as she watched Julia rip right through the paper. "It's a bracelet," she blurted out before Julia had even opened the box it came in. "It has a music-note charm on it. Daddy said you like music. I picked out the nail polish charm."

145

Julia cracked open the box and her hand flew to her chest. "This is gorgeous. Thank you, guys."

"You're welcome," I said, "but you might want to have a look at what else is hiding in the wrapping paper."

Julia frowned, shaking out the paper. The album I'd slid in beneath the box fell out, but she caught it in her hand before it fell. She recognized it immediately and let out a shrill, short scream when she noticed what set it apart from whatever albums of ours she might have had already.

"You had everyone sign it?" she asked me with eyes wider than they should have been able to go without her eyeballs falling out.

I shrugged. "I mean, I do keep in touch with the other guys. It's no big deal."

"No big deal?" she squealed again before tackling me in a hug. "This is a huge deal. Thank you so much."

It really wasn't a huge deal, but arguing about it wouldn't get me anywhere. Despite the fact that I was technically repaying her favor tonight, I'd wanted to do something nice for her.

Thanks to her agreeing to watch Winter on Sunday, I'd had a great fucking night that I wouldn't forget for as long as I lived. The sight of Tiffeny's lips wrapped around my cock and the sound of her moans in my ears had been... *Just. Fuck.*

Julia ran off with the album after fastening the bracelet to her wrist and thanking us again. Tiffeny leaned into my side. "That was really awesome of you to do for her."

I lifted one of my shoulders in another shrug, but a corner of my mouth inched up. "She should be thanking you, really."

She laughed and bumped my shoulder with hers. "If you mean what I think you mean, you're welcome. I'll be sure to let her know that gift was really from me."

Reclaiming Winter's hand, she nodded toward the bar. "I'm going to get us something to drink. You want anything?"

"Just a water, thanks," I said.

I trailed after them to the bar, staying close to Winter throughout the night, but Tiffeny was the one really taking care of her. She got her juice or water whenever she wanted, walked her to the bathroom, made sure she ate, and sat with her while she did.

The way she was looking after her was with as much dedication and devotion as if Winter was her own daughter. It made my heart soar and clench at the same time, but before I could give it much thought, my name was being called from the stage.

"You guys good?" I asked one last time before I took the stage.

Tiffeny grinned with her arm around Winter's shoulders. "We're great. We'll be right here cheering you on. It's your turn to repay the favor, superstar. Rock our socks off."

I groaned, shaking my head at her. "You're not even wearing any socks, but that's not the point. No one says that anymore."

"I do." She shimmied her shoulders, laughing as she waved me off. "Go on. We'll be fine."

I put up my hands in surrender. "Fine, fine. I'm going. See you soon."

The gathered crowd parted for me as I made my way to the stage. I'd stowed my guitar there earlier in the afternoon when the owner had insisted I come by for a very fast soundcheck, so it was waiting for me in its stand.

I picked it up and slung the strap over my shoulder. Walking to the microphone, I channeled Clark and wrapped my fingers around it when I stepped up. "What's going on, guys?"

Julia's friends and family cheered. Some screamed while others whistled or waved their arms. Although the audience was much smaller than I'd been playing to for the last few years, I felt that thrill I'd been missing up onstage as I watched them.

"We're all here to celebrate Julia's birthday. I haven't known her all that long, but she's a great girl, and I'm honored to be sharing the day with her." More cheers. "Okay, so I've been told Hallowed Nights is a favorite of hers, so I'm going to give it a try by myself tonight. You might have to bear with me, seeing as how I'm not Clark and I don't have any of the boys here to back me up, but I'm going to give the acoustic version of our first hit song my best shot."

The crowd went mad, only quieting down when I started strumming the first bars. I'd always loved this song, and it flowed out of me freely and easily, like the last time I'd played it had been this morning instead of months ago.

I'd written it about those early nights when Clark and I had still been trying to get a band together, the nights we'd stayed up drinking, dreaming, and talking shit until the birds started chirping outside. *Great memories.*

The majority of the audience sang along to every word and the experience was strangely haunting and humbling in a way I'd forgotten intimate crowds could be. By the time I played the last note, I was solidly in the zone and enjoying myself too much to stop now.

"Guess you liked that even without the full band, huh?" I smirked, still trying to channel Clark's effortless charm with the audience.

Judging by their wild reaction, faking it till I made it seemed to be working. "I was only supposed to play one song tonight, but there's another one I'd like to do if that's okay with you."

My question was greeted by an overwhelmingly positive response and my smirk morphed into a genuine smile. "This next one isn't well known. In fact, you'll be the first people outside of my family and best friend to hear it. I wrote it for my daughter, Winter. She's here tonight and she'll be the only person here who can sing along to it, but I hope you like it anyway. It's called String Bean. Here we go."

There was a reason I'd never put this song up for release, even though Clark had begged me to. It was deeply personal, about my feelings after Winter was born and how she'd been so small and skinny.

Playing it now felt good, though. Letting these strangers into my innermost thoughts and fears when I'd first become a father wasn't daunting. It was freeing.

When the last note faded, more than a few people—men included —were wiping their eyes and nodding. I lifted my guitar off and set it back on its stand. "Thank you for having me, thank you for listening to me, and happy birthday to our guest of honor, Julia."

The woman in question was standing with Tiffeny and Winter

when I made my way back to them. She sniffled and gave me a hug. "Thank you for that. You were amazing."

"Thanks." I released her and picked Winter up before finally looking fully at Tiffeny for the first time after she'd heard me play. Her eyes were misty and her smile soft. "So, what did you think?"

"You're incredible," she said. "You should definitely sing more often. I love Winter's song. It's beautiful."

So are you. "Do you think I've successfully converted you to being a fan?"

She rolled her eyes, but her lips spread into a wide smile. "You wish, but maybe. Do you have any other obligations here tonight?"

"No," I said. "I promised one song. I did two. Why?"

She looked between Winter and me, the smile still on her lips. "What do you guys say to some late-night ice cream? With the formalities done, the party's bound to start getting out of hand. I don't know about you, but I think I'd rather duck out before that happens."

A part of me suspected she was doing this for Winter, to get her out of here before the party really got into full swing, and I appreciated the hell out of that. "Late-night ice cream sounds great to me."

"And to me too," Winter agreed, then surprised me when she bent in my arms and held hers out to Tiffeny instead. "Will you hold me? I liked sitting with you earlier."

"Of course." Tiffeny glanced at me to check and, when I nodded, opened her arms and took Winter into them.

It did strange things to me to see that, things I wasn't sure how I felt about just yet.

CHAPTER 22

TIFFENY

I flipped the lights on when we walked into my shop, then swept my arm out ahead of me and grinned down at Winter. "The kingdom is yours, my dear. What do you want to do first?"

"Anything?" she asked, clear blue eyes wide and excited.

I nodded. "Anything at all."

Her head swung from side to side as she considered her options. "I want to make a new flavor."

"Sure, what flavor?" I asked as I led her around the counter to the machines.

Callen followed after us. "Are you really going to give a three-year-old free rein? Because that seems dangerous to me."

"Blueberry and Mint Choc Chip," she said, ignoring Callen's warning. "We'll call it Blue Chip."

I sent a wink to Callen and nodded at Winter. "One Blue Chip coming up."

Grabbing one of my sample cups, I opened the display case and mixed a small scoop of each requested flavor. "Try it first. Then tell us what you think."

Winter took the cup and lifted the small plastic spoon to her mouth, savoring the flavor before bouncing enthusiastically. "It's good. Try it."

Callen and I exchanged a look. Then he took two more sample cups off the stack and handed them over. "You might have created a monster. The least you can do is share in the torment."

"Fair enough." I laughed but mixed us a Blue Chip each and passed his cup to him. "Cheers. I look forward to seeing what we're trying next."

He held his cup between us for me to clink mine against it, doing the same with Winter before taking his first bite. I took mine, too.

And honestly? It was better than I thought it would be but still gross.

Callen pulled a face and set his cup down. "Let's try again, sweetheart. I'm not sure about blueberry and mint."

Winter had polished off all of hers. She shrugged at her father. "It wasn't that bad."

Banana and mint was worse, as was cookies and cream with hazelnut, butternut and fig. I laughed at the last one and set down my cup. "You know, I think it would be fine without the fig."

"Agreed," Callen said. "Think we can sit the next one out?"

"I don't know. That's up to Winter."

She looked between us but was distracted by all the flavors she had left to mix. "Sure. I can eat ice cream by myself."

Callen ruffled her hair. "Thanks, my love. I just don't think I'm cut out for all these adventurous choices."

"That's okay, Daddy. I think they're fun."

Callen and I sat down in a booth near the display case, watching as Winter heaped scoops of God only knew what into the next cup. He sighed but couldn't quite hold back a smile. "Have you ever heard that sugar keeps kids awake and turns them into monsters at night?"

"She could never be a monster."

He pursed his lips. "You haven't seen her when she throws a tantrum. Thankfully, they're rare for her, but I once ruined her day by insisting she wear pants in Minnesota in the middle of winter."

"That's it?" I asked, tilting my head and grinning at him. "Because I've heard much worse stories about toddler tantrums."

"Trust me, that was a mild one. I just didn't want to scare you."

"Hit me," I said. "I can take it. What horror stories do you have?"

He chuckled. "She once screamed so loudly after I took a knife she'd found in my dressing room away that I could hear her crying even while I was onstage."

"Still tame. You're attuned to her cries. Of course, you'd hear her."

"There were more than five thousand people in the audience that night," he deadpanned. "And I heard a toddler screaming about a steak knife as we walked out."

"Getting better," I said. "But she was backstage and presumably close by when this happened?"

"Touché." He drummed his fingers on the table. "Okay, how about this? I once left a grocery store with an entire cart of feminine pads because she liked the colors on the packaging. And we'd only gone to get me new deodorant."

I felt my eyes growing wide, but I couldn't stop laughing at the mental image I conjured up. "What did you do with all of them?"

"Donated them eventually," he said, eyes crinkling at the corners. "But not before she got one package open and I walked into a meeting with our manager with a pad stuck to the side of my shoe."

"How did you not notice that?" I laughed, clapping a hand over my mouth.

He shrugged. "Single, sleep-deprived father. I surprised myself when I figured out I'd actually remembered to wear shoes."

My laughter stopped instantly. There was so much out there about single moms that I'd never given much thought to single dads before Callen had confided in me last weekend. A whole week had passed without any more information about Winter's mother and how Callen had become a single father, but I was resolutely waiting for him to tell me in his own time.

"You're a great dad," I said. "I hope you know that. That song you played for her? It was stunning. There should be more fathers out there like you."

"I'm sure there are," he joked. "They just don't write songs about it."

"But you did," I pressed because it didn't feel like any harm could come from wanting to learn more details about a song he'd sung voluntarily. "Tell me about String Bean. You said you wrote it for her?"

"I did," he mused. His eyes became unfocused as he stared at the wall behind me. "I can't even begin to describe to you how I felt when she was born. It was the best feeling ever, but it came with the weight of responsibility like nothing I'd ever felt before."

"I think that's probably normal."

He nodded, but he still didn't look at me. "After we took her home, she wasn't picking up weight like she was supposed to. She lost a lot more than what is normal. I looked at her one day and I couldn't help thinking that she looked like a string bean. She'd gotten taller, but she was so damn skinny."

Callen smiled, but it was a sad smile that didn't quite reach his eyes. "After I put her to bed that night, the lyrics just came to me. I wrote the whole song in less than twenty minutes, music included."

"Wow," I said. I had no idea what went into songwriting, but that seemed really impressive to me. Linking my hands together, I rested my chin on my fingers with my elbows propped on the table. "You must be quite something if you're able to put songs that good together so fast."

"I'm nothing special." He said it in a way that was just honest. He wasn't fishing for compliments or hoping I'd contradict him. "I love music. It's like breathing to me now. It just happens."

"What are your plans with music now?" I asked, inadvertently leaning forward as I waited for his answer. Guys like him belonged to Hollywood and crowds in stadiums, not simple girls from Myrtle Beach.

It hurt to even think about them leaving me, but I had to be realistic. He loved music with a passion and he was obviously good at writing it as well as making it. Whatever had brought him here wasn't going to last forever.

Eventually, he was likely to take off back on the road, recording in LA and doing whatever it was rock stars really did all day. He'd take Winter with him and I'd never hear from them again.

More than anything, that thought convinced me to just enjoy the time we had together. Callen, however, didn't seem to be thinking about hitting the road anytime soon.

"I don't have any plans with music right now. I've got enough money and I just want to spend some time with Winter before she gets mean in her teens, you know?"

"I don't think she'll ever get mean," I said, my eyes darting to the side to find Winter leaning heavily on the display case. Her eyes were half-closed and she looked dead on her feet.

Callen noticed the same thing I did, standing up with a smile shot in my direction. "I think we'd better get going. It's way past someone's bedtime and it seems to be catching up to her."

Winter let Callen pick her up, resting her head on his shoulder while I made quick work of switching off the lights and locking up.

They dropped me off at my house, but before I got out of the car, Winter stirred in her seat. "Bye, Tiffeny. I love you."

Her voice was sleepy but clear. Surprised and taken aback by her declaration, I blinked a few times before I acknowledged my melted heart. "I love you too, sweetheart. See you soon, okay?"

"Okay." She yawned.

When my eyes slid back to Callen's, there was a very forced-looking smile on his lips. He gave me a curt nod, not even trying for a hug.

"I'll call you, Tiffeny. You have a good night now."

"Yeah, you too." I got out of the car, but I watched them drive away. There had been something very wrong with that smile and the coolness in his voice when he told me he'd call me.

Everything had been fine all night, though.

Blowing out a breath, I decided to ignore it. *He's probably just tired.*

CHAPTER 23

CALLEN

"Have a great day, honey," I called to Winter as I dropped her off, waving until she disappeared into the center.

With a heavy sigh, I shifted my car into gear and merged into the traffic. All weekend, it had been a struggle to keep my mind off Tiffeny and on doing things with Winter.

Since it was Monday morning and she was back at school, I finally allowed myself to really think about what was bothering me about Friday night.

Winter had told Tiffeny that she loved her, and she'd meant it. I'd asked her about it on Saturday and she'd confirmed.

Hearing those words out of her mouth was like having someone shove a red-hot brand into my chest. The word it felt like it had seared into my skin was *traitor*.

Logically, I knew it wasn't true. Winter loving a woman who wasn't her mother didn't equate to me betraying Alice. Emotionally, however, it felt like that was exactly what I had done.

Navigating the relationship Winter was forming with Tiffeny was proving as perilous as trying to navigate my own with her. On the one hand, I was glad they got along so well and that Tiffeny loved her, too.

On the other, that part of my heart that still belonged to Alice revolted. It rebelled against the idea that another woman would hear those words from her daughter when Alice herself had never gotten the opportunity to hear them herself.

Lost in the warring parts of my heart and brain, I drove home. It was only when I got there to find an unfamiliar car in my driveway that I snapped out of it.

Furrowing my brow as I parked, I craned my neck to see a figure sitting on the step outside the front door. Unlike the car, the figure was very much familiar.

A wide smile spread on my face as I shut the engine down and hopped out of the car. "Clark? What are you doing here?"

Already in the process of standing up, he walked over to me and offered me his hand while pulling me into a hug. "I came to see you obviously. How's it hanging, man?"

"We're good." I stepped out of his back-thumping hug and fished my house keys out of my pocket. "How about you?"

"Well, it took me a while to find your house, but here I am. I was hoping to catch you before you took Winter to day-care." He followed me in after I unlocked the door.

Stopping in the entrance hall, his eyes swept across the modest space, the pictures and album covers on the walls and the rug beneath his feet. "Wow. Looks like you've really settled in here."

"Yeah, well, what can I say? I was tired of living with a thousand boxes." I shrugged and tossed my keys into the bowl on the side table, jerking my chin in the direction of the kitchen. "You want some coffee? You still haven't told me what you're really doing here."

"Coffee would be great," he said, dragging a hand across his face. "I've been up since three a.m., so make mine extra strong."

"I can do that." Clark took a seat at the island while I flipped on the coffeemaker and grabbed some mugs from the cabinet above it. After getting the sugar and cream ready, I leaned my hip against the counter and faced him. "Why have you been up since three?"

"Last leg of the drive," he said. "I was really hoping to catch a glimpse of my goddaughter this morning. I miss that kid."

"So you got a new car, then?" I asked, tipping my head to the front of the house. "I didn't recognize that one."

"Yeah, the label gave it to me to sweeten the deal during negotiations for a new album. It's an Audi. If you like it, you can have it. I was happy with my truck."

"Why'd you take it?"

He lifted a shoulder. "One of the meetings we had was at this beachside bistro. Jared, you remember him right? The exec? Anyway, he saw me admiring one leaving the parking lot, and the next day, this one arrived on my doorstep. Felt rude to give it back."

I laughed as the pot started filling with coffee. "Being given a car and feeling too bad to give it back? Now that's a different level of first-world problems, my friend."

"Yeah, I know." He flashed me a sheepish grin. "Which brings us full circle to your first question. I'm here because I have this swanky new car and contract, but I really don't want to record without you. I've been in the studio a few times, but something just feels off."

My brows rose. I filled our mugs, fixed the coffee, and handed his over. I joined him at the island, putting my feet up on the rung of the stool. My knee started bouncing because I wasn't sure I liked where this was going. "You came to lure me back to LA? Because I gotta tell you straight up, that's not happening right now."

"You don't have to come back to LA necessarily. I have a tour starting in a few weeks and we can record on the road. Wouldn't be the first time."

With a firm shake of my head, I flashed him a small, apologetic smile. "I can't go back on the road in a few weeks. Winter loves it here. She's really settled in at the day-care center and I just finished unpacking the other day."

Clark's shoulders lowered, and disappointment flashed in his eyes, but he nodded. "I figured you were going to say that, but I had to give it a try."

"Just because I'm saying no to touring and recording right away doesn't mean I can't help you at all. It's like I said. I need some time to sort things out, but I have been writing. There are a few more songs you can record and I can help you fine-tune them to your style before you leave."

"Yeah, okay. That'd be great. It's not having you with me, but I guess it's the next best thing." He took a sip of his coffee and cracked his neck. "What are your plans for today?"

"I was actually going to do some writing, so you've got good timing." As I lifted my head to take a sip of my own, my eyes landed on the light green depths of his. "I'm glad you're here. It's good to see you, even if I have to turn down your offer."

His lips curved into a grin. "I'm glad I'm here, too. I can't wait to see Winter and I'm even excited to spend some time with your sorry ass."

"Hey, my ass isn't sorry. It's hot." I smirked, but it dropped when I saw the surprised expression on his face. His brows were slightly pinched, his lips pursed, and his head fell to the side. "What?"

"Nothing. I just haven't heard a comeback like that from you in a long time. For the record, one's ass can be hot and sorry at the same time, but just hearing you say something like that in that tone makes me think it might not be so sorry anymore. What gives?"

"I met someone," I admitted, then brought up a hand to squeeze the back of my neck.

Clark choked on his coffee and banged his fist against his chest as he lifted his watery eyes to mine. "You what?"

"You heard me."

"Yeah." He grinned and rubbed his finger at the base of his ear. "I'm just not sure what I heard was correct. Long drive, early start. Air pressure differences. Maybe my ears aren't functioning properly because I could've sworn I just heard you say you 'met someone.'"

He made air quotes with his fingers on the last two words, then scooted forward on his seat and propped his elbows on the table.

I laughed. If only his fans knew how much their tattooed, charismatic, supposedly bad-boy idol loved gossip, his reputation would be shattered.

"Calm down, Clark. You look like your tongue is about to loll out and you're going to start panting."

"Any second now," he agreed. "So what gives? Who is this some-one? Have you finally broken your celibacy vows? What does she look like? Do you have a picture?"

Dropping my head back as I laughed, I lifted my hands with my palms out. "Slow down, bud. I'll tell you whatever you want to know, but I can only remember so many questions at a time. Her name is Tiffeny. I don't have a picture, but I really should. She's gorgeous and yes, we've been intimate."

He let out a loud whoop and gave the air a victory punch. It was ridiculous, but his theatrics also made me smile.

"Way to go, Tiffeny," he hollered, his hand cupped over his mouth before he started a slow clap. "My boy's finally back. And I'm here, too. Guess the boys really are back in town, am I right?"

Shaking my head at him, I rolled my eyes. I couldn't help but let out a soft chuckle, though. "Yeah, I guess we are. Just not in the way you're thinking. I'm not about to climb into the bed of every groupie who throws herself at me, and Winter is still my first priority."

"Of course." He scoffed. "But at least you're partway back in the game. You dating her?"

My cheeks puffed up with air as I arched a brow and lifted my shoulders. "I mean, I like her and she likes me. We're seeing where it goes."

"Seeing where it goes?" He brought his fingers up and tapped his chin a couple of times before giving me a nod. "I suppose that's better than nothing. When are you seeing her again?"

Damn it. I really was going to have to go there, talking about my feelings and shit that was bothering me. *Fuck.* "I don't know."

"Why don't you know?" He narrowed his eyes at me. "Seeing where things go kind of requires actually seeing her, doesn't it?"

I blew out a frustrated breath. "Yeah, but we went out on Friday night. Winter was with us. When we dropped Tiffeny off, Winter told her she loved her. It freaked me out a little."

He stuck his bottom lip out and scratched his head, then frowned at me. "Okay, why is that a bad thing? You definitely said that like it's a bad thing, but I can't figure out why. It's good for Winter to have a positive female influence in her life, unless you're telling me Tiffeny isn't a positive influence."

"No," I said firmly. "No, it's not that. Tiffeny's great and she's definitely a positive influence. I just don't think Winter needs a woman in her life. It's too soon and I don't want her getting confused."

"What are you going to do?" he asked after a brief pause. "Are you so freaked out you're going to stop seeing her?"

"No." I sighed. "Maybe. I don't know. I don't want to stop seeing her, but I also want to do the right thing by Winter."

Clark reached across the island and gave my shoulders a quick squeeze. "You'll figure it out. In the meantime, I'm going to stick around here for a bit. We can work together and I can meet this Tiffeny of yours."

"Sounds good," I said. "It'll be nice to have you around again."

Maybe I hadn't figured out what to do about Tiffeny and Winter's feelings about her, but it really was good to have Clark around. Telling him what was going on had lifted a weight off my shoulders and made it easier to breathe again.

Women had the right idea about most things, I'd realized a long time ago. I was starting to think they were right about talking about feelings, too. Not that I'd ever admit it out loud, least of all to Clark.

CHAPTER 24

TIFFENY

"I'm so hungover," Julia complained as she slid into the seat across from me. "I'm never drinking all weekend for my birthday again."

"Well, at least that's a more realistic promise to make yourself than swearing never to drink again at all." I lifted my glass of water to my lips and let it hang there. "Was it at least worth it?"

She pushed her giant sunglasses into her fiery hair now that she was inside the cafe where we had arranged to meet for breakfast, letting me see the excitement in her red-rimmed eyes.

"Yeah, totally worth it. I'm so happy Callen sang. It was the cherry on top of the best birthday ever." She grinned and managed to waggle her brows at me, even as she massaged her temples with her fingers. "You guys disappeared early on Friday night. Did you have your own private after-party?"

"Not in the way you're thinking." I laughed. "Winter was there with us, remember?"

"And?" She scoffed. "Kids go to sleep earlier than adults. It's like, a universal fact."

"Really? I think there are millions of parents out there who would vehemently disagree with that statement."

She waved her hand dismissively. "Okay, maybe. But I know Winter has a strict bedtime. I've had to make her stick to it. Twice."

"Callen let her stay up later to come to your party so she could hear him sing. We went to get some ice cream after that. Then they took me home."

"That's a disappointment." She swigged the water I'd ordered for her before she arrived, draining the glass in one long gulp. Wiping her mouth with the back of her hand, she held the glass up to a passing waitress to signal she wanted another. "At least you don't feel like death warmed over today, so that's a win for you."

"True." I smiled sympathetically. "The rest of you guys carried on all weekend then?"

She groaned and nodded before she buried her head in her hands, her elbows propped up on the table. "Unfortunately, yes. You'd think I was old enough by now not to make rookie mistakes, but I did."

"What did you do?" I'd never been a major partier, but I'd had a lost weekend myself here and there.

A tiny, nagging corner of my brain thought that staying and partying with them would have been a better choice than going to get ice cream with Winter and Callen. An epic hangover probably would have been significantly better than the doubts and uncertainty I'd been having since they dropped me off.

Thinking about that was only going to bring me down. I prompted Julia again instead. "I can't wait to hear all the sordid tales about what you guys got up to."

"It wasn't that sordid." She sighed dramatically but then smirked. "Okay, maybe there were some sordid parts. If Callen dropped you off after ice cream, why didn't you come join us again?"

"Tell me the juicy parts first. Then we can talk about that. Think of me giving you free rein to gossip as much as you want to as another birthday gift."

She clapped her hands together gleefully, then rubbed her palms like some kind of evil villain in a movie. Mirth danced in her eyes as she leaned forward. "Okay, so you know how Tom, Dick, and Harry were all there?"

"The triplets whose mom thought she was hilarious when she named them? Sure, I saw them." I'd only had eyes for Callen most of the night, but I'd done the polite thing and greeted the people I knew. "What happened?"

"After we left the bar, we decided to go to the beach. Harry said he had some vodka in his car, so we thought we'd take the party there."

"The way you phrased that makes me think the party never made it to the beach?" My worries about the way Friday night had ended faded a little as I immersed myself in Julia's story. The triplets, while they didn't hold a candle to Callen, were all cute in their own right. They were also living proof that mostly, blonds really did have more fun. Which was why their escapades were a great distraction. "What did they do this time?"

She giggled, her expression far away for a moment as she remembered. "Tom decided it was a good idea to grab a garden gnome from a yard near the beach after we parked."

"Oh no." People with garden gnomes around here were usually very, very protective of them. It was like they belonged to a secret cult where scary-looking clay people were sacred. I'd never understood it and I never would. "Please tell me he didn't."

"I wish I could," she said. The corners of her mouth pressed in like she was trying not to smile. "But he did. Richard, of course, decided that one gnome would be lonely without a friend, so he took one, too."

I groaned. "I'm assuming Harry didn't let his brothers outshine him?"

"He didn't." She laughed. "Needless to say, it was a terrible idea. We got caught, the police were called, and we spent several hours at the station getting them out. They felt terrible about it all, so they invited the rest of us back to their place and we crashed for a few hours. But then they woke us up with Mimosas and tequila and the party was back on."

"Sounds like fun," I said. "And possible liver damage, but still fun."

"Yeah, it was." She raised an inquisitive brow at me. "Tom asked about you."

"He did?" The triplets were the subject of many crushes and fantasies around here and always had been.

I'd known them forever though, and I'd never thought of any of them as more than a friend. Actually, even *friend* was a stretch. *Long-time acquaintance* was more accurate.

Before I'd met Callen, I might have been mildly curious about what exactly Tom had said to Julia about me. As it was, however, I really didn't care.

No one I'd ever met had the effect on me Callen did. He made my heart beat faster and my palms sweaty but not in a bad way. He made me laugh.

I felt special when I was around him, like I was the only woman he cared to look at or even sit and talk to. I even got butterflies whenever we were together. Not those tiny, every day, run-of-the-mill type either. *Big-ass freaking butterflies with the wingspan of a manta ray.*

So it didn't matter that Tom had asked me about me. If anything, it made me feel a little guilty for some stupid reason. Like I belonged to Callen and this was somehow a betrayal to him, despite the fact that the only person I truly belonged to was myself.

A deep sigh escaped me as she nodded, enthusiasm making her eyes bright. "Yes, he did. Harry and I might be going out on a date soon. How would you feel about turning it into a double?"

"I'm not interested," I said without hesitating. "Before you ask, no, I'm not going on a date with another guy, not even for you."

She rolled her eyes at me with a sly smile on her lips. "I wasn't gonna ask. In fact, I've already told him you're not interested. I just thought I'd take a chance, since you got all weird when I asked about Callen earlier and then promptly changed the topic."

"I wanted to hear how your birthday went," I protested, but it was weak. Even I knew it.

Julia gave me a look that said she knew it as well. "I've let you stall long enough. As much as I want to talk about the rest of our escapades over the weekend, I want to know why he dropped you off so early."

"It wasn't that early. It was past ten-thirty by the time we got to my place."

"Shock. Horror." She gasped and pressed her hand to her mouth. "Past ten on a Friday night? How could I possibly have said that was early for an unattached twenty-something like yourself to go to bed?"

"I'm not entirely unattached," I pointed out, then realized that I was being dilatory for no good reason. Julia wasn't going to let this go. "We ducked out of your party before it got too wild and went to the shop for some late-night ice cream. Winter was practically asleep on her feet a while after we got there, so we went home."

"But you didn't go home together, obviously?"

"No, he's uncomfortable doing anything like that with Winter around. I get it, though. I really don't blame him."

She rocked her head from side to side, then nodded. "Yeah, I think I get it too. It's probably harder to understand since we're not parents ourselves, but it makes sense. It doesn't explain why you didn't come back to join up with us again or why you tried to skip over the topic earlier, though."

"I thought about coming back to you." I really had considered it for about a minute after I'd walked into my house. "But I'd have been a downer at the party and I didn't want to do that to you."

"I knew there was something you weren't telling me." A protective gleam came into her eyes. "What did he do? Did he hurt you? I'll cut his balls off if he did, but don't worry. I wouldn't do it when Winter was around."

"No. Why would you even ask that? He didn't hurt me. Also, we've talked about the acceptability, or lack thereof, of violence." I shook my head. "You don't need to cut his balls off anyway because he really didn't hurt me. I think it might have been the other way around actually."

Her eyes widened in disbelief, her eyebrows jumping high up on her forehead. "I can't believe you would do something that could hurt him."

"I'm not sure if I did. When they dropped me off, like I said, Winter was already sleepy. She told me she loved me when I got out of the car, and I think that it made Callen uncomfortable. It might even have hurt him. I just don't know."

Julia's posture relaxed, her frown disappeared, and an easygoing smile spread on her lips. "Is that what you're so worried about? Girl. Chill. Kids say 'I love you' to anyone. I have a niece who used to say it to the UPS guy. It's not a big deal."

I chewed on my lower lip. "Really? You think so? Because it looked like it bothered him."

"He was probably just tired," she said, confidence giving her voice strength.

"That's what I thought at first. I just hope we're right."

"We *are* right." She held my gaze. "I wish you'd have told me over the weekend you were worried about this. You could have saved yourself the headache of spending the weekend mulling it over."

"And given myself a headache by drinking with you instead?"

She winked at me. "Exactly. Now can we order? I need to get a ton of bacon into me if I'm going to be able to get through all my clients today."

Julia and I ate our way through a huge mound of bacon, pancakes, and scrambled eggs, sucking down a virgin Bloody Mary each before we took off to open our shops. As I flipped the sign on my door to open, my phone rang.

I pulled it out of my pocket and scrunched up my nose when I saw it was my mother. I had to answer, unless I wanted her to make another unexpected visit to my place of work.

"Hey, Mom, what's up?"

"Tiffeny. Hi, darling. Nothing is up. I am doing well however. How are you?"

I bit my tongue against a retort at her lesson in etiquette. "I'm fine."

"Good. Are you still seeing that Callen Grimes?"

"Yes, Mother." I hoped she wasn't about to invite us to dinner again. Julia had set my mind at ease over the whole "I love you" thing, but I'd still feel a little weird calling him up to ask about dinner with my parents before we'd gotten a chance to talk about it.

"Excellent," she said, surprising the living daylights out of me. "I've looked him up and he's rather famous. His former band was quite successful. Did you know?"

"Yes, Mom." *So that's what's up.* "I'm assuming that's why it sounds like you're so much more supportive of our relationship now?"

"You know what I say about making assumptions, my dear, but yes. In this case, you are correct. He's a much better match for you than I initially realized."

"Thank you," I said, but I doubted she'd pay any attention to the sarcasm in my voice. "Was that all you wanted to talk about?"

"No. Callen seemed quite taken with you at dinner the other night and I wanted to ask you not to screw things up with him like you've managed to do in every other facet of your life. He would make a good partner for you to make a future with."

At first, I thought I'd heard her wrong. *It really isn't like her to say* screw *things up.*

Then I realized this was my mother and that saying something so rude and hurtful was just like her. Blood boiled in my veins and rang in my ears.

I squeezed my eyes shut and forced myself to take a deep breath in a deliberate attempt to calm down. If I didn't, I was going to say something I'd regret before this call ended.

It felt like she'd slapped me across the face, but she'd still raised me better than that. *Or at least, my nannies had.* "Yes, Mother. Thank you. I'll try my best. Goodbye."

I hung up the phone and tossed it down on the counter, sinking down onto my haunches and covering my face with my hands. I let out a muffled shout of frustration before standing back up.

I didn't know exactly where I stood with Callen right now, but everything felt okay. If one of us was going to screw it up, why did my mother automatically assume it would be me?

CHAPTER 25

CALLEN

"Uncle Clark," Winter cried out when she found him in our kitchen on Wednesday morning. "You're here!"

"I'm here, kiddo." He dropped off his stool and opened his tattooed arms up wide. A giant smile appeared on his lips as she smacked into his chest. "It's so good to see you. It's been too long."

"So long," she agreed. "We haven't seen you since we moved."

"I know, baby girl." Releasing her, he ran his fingers through her loose hair and cupped her face to press a kiss to her forehead. "That's why I came. I missed you too much. How are you?"

"I'm good." She wound her arms around his neck again before clambering onto her stool. "It's nice here."

"Yeah?" He grinned as he took his place again, wrapping his fingers around his steaming mug of coffee. "Glad to hear it, even if it means I had to follow you across the country to get to see you."

"Please say you're not leaving soon," she said, the corners of her mouth already turning down in anticipation of his answer.

Winter had gotten so used to all of us constantly being on the go that I knew she expected Clark to leave within the next few days. It was a not-so-subtle reminder of why it had been the right thing to do to turn him down, even if I had found myself doubting my decision once or twice over the past two days.

Clark exchanged a look with me and then shook his head. "I'm planning on staying for a few weeks actually."

She blinked, then threw both arms into the air while her lips split into a massive smile. "Yay! You have to come see my classroom and meet all my friends. And my teacher."

"I definitely will, honey," he promised as he sipped his coffee. For all his faults, he was extremely devoted to Winter.

I didn't doubt for a second that he really had come here to spend some time with her as well as trying to lure me back to work. He shifted in his seat so he was facing her. "That's why I came by this morning. I was hoping to see you before you left and then come with you all to drop you off today. How's that sound?"

"Yes." I nearly rolled my eyes at how excited she was about Clark, but it was too sweet to go through with it. "We have a vegetable garden especially for our class. I watered the squash yesterday."

"You did? Wow. You'll have to teach me how to grow vegetables. I think it'd be pretty neat to have my own vegetable garden."

I snorted, raising a brow at him. "Who would attend to all your vegetables while you're on tour?"

He scratched his chin with his middle finger as he turned his head toward me, flipping me off discreetly. "Maybe I'll make one on the roof of the tour bus when we buy one. Ever thought of that?"

"The roof is rounded," I deadpanned.

"I can always request they change that," he retorted, but then a serious expression formed on his sharp features. "Seriously, if it'll get you back, I'll give the Audi back and get them to get us a tour bus instead."

"Keep the bus," I said and crossed the room to get the cereal and three bowls. At least that was one breakfast food no one could fuck up. After swiping the milk from the counter behind me, I set everything down on the island. "Okay, guys. Breakfast is the most important meal of the day, so let's dig in, shall we?"

Clark shot me a look that let me know he wasn't done talking about this, while I just shook my head to say *not now*. If I ever considered going back on the road, I wouldn't break it to Winter like that.

He nodded his understanding. "Tell me about your friends, baby girl. You said you'd made some at your day-care center?"

Clark and Winter spent the rest of breakfast catching up. After coming to see me on Monday and looking over a few of my new songs, he'd had to get settled and attend a bunch of meetings online.

The label had also rented him space at a local studio so he could keep working on recording. Between that and making arrangements for longer-term accommodation at his hotel, he hadn't been able to come see Winter until this morning.

I let the two of them chat as long as I could before we had to leave. "Okay, guys. Time's up. We have to get going."

Surprisingly, Winter didn't complain. She got up and fetched her backpack before walking to the car with Clark hot on her heels. After strapping her into her seat, he climbed into the front with me.

"Tiffeny isn't a friend from school, but you have to meet her as well," Winter said as we backed out of the driveway, continuing their conversation from the kitchen. "She's the best. Daddy is friends with her, too. We get free ice cream from her shop."

"Really?" he asked, a mischievous gleam in his eyes. "I'd love to hear more about Tiffeny. What's she like?"

I'd already faced the inquisition, but it looked like he still wasn't satisfied. I narrowed my eyes at him in the rearview mirror as a warning, but he ignored me. "Tell me about her."

"She's so cool," Winter said. "She's nice and funny and really, really pretty."

"Sounds like someone I should meet," he said with a smirk that made me want to rip his balls off.

Despite my recent misgivings about how a relationship with her could affect Winter in the long run, a primitive caveman deep inside my chest growled, *Mine*. Clark would never go after her—I knew that as well as I knew my own name—but my reaction to him showing an interest in her with *that* smirk on his face was primal.

He chuckled when he saw what was sure to be the murderous

expression on my face. "Yeah, I'm definitely looking forward to meeting her."

I shot him another glare, but Winter was already talking again and didn't keep quiet about how great Tiffeny was until we got to the day-care center. She insisted on taking Clark on a tour before they got started for the day.

He went along willingly, and when he dropped back into the passenger seat after they were done, he crossed his arms. "I think that maybe's it's time I meet this Tiffeny of yours. Don't you think?"

Considering the protective surge that had flared in my gut earlier, I didn't think.

But I knew I was being idiotic and that in reality, I wasn't a damn caveman, so I gave in. "Sure. Let's go swing by her shop."

Tiffeny looked up when the bell jingled as we walked in. Her lips curled into a wide smile that lit up her eyes when she saw me, but I didn't see so much as a flash of recognition there for Clark. It was weird seeing someone not go starstruck by him as soon as he entered the room.

"Hi." I walked right up to her and pulled her in for a hug. She buried her head in my chest and looped her arms around my neck, the sweet, nutty smell of her shampoo wafting from her hair. I wasn't ashamed or embarrassed when I breathed in a little deeper. "How are you?"

"I'm good," she said, her voice slightly muffled by my shirt before she took a step away and tipped her head back. Questions darkened her blue eyes, but she didn't ask what I knew she wanted to, like why she hadn't heard much from me since Friday night. "You?"

"Good." I took her chin in my hand and planted a single, chaste kiss on her lips before jerking my chin at Clark. "This is Clark, by the way. My best friend. Clark, Tiffeny."

"It's nice to meet you," he said, extending a hand toward her. "In the interest of getting it out of the way, would you like a picture with me or my autograph?"

"No." She frowned, her head pulling back as those blue eyes took him in while she shook his hand. "You're the lead singer, right? Front-man. Whatever it's called."

So she had recognized him. She just didn't care about who he was. I liked that. Laughing at how taken aback he was, I clapped him on the shoulder. "What'd I tell you? She's special."

The tops of Tiffeny's cheeks became streaked with red while Clark observed her with wide eyes. "So you're the unicorn, huh?"

"Unicorn?" She frowned and pursed her lips to the side. "I mean, I've had a few dreams about being a unicorn and more than a few about being able to fly, but as far as know, I'm still just a plain old human."

Clark's eyes widened even further. Then he busted out laughing and let his trademark swagger melt away as he collapsed into a booth. It left just Clark behind, and I was thankful for that. I wanted to see how they would get along as themselves, not with Clark's persona in place.

"I like you," he said between laughs. "I can see why the Grimes family holds you in such high esteem."

She shrugged, but there was laughter dancing in her eyes as well. "Thank you. I'm here every day if you need free entertainment. Now, what can I get you? Ice cream is compulsory here."

His gaze slid to the blackboard above the counter displaying the daily offering. "You'll find no complaints about having to eat ice cream from me. I'll have two scoops of salted caramel, one banana toffee, and two vanilla pepper."

"All in the same cup?" Her brows lifted. "Because I'm not sure I can allow you to do that with my creations."

"You're saying no to me?" It looked like his jaw had been unhooked from his body. "You really are a unicorn. Alrighty then. Three separate cups, but I still want to try them all."

"You got it." She swung her gaze to me. "Let me guess. Double scoop butter pecan?"

"Yeah, but I'll also try the vanilla pepper. I'm not sure if it sounds awful or awesome."

"Hopefully awesome." She tucked a lock of her loose hair behind her ear and shrugged, a smile playing at the corners of her lips as she winked at me. "It's the first time I've made it and you're the first people to try it, so I'm afraid you're my guinea pigs today."

"Bring it on," Clark said and patted his stomach. "I'll try every flavor you've got, as long as it's not kale."

"Ah, you must be fresh off the plane from LA." She was still smiling. "Poor you. Don't worry. I wouldn't dream of sullying my shop with kale."

Clark's laughter followed us when I walked with her to fill our order, my hand on the small of her back because I just couldn't *not* be touching her. I was seriously in danger of developing a Tiffeny addiction.

Being in her presence again, it was difficult to imagine that I'd spent the last few days wondering if we had any kind of future together. With her right next to me, smiling and bantering with Clark as she filled his cups, I couldn't imagine not having a future with her.

I still wasn't ready to drop down on one knee for her or anything as serious as that, but I sure as fuck wasn't ready to give her up. If I was being honest with myself, I'd have admitted days ago that doing it now would've hurt Winter even worse than if Tiffeny and I eventually didn't work out.

There wouldn't have been any real reason I'd have been able to give either girl for doing what I was doing, and they'd both just have ended up hurt, pissed, or both.

I leaned into her, brushed a kiss to her cheek, and was surprised when she turned at the last second to catch my lips.

She smirked up at me. "Somebody missed me, huh?"

"Yeah, but I know you missed me more. You should have seen your face when we walked in here."

Clark groaned. "Can I have my ice cream before you two disappear into the back to reunite passionately?"

"We're not going to reunite passionately." Tiffeny scoffed. "We were just going to drool over each other right into your ice cream."

He froze, blinking at Tiffeny like he couldn't believe she was real before he was laughing again. He even slapped his knee this time.

She gave me a sidelong glance as we carried the filled cups to the table. "What's with him? He keeps looking at me like I'm crazy."

"He doesn't think you're crazy. You're just the first person who has treated him like he's a real, normal person in a very long time."

"But he is a real, normal person, isn't he?" she asked.

"Yeah, he is," Clark said, his laughter subsiding. "But he doesn't get treated like it by anyone but Callen, Winter, and the guys very often."

Before I could explain, Tiffeny's landlord—or douchelord, as I thought of him—shoved his way through the doors. "What is going on in here?"

"I'm serving customers," Tiffeny said, but her voice rose at the end like she was asking a question. Her chin came up then and all traces of good-natured laughter and banter disappeared. "What can I do for you, Mr. Nicholson?"

A cool, almost cruel smile lifted his lips as he slid his gaze to Clark and me. "If you think these guys being here is going to intimidate me, you're wrong. You and I are going to spend some time *alone* together soon. It's hardly fair that you're giving it away for free to these two when I'm offering something in return."

"You know, I didn't think it was possible for you to be more of an asshole than you were the last time. You've just proven me wrong." My fists clenched at my sides and my blood started simmering. "Tiffeny isn't spending any time with you unless she wants to, and in case you haven't noticed, the lady said no. Do yourself a favor and fuck off before I make you, okay?"

The douchelord's face turned white, then almost purple as he pierced Tiffeny with a glare. "Your rent just doubled, young lady."

Clark was at my side in a heartbeat, his arm shooting out and keeping me in place. He knew I was about to get beyond pissed off and stepped in to diffuse the situation.

After having known him for more than half my life, I used to think there was nothing Clark could do to surprise me anymore. He'd proven that assumption wrong so many times, I'd stopped making it years ago.

Regardless, when he pulled wads of cash out of the inner pocket of his leather jacket, even I had to raise an eyebrow. His voice had a dangerous, cutting edge to it when he stepped forward and got in Nicholson's face.

"How much is her rent for six months?" he asked.

Nicholson gave him a much higher number than I thought was justified for the space Tiffeny occupied, but Clark didn't try to negotiate or bat an eye. He simply licked a thumb and started counting.

When he had a fairly fat lump of bills in his hand, he swiftly lifted the lapel of the other man's jacket and slid it into his pocket. He even patted over the cash as he let the jacket fall back into place.

"That's her rent for the next six months. Do us all a favor and get the fuck out of here like my friend suggested." When Nicholson didn't move, Clark's lips curved into a smirk and his eyes turned to ice. "Or are we going to have a problem?"

CHAPTER 26

TIFFENY

I was positively reeling as the door slammed shut behind Nicholson. It was like the last few minutes had been a dream, a fucked-up dream where my landlord had propositioned me in front of my sort-of boyfriend and his best friend, but a dream nonetheless.

My hands shook. It felt like I couldn't quite drag enough air into my lungs. *What the hell was that?*

A big, strong hand closed on my shoulder before I was pulled against a wide chest. Giving myself a mental shake, I blinked and looked up into forest-green eyes. Callen's brow was furrowed with concern. "You okay?"

I nodded, releasing a shaky breath. "Yeah, I'm fine. I guess I just can't believe he went that far, you know? It's not every day a girl gets extorted."

"That guy's an asshole," Clark growled behind me.

I spun around in the circle of Callen's arms, coming face to face with the man who'd just forked out thousands of dollars for me. "Thank you. I don't even know what to say except that I'll pay you back every cent. I promise."

"No, you won't. Really, that was the best thing I could have done with that money. It would have gone to much less honorable causes if

I hadn't used it on your shop." He waved his hand, winking at me before his expression darkened and his eyes slid up from mine to meet Callen's. "We're going to have to do something about him."

"I know," he said, his deep voice rumbling in my chest from how tightly he held me. "Let me work something out."

Gently pushing his arms away from my waist, I stepped away from him and shook my head firmly. "You've both done way more than enough for me. I'm not letting you get any more involved in my problems than you already are."

Clark opened his mouth, but I shut him down. "No, that's the end of it. I'll take care of it myself. I do want to do something to thank you, though. Have you got time for lunch? My treat."

Both of the *rock stars* standing in my humble ice-cream shop nodded, and for a second, it struck me how bizarre the situation was. There were two honest-to-God celebrities standing in the middle of my store, I was seeing one of them, and they'd just defended me against a major creep trying to extort me and turn me into a prostitute at the same time. Then they proceeded to pay my rent for the next six months.

What the hell happened to my quiet, boring life?

On the way to the restaurant, I tried to bring up paying Clark back again, but he wouldn't hear of it. I wasn't going to let it go, but I dropped it for the moment. Somehow, I would get his banking details and pay him back anyway.

There was probably so much money in his account that he wouldn't even notice, but I'd still know I'd done the right thing. *Speaking of which.* "Tell me if this is asking for too much information, but how the hell did you just happen to have that much money on you?"

Clark lifted a shoulder and smirked. "I signed a deal on a new album I'm recording and that was some of the advance I got. It's part of the reason I'm here."

Callen slid into a booth at the beach-side cafe I'd chosen for lunch. "I think she meant to ask why you had it all in your pocket."

177

He laughed, giving us another shrug. "I like to know I'm covered in the event the urge to do or buy something takes me."

"You know you've got a card for that, right?" I asked.

"Yeah, well, some establishments I like to visit prefer cash." He winked. It seemed to be something he did often, which would have made him a total ass if he didn't pull it off so well.

The man was smooth and charismatic as all hell. It wasn't really my thing, but it was easy to see why he was as popular as he was.

Plus, he was genuinely nice, which had come as a bit of a surprise.

Clearing his throat, he shifted his attention to Callen again. "I have your half of said advance as well, by the way."

"I haven't done anything, so keep it." He picked up the menu and looked at Clark over the top of it. "I'm not taking *your* money."

"Think of it as incentive for helping me with the album," Clark said, a smirk tugging at the corner of his lips as he leaned forward. "You know you are going to and you know you already have. Therefore, it's not *my* money. It's yours."

Confusion prickled at the back of my mind. As far as I knew, Callen didn't have any plans relating to music at the moment. I had asked him about it just the other night, but the way Clark was talking made it sound like Callen was working on his album with him.

Raising my brows in question as I glanced over at him, I frowned. "You're working on his album?"

He sighed, dragged a hand across the stubble on his jaw, and sent Clark a sharp look. "No, I'm not. I've written some songs he can use if he wants, but that's it."

"That's a lot," Clark said. "It's kind of hard to release an album with no songs on it."

"What are you going to have to eat?" Callen asked, very obvious in his attempt to redirect the conversation. "I'm thinking of going with a cheese and bacon burger with a salad."

"Dude, you might as well leave the salad if you're having that burger. Just order fries and get it over with." He rolled his green eyes, his amusement showing in the quirk of his lips. "I'll have the same, but

I'm going with a double burger and extra fries. If you're going to have a heart attack, so am I."

"I'm not going to have a heart attack from one burger. If anything, I'm going to have one the first time Winter goes out on a date."

"Keep eating like this and you'll have that heart attack before she ever gets asked out. Shit, since she comes to me if anything happens to you, maybe I shouldn't get the burger."

"Get the damn burger," Callen said. "You're going on tour soon. You'll get enough exercise to work off your one transgression."

Clark's expression brightened. "You're right. I'll be getting tons of exercise both on and off stage."

Callen chuckled and shook his head at his friend. "Yeah, I don't think a heart attack is going to get you. It'll be an STD."

Clark clutched his chest in faux outrage. "How could you? You know I always wrap it up."

"Yeah, but those things can fail, and at the rate you go through them, it's only a matter of time before it happens to you."

"Hasn't happened to me yet." He turned to me. "Ignore him. I'm not nearly as bad as he makes me out to be. You need to give me some fresh dirt on him, though. He hasn't given me anything to give him shit back about in a long time."

I smiled coyly and tapped the menu lying on the table in front of me. "You know, I think I'll have a burger too."

"Good choice, babe." Callen draped his arm over my shoulders and pressed a soft kiss to my temple before shooting his friend a shit-eating grin. "My secrets are safe with her."

"Oh, I see how it is." Clark pouted, winked at me again, and then turned to give the waitress approaching our table a megawatt smile. "We'll have three double bacon cheeseburgers with fries, extra fries, and I'll have a beer."

"Me too," Callen said.

"Me three." I picked up my menu to hand it to the waitress, but she was staring down at Clark with stars in her eyes. A flush crept onto her cheeks, and her lips parted, but it seemed like she was too starstruck to say anything.

Suddenly, it made a lot more sense why the guys had been so surprised about the way I had treated Clark. If this was the reaction he usually got from strangers, I now understood why they'd made such a big deal over me not making a big deal about him.

Clark's smile didn't fade, but I saw a flash of something that looked a lot like disappointment in his eyes before he shook it off. As if someone had flipped a switch in him, he was suddenly all cocky confidence and smooth swagger.

"Hey, sweetheart, you a fan?"

She nodded, still without uttering a single word. Or taking down our order for that matter. Clark got to his feet and I saw her knees buckle at his proximity.

Thankfully, he saw it too and slid his arm around her waist. "Would you like an autograph or a picture? Maybe both?"

Her brown eyes widened as she nodded enthusiastically. With trembling hands, she pulled her phone out of the front pocket of her apron and handed it over to him.

Clark pulled her in closer, turned that smile of his on the camera, and snapped a few pictures before handing it back to her. When that was done, he bent over and dug around in the pocket of his leather jacket again, coming back with a sharpie.

"Where do you want it?"

She pulled down the collar of her pale yellow dress and shamelessly exposed the top of her breast. Clark, again, didn't seem even vaguely surprised. He signed her boob, giving her a smirk that made her knees buckle all over again.

He didn't catch her this time and she reached out to grab the tabletop with one hand, steadying herself as she blinked slowly. Clark sat back down. "You know Callen as well, right?"

The man in question shot him a glare but then forced a grin when the waitress seemed to notice him for the first time and nodded again. Clark ignored Callen as he looked up at her. "Would you like the same from him?"

Wordlessly nodding once more, leaving me to get seriously worried about the effect they were having on her, Callen scooted out of the booth. He took the sharpie from Callen and the phone from the waitress, rushing through the same process Clark had handled with practiced finesse.

When he was done, he sat down but scooted over until his side was pressed to mine. He hung his arm over my shoulders once more before turning his head toward their number-one fan. Opening his mouth, he looked relieved when Clark jumped in to speak instead.

"So, how about those burgers?"

She performed her signature nod again and scurried away. Clark laughed, but Callen looked a little sick.

"Man, I was worried I'd lost my touch earlier with you," Clark said. "But it looks like you really just are a unicorn."

Callen's jaw clenched, but I let my hand glide over to his thigh and squeezed it before raising a brow at his jacket. "That thing is like Mary Poppins's handbag. What else have you got in there? A sharpie, several thousand dollars..."

"Wouldn't you like to know?" he quipped.

"I would actually. Do you also carry signed headshots in there?" My phone buzzed on the table and Julia's name appeared on my screen. I answered it quickly. "Hey, what's up?"

"Nothing much. Just checking in. Where are you? I saw you closed up early."

"Yeah, I'm coming back later. I'm just having lunch at Tony's with Callen and some guy named Clark." My smile morphed into a smirk when I met his eyes, and he narrowed his.

"Some guy named Clark, as in *the* Clark McMann?" she screamed into the phone, causing me to pull it away from my ear. When I brought it back, Julia had hung up the phone.

"What was that all about?" Clark asked.

"You'll see."

Five minutes later, we were in the middle of talking about some of the antics the guys had gotten up to when they were younger. Julia barreled into the cafe with bright red cheeks and her flaming hair flying behind her, her eyes wild as she scanned the room.

When she spotted us, she made a beeline for our table and threw herself into the empty seat beside Clark. Without acknowledging either me or Callen, she turned to him and stuck out her hand.

"Clark McMann, it's so very nice to meet you. I'm Julia, Tiffeny's best friend and the girl who just left a client in the booth so I could come over here."

This time, he did seem surprised. But only for a second. It seemed nothing could rattle his cage too much.

A wide grin spread his lips as he reached for her hand. He shook it slowly. "It's nice to meet you too, Julia. I'm Callen's best friend, so it looks like we're going to be spending some time together before I leave. That okay with you?"

"Absolutely." She didn't hesitate to start asking him a thousand questions.

Clark answered each one while Callen leaned in to whisper in my ear. "And that right there is why I knew right away you were one in a million. Thank you for being you."

I melted into a puddle of goo and kissed the forearm resting on my shoulders, unsure how to react to that after everything.

Clark and Julia hit it off like a house on fire, leaving time for me to get caught up with Callen. While we were eating our burgers, Clark's gaze drifted between Callen's and me, then to Julia. He whispered something to her. She obviously agreed. Then he turned back to us.

"Julia and I can watch Winter tomorrow night if you guys want to go get some dinner."

Callen cocked his head, searching for something before he shook his head, but he said, "Yeah, sure. That should be fine. If it's okay with you?"

If it's okay with me? Sure, because I was going to turn down a date with a super-hot, amazing man I really liked, who also just so happened to be a tattooed rock star and a sex god? Yeah, right.

CHAPTER 27

CALLEN

"So what was that between you and Clark yesterday after he offered to watch Winter tonight?" Tiffeny asked.

She sat across the table from me at a small Mexican place she'd suggested for dinner, her head tilted as she waited for my answer.

The restaurant was casual, with oil lamps on the tables, colorful rugs hanging on the walls, and plastic furniture. I dug it, but what I dug more was that Tiffeny hadn't dressed up for our date.

She was wearing a black, tight-fitting T-shirt with a V-neck that was cut deep enough to offer glimpses of her cleavage as she shifted. Which was why I was having a hell of a time trying to focus my attention on her eyes and what she was saying.

"Callen?" she asked, a frown pulling her eyebrows together as she leaned forward. "Are you okay?"

It took everything I had to keep my gaze from falling down her shirt. I cleared my throat and put a hand in my lap to press it against my rapidly growing dick. "Yeah, I'm fine. I just really like that shirt."

Her cheeks took on a rosy hue in the soft lamplight, a shy smile spreading her lips. "Really? My shirt is what's making you look like you're lost in space?"

"You have no idea how fucking hot you look, do you?" I leaned over and cupped her flushed cheek, watching as she pulled her bottom lip between her teeth.

Captivating blue eyes on mine, she shrugged. "Maybe I do and that's why I chose this shirt. That being said, you're one to talk. You always look good."

"What?" I lifted my new blue T-shirt away from my body. "This old thing?"

Tiffeny laughed. "Yeah, that old thing. Anyway, now that we've established you are, in fact, capable of speech and not sick but just horny, are you going to answer my question?"

"There was nothing really going on, but you know he only offered to watch Winter for us tonight so he could get to know Julia better, right? I might be horny, but I guarantee I'm not the only one."

"You mean he didn't genuinely only want to give his friend the night off to go on a date and to spend some time with the goddaughter he adores?" She batted her long, dark lashes. "Well, I never."

"Yeah, all his intentions were noble all right." I chuckled. "I hope your friend knows what she's in for."

"I'm pretty sure Julia would be in for anything with him, so I don't feel too bad about taking them up on their offer."

"Neither do I." A server delivered our nachos to the table, also bringing a pitcher of beer and two glasses.

He set the nachos down, filled the glasses, and asked if we needed anything else before he hurried away. Tiffeny plucked a nacho off the plate and popped it in her mouth, achieving the impossible by even making eating nachos look sexy.

Christ, there's something wrong with me.

Ever since I'd realized I wasn't about to give her up, it was like my mind was stuck in an infinite loop and every one of the thoughts in that loop involved Tiffeny. Some of them were dirty, but most weren't. I'd even written a song about her, not that anyone except for me knew or ever would know about that.

After she swallowed the nacho, she took a sip of her beer and sat back, smiling at me. "I didn't know you were working on Clark's album."

"That's because I'm not working on it," I said before taking a long pull of my own beer. "Like I said, I've only written a few songs for him."

"Songs he's obviously willing to pay you for, which kind of means you're working with him."

I chuckled and popped some nachos into my mouth. They were cheesy, crunchy, and spicy. The perfect blend.

"Yeah, if you look at it that way, then I guess I am. I'm not recording with him, though. It's his album."

"That may be true, but he already said he's putting your name on it as well."

"It's only going on to credit the songs I wrote, nothing more." I'd fought him on that, but he insisted on having my name on the album. Credit having to be given where it was due and all.

Thankfully, it wasn't like anyone ever actually checked who wrote which song on an album. Slapping my name down next to the songs I wrote wouldn't affect the relative anonymity I had going on in Myrtle Beach and wouldn't thrust me into the press.

"Well, I, for one, can't wait to hear them." She smiled and wagged her brows at me. "What are you planning on doing with your unexpected windfall? Take an exotic vacation, buy a sports car, go on a shopping trip?"

I raised one shoulder. "I'll probably just set it aside for Winter. I think we've traveled enough this year. Taking a vacation doesn't really appeal to me at the moment and we don't need a new car or anything else. Besides, sports cars don't take car seats, which means I'll have to wait until Winter's out of one to indulge in any midlife crisis."

Drumming two of her fingers against her chin, she narrowed her eyes in thought. "I wonder what a rock star's midlife crisis looks like?"

"You've seen it in the news a lot. Usually, it involves drugs, booze, parties, fast cars, and faster women. Since I'm a much tamer, more responsible rock star, mine will probably be limited to the fast cars.

Hell, I won't even be a rock star anymore by then. I'm not even sure I'm one now."

"You'll always be a rock star to me," she said, reaching out to pat my hand as she flashed me a playful smile. "My tame, responsible rock star who's a great dad and values his life and daughter too much to mess around with that other stuff."

"I didn't say tame. I said *tamer*. Saying I'm tame and responsible makes me sound lame. God, now I'm even rhyming. Maybe I *am* lame."

"You're a songwriter. Isn't rhyming in your blood?" She popped another nacho in her mouth, chewing as she kept her eyes on mine, waiting for my answer.

"Songwriting isn't all rhyming, but I guess there is a fair amount of it involved." I shrugged. "I've never really had to think about it that way. Songs just kind of—I don't know—they just come to me and insist to be let out."

"I'm impressed." She dabbed the corner of her mouth with a paper napkin. "I've never written a song in my life, and I don't think I will, but I can't imagine it comes that easily to everyone. Do you think you'll keep doing that? Writing songs even if you don't get to be the one to perform them?"

"I love performing." I frowned. "Or I used to anyway. I think song-writing is probably a better option for me than touring all the time, though."

"Well, if it pays as well as it seems to, it certainly seems like a good alternative." She put her fingers around the edge of her glass and spun it slowly on the table, her gaze on the swirling amber liquid inside. "Will you miss performing and touring?"

Should've seen that one coming. I filled my lungs with air and held it there while I mulled over the question. It felt like the answer should have been easy, but if I really thought about it, it wasn't.

Eventually, I settled on the only truth I could offer unequivocally. "Performing used to be my life, but being on the road is tough. Winter misses out on a lot of social interaction, even though I try to get nannies and sitters who can keep her up to date developmentally.

There are other kids on tour with us. Some of the crew and roadies bring theirs too. It's just not the same, though."

I shook myself out of my thoughts because if I was honest, I did miss it sometimes. "Enough about me. What about you? What does your future look like?"

"If I'm lucky, it looks a lot like my life does right now," she said, a serene smile appearing on her lips as she leaned back in her chair. "I love how things are at the moment. I have my shop, a great friendship with Julia, and some other friends I can do stuff with when she's busy. I'm getting to spend some time with you and Winter. All around, I think the only thing I'd like to work on is getting a few more contracts like the one I have with the day-care center. If I can do that, my rent will be taken care of, regardless of what Nicholson does next. Then life will be good."

"You've got it all figured out, huh?" *Damn it, I wish I could be that content and at peace with where I am at the moment.* "I'm almost jealous."

"You?" She arched a dark brow. "You're a rock star with more money and talent than you know what to do with. How can you be jealous of me?"

"I said *almost* jealous, but that's still an easy question to answer. You're self-assured, independent, you've built a life you are proud of and can build a future on. That's no small thing."

"Yeah, maybe." She dropped her head to one side, her gaze narrowing on mine. "But you know music is your future. I heard all those people singing along to your songs at Julia's party. You've definitely built something you can be proud of, so we're not that different in that respect. You just need to figure out which direction your music is taking you. I only figured out the bulk weekly contract thing recently and decided to do more of that in the future. All you need to do is figure out what your proverbial 'bulk weekly contract' is."

"True, but somehow, we've managed to start talking about me again." I raised my glass and let it hang in the air between us. "Here's to us no longer talking about what the future might hold and focusing on the here and now instead."

"Cheers." She smiled and clinked her beer against mine before taking a long sip and swallowing. Then she glanced down at her menu. "Speaking of the here and now, we'd better order. What are you going to have?"

Tiffeny and I kept the conversation light after that, just getting to know each other better. When our meals were eaten and our bill was paid, we left the restaurant hand in hand.

"I should probably be getting home soon, but let me call Clark and find out how things are going. If they're okay there, maybe we can grab dessert from somewhere."

"There's a great ice-cream place near here." Her eyes sparkled in the moonlight as she looked up at me on the sidewalk. "I happen to have the keys for it on me. No idea why the owner would let me have them. She must be crazy."

"She must be." I laughed as I pulled my phone out of my pocket and dialed someone on my speed dial. Clark picked up not a minute later. "Hey, bro. How's the date going?"

"Good. We just finished dinner, so I'll be home soon. I just wanted to check in on you guys."

Clark scoffed. "You will not be home soon. Stay the night with Tiffeny, Cal. It's been a long time and you deserve a proper break. Jules and I have got this. Winter is in bed, and we're watching a movie. There's no need to rush."

Translation: *his* date wasn't done yet. I had to admit, though, the idea of getting to spend the night with Tiffeny was tempting. If there was anyone I trusted to have them stay over with Winter, it was Clark. I knew he would take care of her like she was his own. He always had.

"I'll think about it," I said finally. As much as I knew Winter would be fine, I didn't know if I would be. I hadn't spent a whole night away from her in a long-ass time. "Either way, you guys are welcome to take a guest room even if I end up coming home."

"Don't come home," he said, then sighed. "But you got it. At least try, okay?"

"Okay." We hung up and I grinned at Tiffeny. "They said to spend the night together."

She tapped the corner of her mouth as she smirked up at me. "You know, now that I think about it, I'm pretty sure I have some ice cream at home. Want to get dessert at my house?"

"Fuck yes." I pushed my worries to the back of my mind and followed my own request from earlier to focus on the here and now. Taking her hand in mine and winding our fingers together, I led her to my car. "You know, now that *I* think about it, there's something else I'd much rather have for dessert."

Her fingers tightened on my hand and her tongue swept across her bottom lip. "Same."

We made it to her house as fast as I could get us there. As soon as we were in her entrance hall, I kicked the door shut and her lips were on mine.

"Wait," she murmured between kisses, putting her hands on my chest and pushing back gently. I obliged immediately, keeping my arms around her waist as I raised a brow and looked into her hooded eyes. Her gaze darted from one of my eyes to the other and I could practically see the wheels turning in her head.

"What's wrong?" I asked, running my fingers lightly up and down her sides. "We don't have to do anything if you don't want to."

"It's not that. Trust me. I do want to. There's just something I wanted to say first." She licked her lips, but it was more of a nervous tick this time. I let her think, keeping quiet despite my body's demands to get her to hurry up.

"I know we said we're only focusing on the here and now tonight, but I wanted you to know I'm okay with that being how things are between us. Not just for tonight. You've got some stuff to figure out and I don't want to be an added weight or an extra pressure. This thing between us doesn't have to be anything more than it is. I'm okay with it just being what it is."

"Okay." My eyes dropped to her lips.

At some point, I was going to have to come clean to her about the way I felt, but I didn't have to get into all of it right then. I ran my fingers across her jaw and tucked a lock of hair behind her ear, my gaze never leaving hers. "You could never be an added weight or extra pressure, but thank you for saying that. Was there anything else?"

When she shook her head, my lips crashed back down to hers, and everything outside of the two of us and what was about to happen ceased to exist. I appreciated that she was trying to make things easier on me, but she didn't need to.

Ever since I'd gotten my head straight and my doubts about being with her sorted out, she was the easiest decision to make. Being with her felt right, and that was all there was to it.

Fuck it. Maybe I should just show her how I feel. Even if I can't say it yet.

CHAPTER 28

TIFFENY

Callen's hand slid to the small of my back and he pressed his hips against mine ever so lightly. Our chests pressed together and he slowed our kiss from the fiery way it had started, eventually bringing his forehead to mine. His eyes met mine, holding my gaze before he scanned my face.

His thumb grazed the side of my jaw, rubbing back toward my ear. He kissed my cheeks, my jaw, and my eyelids before finally moving back to my mouth. When his lips landed back on mine, the kiss was gentler than it had been before.

He brought his hands to my hips and squeezed as he started walking us backward. As he had the last time we'd been there, he kept going until my back hit the wall.

"I want to start on the bed this time," he murmured between kisses, nipping my lower lip and pulling on it until I moaned. "Come on."

Somehow, we managed to make it to my bedroom without ever fully breaking our kiss, any bones, or any furniture. We even managed to get our clothes off before falling onto my bed while still making out.

There was an urgency growing in me that I couldn't stop. My legs wrapped around his hips as we lay back on the bed. I positioned myself so his cock slid against my wet folds and his heavy tip rested against my swollen clit.

I gasped at the contact and Callen let out a low moan. "This wasn't exactly what I had in mind."

"What did you have in mind then? Ice cream?" My heart thundered against my ribs. "Because I have to tell you if you stop now, you're going to have to get it from somewhere else."

He kissed the tip of my nose and propped his elbows on the bed next to my head, his face only inches from mine and his chest heaving. "Believe me, I'm not interested in getting anything from anywhere other than you. I'm not stopping. I'm just switching things up."

A smirk curved his lips. Then he cupped my ass and lowered himself down the length of my body. He used his knees to spread my legs farther apart, making space for his shoulders as his head hovered above my pussy.

A moment later, his tongue landed on my clit, circling it before his lips closed around me and he sucked. I writhed beneath him, glad that his hands were on my hips or else it felt like I would start floating. Shaking as he kept licking and teasing me to the edge of oblivion, I gripped his head and arched my head into the pillow.

"Callen, I—" Cut off by my own moans, I bucked my hips into his mouth. One long finger curled into me in response, driving me right over that edge.

I came so hard, I wondered momentarily if we were having an earthquake. Callen's head between my legs as they formed a vise around it made it seem unlikely, but holy hell, it felt like it.

My breaths were unsteady as I finally descended back to earth, seeing him sitting up with a goofy grin on his face. "Definitely much better than ice cream. Even yours. I'm not even sorry to say it."

"I'm not sorry to hear it, either," I managed to say while trying to catch my breath. "But it's my turn for dessert now."

Heat flashed in his eyes, and I saw his cock move, but he shook his head. "Nope, I wasn't done yet."

"Not fair." I did my best to pout, but it was kind of hard, given how sated I was. "What about my dessert?"

"Compromise?" he asked, a wicked, devilish-looking grin spreading on his lips.

My heart stuttered, but I couldn't deny being curious about what he was going to suggest. "Okay, what kind of compromise?"

In a flash, he turned around to straddle my face, with his nestled between my legs. Suddenly completely clear on what he wanted, I stuck my tongue out to lick the underside of his tip while I wound my arms around his ass.

"Oh, this," I said, my lips brushing over his warm skin as I did.

"Yeah, this," he groaned, then lowered his head and lapped at me like I really was an ice-cream cone. Taking him into my mouth, I released one of my arms around him to wrap my hand around his shaft and stroke the part of him I couldn't fit in my mouth.

Every one of his moans vibrated against me, working with his fingers and tongue to catapult me right back to that blissful edge. Callen's cock sliding between my lips heightened the sensation, until suddenly it was gone.

As was the exquisite pleasure that had just been about to wash over me. I blinked in surprise, lifting my shoulders to see what the hell was going on.

Callen was already in the process of rolling on a condom. Then he lay down with his back on the mattress and reached for me. His grip was rough on my hips as he moved me to straddle him, his eyes burning into mine.

"Couldn't wait any longer," he gritted out as I lowered myself down on his rock-hard erection. Pleasure swept through me again as he stretched me out and started thrusting.

It wasn't long before I reached my peak and my entire body started vibrating like a tuning fork that had been struck against a star. Callen flipped us over at some point, his hips never once stopping their wild thrusting.

I felt him tense and tremble, my name on his lips as his eyelids fluttered and his jaw clenched. His stomach dipped against mine, and I felt him twitch deep inside me as he finally found his own release.

Callen let out a long groan, his face coming down to rest in the crook of my neck. His labored breaths fanned out across my skin, leaving goosebumps as he trembled above me.

We stayed like that for a long time until he finally had to get up to take care of the condom. When he came back to bed, his dark black hair was all messed up from having my fingers in it and he looked so damn sexy I almost lunged for him again.

I held back though, since despite what it might have looked like when I was with him, I wasn't actually a nymphomaniac. Opening my arms for him instead, I wrapped one around his neck as he came to lie back with his head on my chest.

I stroked my fingers through his hair, secretly reveling in messing it up even more. Smiling up at the ceiling in the darkness, I felt him stiffen at my side.

"What's up?"

"I almost just dozed off," he murmured, his voice thick and sleepy. "That feels so damn good."

"You're allowed to doze off tonight, remember? Sleep, baby. It's okay." I closed my own eyes, but when he still hadn't relaxed a few minutes later, I propped myself up on my elbow and slid a finger under his chin to get him to look up at me. "You can't relax, can you? You're thinking about getting back to Winter."

He nodded, a sheepish smile curling its way onto his lips. "I'm sorry. It's not that I don't want to fall asleep with you, hold you all night, and wake up next to you in the morning. It's just that I can't help it."

"That's okay," I said. "I admire how good of a father you are to her. You don't have to stay if you'd feel more comfortable going."

A thoughtful expression darkened his eyes. After a beat, he laced our fingers together. "What if you come with me?"

"Come with you?" My teeth sank into my bottom lip as I raised both brows at him. "As in, come spend the night at your house?"

"Yes." His tone was decisive now, determined. "I want to sleep next to you. I just want to be there for Winter when she wakes up in the morning, too."

"Okay, but you know that means she's going to know I spent the night at your house?" I knew she wouldn't at all understand what that implied yet, but still. "Are you sure you're ready for that?"

He gave a single, firm nod, then smirked as he hopped out of bed and put his clothes back on. "She knows friends have sleepovers, but you'd better bring some pajamas. As much as I'd like you naked all night, there's a very good chance she'll be getting into bed with us in the morning."

"Duly noted," I said. Climbing out of bed, I got dressed and packed a small overnight bag, but my thoughts were all in a haze.

Just a little while ago, I'd told him I was okay with this being what it was. Then he went and upped the ante on me by inviting me over to sleep at his house. With Winter there. I wasn't about to complain about it. I was just a little bit confused.

Getting into it and asking a million questions would just ruin the mood, though, which was the last thing I wanted to do. We were both happy, relaxed, and enjoying each other. Both of us wanted to spend the night together and I was excited about getting to see Winter in the morning.

I'd told him I was okay with this being what it was, and if it was *this*, that was pretty freaking awesome. So I didn't ask my questions. I simply took his hand when he offered it and followed him out the door once again. Callen drove his car while I followed so I could get to work in the morning.

The house was dark and quiet when we got there, both Julia and Clark's cars still in the driveway. I arched a brow at Callen when we snuck past the guest rooms, only one of which had the door closed, and he winked as he pulled me past it and into his bedroom.

"Want to get ready for bed, or would you like something to drink first?" he asked once the door was securely shut behind us.

"Let's get ready for bed." Drinking together was something we could do all the time. Just lying in bed together? Not so much.

Callen grinned and inclined his head toward the bathroom. "Good choice. You go first and I'll get cleaned up once you're done."

After extracting a small bag with my toothbrush and toiletries in it, I lifted my eyes to his. "I'm pretty sure that at this point, you don't need to be worried about seeing me change into my pajamas. You've seen a hell of a lot more of me than that."

He shrugged, nodded, and came into the bathroom with me. It was strange how intensely intimate it felt going through our nightly routines together when he'd been buried inside me numerous times, but somehow, it still did.

There was a certain domesticity to this that was comfortable and unfamiliar all at the same time. If Callen felt the same way, he didn't show it or say anything about it.

Once we were done in the bathroom, he put on a pair of drawstring pants and turned the comforter down, climbing into bed and patting the open space on the other side for me. I didn't hesitate, even as I wondered if this was more difficult for him than he was making it seem.

I'd never been in a relationship where this happened regularly, but I had a feeling he had. He might not have told me very much about Winter's mother, but doing all this together seemed to come naturally to him.

He even kissed me on the forehead when I climbed into bed with him. Then he turned me over in his arms so my back was against his front. He hauled me as close I could get to him, planted another kiss between my shoulder blades, and cuddled into my back.

"Good night, Tiffeny," he whispered, releasing a contented little breath as he fitted his legs to the backs of mine. "Sleep tight."

"You too," I replied, but it took me a lot longer to fall asleep than it did him. There were so many thoughts tumbling through my head, but there was one incredulous one I kept coming back to.

Callen Grimes likes to cuddle, and he wants to do it with me.

CHAPTER 29

CALLEN

"Daddy?" Winter's soft voice asked right up against my ear the next morning. "Wake up, Daddy."

My eyelids cracked open and I reached for her automatically to help her climb into my bed. It took me a second to realize there was something warm already pressed tightly against my side, and with Winter in front of me, that meant—

It all came rushing back then. Tiffeny was in bed with me. At my house. With Winter about to get into bed with us. *Fuck.*

We were both fully clothed, thank God. *But still.*

What had seemed like such a good idea in the dark of night suddenly didn't seem so great anymore in the bright sunshine streaming through the wide windows. *No. It was a good idea. Don't second-guess yourself.*

Releasing a deep breath, I helped Winter the same way I did almost every morning, but I was wide awake this time. Carefully keeping my gaze locked on her, I waited for her reaction to finding Tiffeny in my bed.

She frowned at first, then recognized her. Air caught in my throat, and my heart started pounding, but then she broke out in a wide grin and wiggled her way in between us.

Tiffeny stirred, which had my heart racing again as I waited for her reaction, too. *Christ. It's not even eight in the morning yet.*

It was way too early for these kinds of nerves.

Tiffeny smiled and lifted her arm to make space for Winter. "Good morning, sweetheart. How'd you sleep?"

I blinked twice in rapid succession. Tiffeny hadn't skipped a damn beat, hadn't seemed flustered or uncertain about what to do. It was like she did this with us every morning.

My daughter didn't bat an eye, either. "I slept so good. Julia and Uncle Clark lay with me until I fell asleep and then I dreamed about the pirate game we played."

"Pirate game?" I asked, my heart rate finally returning to normal as I turned to face both my girls. Tiffeny lay on her side, facing me as well, while Winter lay on her back with her hands on her tummy.

"We pretended to be pirates," she explained excitedly. "There was treasure in the pool and everything."

"That explains why there weren't any toys downstairs last night. They're all outside, aren't they?"

She nodded. "We gathered all the treasure and put it on the deck under the chair for safekeeping."

"Of course, you did." I smiled, shaking my head against the pillow. "Let me guess. It was Uncle Clark's idea to stash it there?"

"Yes. It was a great idea. We didn't want the bad guys to get their hands on it again."

"Smart," Tiffeny said. "Speaking of Clark and Julia, do you think they're still here?"

"I can't hear anything, but Clark won't leave if I don't give him coffee and something to eat," I said.

Her brows rose, a small smile playing at the corners of her lips. "He trusts you to cook for him? Brave man. It's only Friday. I'm sure he still needs to work today."

I snorted out a laugh but nodded and sat up. "Even I can scramble an egg. It's not very hard. You just break it and stir it all up."

"That's not really all there is to it." She wriggled her nose and winked at Winter. "But okay. Let's go make some scrambled eggs. And then I need to get to the shop."

"Will you show me how you make them?" Winter asked.

"Sure, honey," she replied as she got out of bed and sashayed out of the room with Winter following after her.

A lump formed in my throat as I watched them leave together. Holy fuck. *It really is like they've done this a thousand times before.*

Before I could give a name to the emotion that caused said lump, I cleared my throat and went after them. Tiffeny was already pulling out a pot from the cabinet under the stove when I got to the kitchen, while Clark and Julia looked mighty cozy sipping cups of coffee at the island.

"Good morning." Clark smirked when I walked in. "Coffee? I made it extra strong in case you didn't get much sleep last night."

"I'm assuming you made it that way for yourself then?" I shot back.

Clark shrugged in that *what you gonna do* way, and Julia's cheeks reddened. Tiffeny's gaze jerked up from where she'd been fiddling with the stove and landed squarely on Julia's, her eyes wide.

"What?" Julia asked, her voice sweet as she batted her lashes innocently. "We were playing pirates till late."

"Clark let you stay up past your bedtime, didn't he?" I asked Winter, who was getting a box of juice from the fridge.

She froze, looking over at Clark for help, but the truth was written all over her face. As always though, he had her back. "It wasn't that far past her bedtime. Besides, it was the first time in forever I got to spend time with the kid properly. Can you really blame me for wanting an extra hour?"

Sincerity rang clearly in his voice, and I caved, especially because I knew he'd be going on tour again soon and didn't know when he'd get to see her again. "Fine, I guess I understand. This one time only."

"Anyone want some toast?" Tiffeny asked after exchanging a loaded look with Julia, who nodded but also smiled at her.

Tiffeny rolled her eyes before turning them on us. "Guys? Winter?"

"Yes, please," Clark said. "Four pieces."

"Four?" Her brows jumped, but then she shrugged. "Fine. Pretty soon, you'll be back to eating kale all day, so you better get your carbs in now."

Clark groaned and hid his face in his hands while Winter and I started on the toast. Julia and Tiffeny talked as she cooked. Julia got out plates and Clark chimed in every once in a while.

Tiffeny turned to Winter before she started cracking the eggs into the bowl. "Want to come help me, sweetheart?"

Her head bounced up and down enthusiastically. Tiffeny picked her up and set her down on the counter before handing her an egg. "Right, now you smack it like this, then crack it into the bowl, okay?"

She demonstrated under Winter's careful gaze while I envisioned us having to dig out a whole bunch of eggshells from the mixture. Surprisingly, Winter managed all right under Tiffeny's supervision, and in no time, we were dishing up.

After breakfast, Clark and Julia were washing up when Winter walked over to Tiffeny. "Can you help me get ready for day-care?"

"Of course." She picked up her coffee mug and walked to Winter's room with her, disappearing a moment later.

My heart gave another strange pang. I couldn't believe how seamlessly this morning was going, how normal it all felt when it was all of our first times in this situation.

Clark stepped around the kitchen island when he was done washing up and squeezed my shoulder, keeping his voice low. "Stop overthinking it, man."

Before I could reply, Julia finished drying the last plate and turned with a bright smile on her face. "Okay, well, will you tell Tiffeny I'll see her later? I need to get home, get ready, and get to work."

"Yeah, I've got to go too," Clark said, the corners of his mouth dipping down as his eyes met mine. "I have to get ready to do an interview in about an hour. Solo, since you won't agree to do this with me."

I punched him in the shoulder. "Hey, you wanted to keep recording. Go be a superstar. I'm happy here in my little corner of obscurity."

Julia looked at me like I'd grown another head, grabbing her purse as she breezed by us to pause in the doorway. "For the record, I'm happy you're happy here because it makes my friend happy to have you here. Also, don't you dare quit music all together."

Clark laughed, elbowed me, and then followed her out, calling from the front door. "Listen to her, man. Don't quit."

The door slammed behind them and I sighed. Winter came back into the kitchen then, her backpack on and wearing the cutest little jeans with a bright pink shirt.

Tiffeny came up behind her, a hair tie in one hand and a brush in the other. She handed them over to me. "I've got to go or else I'm going to be so late to the center this morning. I still have a million things to do before I'll be ready to deliver."

She pressed a kiss to the top of Winter's head. "Bye, honey. I'll see you later."

Seemingly without stopping to think about it, she offered me a smile, came to stand close enough that she could kiss my cheek without Winter seeing it, and then tossed her hand up in a friendly wave. "Later, Callen. Have a good day."

A few seconds later, the door clicked shut and the kitchen was thrown into silence for the first time this morning. I motioned for Winter to come closer. "What do you want to do with your hair today?"

She came to stand between my legs where I was still sitting on my stool, but she didn't say anything. She simply shrugged her little shoulders.

"Okay, a plain ponytail it is," I said, expecting that to elicit some kind of response from her. When it didn't, I frowned and gently turned her to face me. "What's going on, String Bean?"

She chewed on the inside of her cheek, her eyes wide and shining when she looked up at me. "Is Tiffeny my mommy?"

The world came crashing down around me with that one question. Every doubt I'd had came into laser-sharp focus, and an inferno of regret lit up my insides. A string of curses reverberated around my brain and something inside me screamed in protest to having to have this conversation with her right now.

I'm just not ready. Not yet.

Another, snarkier part of me piped up next. *Yeah, well, you brought this on yourself. Suck it the fuck up.*

With Winter's wide eyes still trained on mine, my shoulders fell and I shook my head. "No, baby. She's not your mommy."

"Where is my mommy?" she asked. Sadness dimmed her eyes and the smile that had been so bright just a minute ago was gone.

I stroked a hand through her soft hair and felt my heart crack in half. "She's not here and she won't be coming back, sweetheart."

Dropping off the stool, I lowered myself to my haunches and pulled her against me for a tight hug. Although I didn't know if it was more for her benefit or my own.

Winter sighed, her small chest rising and falling against mine. "I wish Tiffeny was my mommy."

"No one will ever be your mommy," I whispered fiercely, tears that I refused to shed right then setting the backs of my eyeballs on fire. "Your mommy was the greatest person in the world, and there will never be anyone that can replace her."

I knew Winter wouldn't understand what I was telling her then, but I'd made myself a promise never to lie to her about Alice. I wasn't about to start doing just that the first time she asked.

Alice really had been the greatest fucking person and she would have been the best mother the planet had ever seen. Hell, she had been —for however brief a time.

Winter deserved to know that. There was no replacing what she'd lost, and I was so fucking sorry about that.

In the space of those few minutes, because of that one question, my heart was blown to smithereens again. And this time, it didn't feel like it would be any easier to put it back together.

CHAPTER 30

TIFFENY

"We've had such positive responses from the parents and the kids about this initiative," the manager at the day-care center said.

She stood next to me at the table set up in the shade of that beautiful old tree, smiling as she set her hand on my arm. "I know it's only been a couple of months, but we'd like to assure you we'll be renewing our contract when the term is up."

"I'm very happy to hear that." A grin as wide as the country spread on my face. If there was anything that could have made the day any better, it was this.

It had started out as one of the best days of my life, and so far, it was still delivering. I was flying so high, nothing could get me down.

Sleeping in Callen's arms, waking up to Winter's sweet face, having breakfast with everyone, and now this? Life couldn't get much better.

"Would you be willing to travel a little further?" she asked as we watched the kids lining up. Winter's class wasn't out yet, but I kept watching out for her.

Forcing my brain to keep its attention on what the woman was saying, I averted my gaze from the mass of kids in front of me and fixed it on hers. "Of course, what did you have in mind?"

Just then, I caught a whiff of what smelled like grilling meat and my stomach lurched as I sniffed the air. The manager sighed as she noticed what I was doing, a sharp frown tugging at her brows. "Sorry about the smoke. It's our neighbors. They have a cookout once every few months to incentivize their employees. I've asked them not to do it while the kids are outside, but it seems they've forgotten. Again. Anyway, what I wanted to talk to you about—"

Something hooked behind my navel and it was all I could do not to be sick all over the woman who was trying to help me with my business. I saw her lips moving, but blood roared in my ears, and I couldn't hear what she was saying.

My stomach rolled and I clamped a hand over my mouth, feeling my cheeks pale. "I'm so sorry. I have to go. I don't feel so well."

"You don't look so well, either. Do you want our nurse to check you out?" She frowned, concern flashing in her eyes.

I started to shake my head, but even that made the nausea worse. "I'm fine. It has to be something I ate. I'll see you next week."

Practically running to my car, even though my legs felt like they were made of jelly, I stopped before I got in and pressed my forehead to the cold metal of the roof. I gulped in lungfuls of air, and finally, my head cleared, and I didn't have to fight off the urge to heave quite so hard anymore.

Weird. I wasn't one to feel ill very often. In fact, I couldn't remember the last time I'd gotten sick. I didn't even keep any pills in my house other than something mild for headaches, which I also only used on the rare occasion that Julia and I had one glass of wine too many.

Many people I knew wanted their mothers when they got sick. Me? I wanted my mother's housekeeper. Elena was a whiz at knowing what was wrong by just looking at you, and she'd never steered me wrong. Probably because she had four children, and her tenth grandchild had been born just a couple of months ago. She always said she'd seen it all and could name the symptoms of all the most common ailments off the top of her head.

Thankfully, my mother's house wasn't very far away, and while she wouldn't be home, Elena would be. My stomach rolled every couple of minutes as I drove there, but at least I managed not to be sick in my own car.

To my surprise, my mother's car was in the driveway when I arrived. I parked behind her, got out, and let myself in, walking straight to the kitchen. Another surprise when I pushed open the door to find Mom in there, but not Elena.

"Hi, Mom," I said weakly. "Elena around?"

With a shake of her head, she frowned and looked me up and down. "No, she's out. One of those grandchildren of hers needed something. What's wrong with you?"

"I just need some medicine. I didn't feel like seeing a doctor or explaining to a pharmacist how I felt when she always knows what to give."

She crossed her arms over her chest, her gaze once more picking me apart. "How are you feeling exactly? Maybe I can help. I am your mother, after all."

Barely, I wanted to retort. But I bit the tip of my tongue. I needed help, and if I didn't get it, I was probably going to barf on the kitchen floor. There was no way Mommy Dearest would ever let me live that down.

I gritted my teeth instead and fought against another swell of nausea as I spat out my symptoms. "I feel sick, I was dizzy earlier, and I feel really bloated."

Also, as I crossed my arms, my boobs felt tender. "I think maybe it's just my period."

Something flashed in my mother's eyes and she gave her tongue a quick swipe along her thin lips. "What made you feel sick?"

"I don't know. I thought it was something I ate. I did eat Mexican last night, but I've been to that place before, and I've never gotten sick from the food."

"Okay, but what were you doing when you first started feeling it?"

Her jaw tightened and there was this knowing light in her eyes that made me throw my hands up.

"I was delivering ice cream to a day-care center, Mom. I wasn't doing anything wrong. Contrary to what you might believe, I don't spend my days slacking off and getting drunk or whatever the hell you think." I slammed my hand over my mouth, my eyes widening.

I'd always had difficulty standing up to her. Mouthing off to her was unheard of.

The flash of anger and irritation that had just gotten me so riled up was gone as fast as it had hit. My jaw slackened. *I can't believe I just did that.*

Absently nodding to herself, my mom lifted a hand to her neck. She just blinked at the floor for a minute, which wasn't a place she ever looked. I braced myself to take whatever was about to come my way.

It wasn't going to be pretty. That was for sure. If I'd been holding back, it only stood to reason that she had been too, no matter how nasty she'd been to me in the past.

What I wasn't expecting was laughter. But that was what I got.

She started laughing while she was still looking down. Then she arched an elegant brow at me. "You don't need Elena to tell you what's wrong with you, darling. I can tell you that. You're pregnant."

"I'm..." I trailed off. Then I understood why she'd laughed. Pursing my lips, I rolled my eyes at her. "Sure, Mom. Very funny. There's no way I'm pregnant and no way you'd know before I did."

"You might think there's no way, but I can tell." Her voice was unwavering, the expression in her eyes resolute. There wasn't a trace of amusement anywhere, despite the laughter. "I know you dropped out of law school, but surely, you remember sex ed. If I'm not mistaken, that was taught in high school. If you're sexually active, there's always a way."

"But..." *But what, Tiff?*

While I wanted nothing more than to argue with my mother, she did have a valid point. Callen and I were sexually active, which meant it wasn't impossible. We'd always used protection, but that first time, the condom had torn, and even the times it hadn't, it didn't mean it hadn't failed somehow.

My head spun and my stomach rolled again. Blood pounded in my ears harder than before and my heart galloped so hard it felt like my ribs might crack.

Mentally trying to add up days since my last period, I came up blank. Everything felt like a blur and my knees felt weak.

When I lifted my eyes back to my mother's, there was a strange kind of understanding in hers. "What you just described as your symptoms, combined with that sudden outburst of yours, was exactly how I felt the day I found out about you. Trust me, darling. You're pregnant. We'd better get you some vitamins."

"Sure. Yeah. Vitamins." I didn't know what to do. The world was spinning faster than it should have been and white spots danced across my vision.

The tips of fingers went ice cold, and before I could stop it, I felt bile rising in the back of my throat. Making a mad dash for my mother's guest bathroom, I made it just in time to fall to my knees beside her toilet.

When I eventually got back to the kitchen after rinsing out my mouth and splashing cold water on my face, my mother was standing with her hip against the counter waiting for me. "Well, that settles it. I hope it's with that rich musician. Lord knows you're going to need someone who can provide for you now."

In total shock, I could only stare at her before I spun around and raced back to my car. I might not have any idea what to do, but I knew what I *wasn't* going to do. I wasn't about to stand there listening to my mother talk about how I wouldn't be able to provide for this *baby* myself.

Holy shit. Holy fuck. I just thought about a baby. My baby. Crap. *I'm going to puke again.*

CHAPTER 31

CALLEN

"Who's that, Daddy?" Winter asked when we heard a knock at our door on Saturday morning.

We were both in the living room, both still in our pajamas. Winter was drawing in a coloring book on the coffee table while I was sitting on the couch, doing nothing but staring.

My guitar lay next to me, but I didn't touch it. I hadn't been able to get anything done on it since Winter asked that question yesterday morning. It had been twenty-four hours, and I was still reeling.

Having cycled through too many emotions to even try remembering them all, I was numb now. I'd barely even processed that the sound at the door was a knock until Winter had asked who was there.

Another question I can't answer to her satisfaction, I thought bitterly. I knew it made no sense, but not much did right then. "I don't know, sweetheart. Let me go check."

Lead formed a ball at the pit of my stomach. If it was Tiffany, I didn't know what I was going to do. I hadn't heard from her since she'd left, but that didn't mean she couldn't be stopping by.

Blowing out a heavy sigh of relief after I swung the door open, I scratched the back of my head. "Thank God it's you."

Clark opened his mouth, presumably to throw out some smart-ass retort, then thought better of it. His eyes dropped down the length of my body instead, and his jaw tightened. "What happened?"

"I have no idea what you're talking about." I glanced down at the tattered shirt I'd had on since yesterday, the holey shorts, and my bare feet. "I haven't showered yet."

"No shit." He stepped into the house around me, threw his sunglasses and keys onto the side table, and pierced me with a dark look. "What happened, Callen? This is like looking through a fucking mirror to what you looked like over a year ago."

I dragged my fingers through my hair and swallowed, my voice coming out raspy. "Winter's in the living room."

"Okay." His expression softened and he even managed a smile before he strode over to her. I followed but with far less of an idea about what was going on.

Winter grinned when she looked up and saw him, jumping to her feet and throwing her arms around his shoulders. "Uncle Clark! Are you here to play pirates again?"

"No, sweetie pie. I actually came to talk to your Daddy, but do you remember Julia made you those extra treasure maps the other day?"

She nodded. "Yes. She said I could look for treasure every day if I wanted to."

"Exactly. Why don't you go grab one of those from your room and go on a hunt while Daddy and I talk?"

"Okay." She ran off and I frowned after her, wondering why it was that children were never that easy or obedient with their parents.

Clark didn't answer when I asked him, though. He grabbed my wrist, dragged me into the kitchen, sat me down, and handed me a beer. When he'd popped the top off one for himself, he fixed his gaze to mine.

"Now talk. You look the same way you did six months after she died, and whatever happened now can't have been nearly that bad."

"It's not the same as losing her," I said because it honestly wasn't. "It's just..."

He gave me a minute, and when I still didn't continue, he gave me another. Clark had been through a lot with me. He'd learned how to deal with me when I got like this, and he knew when to push me.

Another few deep breaths later, I admitted the awful truth. "I didn't lose her again, but I replaced her. Losing her wasn't my choice, but replacing her? That was."

"What the fuck are you talking about?" he asked, a frown deeper than the Grand Canyon on his forehead.

"Tiffeny." I nearly choked on her name. "Winter asked me if she was her mother after you guys left yesterday."

"Shit." Clark deflated, all bravado vanishing as he set down the beer to scrub his hands repeatedly over his face. "Fuck, bro. I don't even know what to say to that."

"Welcome to the club. I didn't know either."

"What did you say?" he asked.

"Just that Tiffeny wasn't her mother and no one else would ever be." My voice cracked then. "I also told her that her mother was the greatest woman in the world. I don't want Winter growing up thinking Tiffeny is her mother, man. How could I betray Alice's memory that way? Tiffeny is fucking fantastic, but regardless of how I feel about her, she's not Alice. Alice is and always will be Winter's mom, but how the fuck am I supposed to explain that to a three-year-old?"

"You're not," he said quietly. "You're not supposed to have to explain stuff like this when your kids are so young because they're not supposed to lose their parents before they can even know who they are."

Clark knew how much Alice had meant to me, but he also knew better than to try telling me shit like how she was in a better place. I knew that, but it didn't help me feel any fucking better. So he validated what I did feel instead. "It's just so fucking unfair, man. She was in the prime of her life, a new mom. Why her?"

He shook his head, not even trying to give me an empty answer. Instead, he just sat there with me while I breathed deeply, trying to banish the demons flying around in my head.

"Look," he said eventually. "After my interview yesterday, I spoke to my new manager. Guy called Guy. You'd like him. Anyway, I told him I wasn't ready to jump into a full-fledged tour as a solo artist without an album of my own released yet, and he agreed."

"What?" I frowned, confused as to why he was bringing this up now. "Why are you telling me?"

"Because we've decided to do a short, acoustic tour of the album as it releases. You wrote all the songs on it, whether recently or months ago. The album drops in a few days. Then the tour kicks off. Like I said, it'll be short and totally acoustic."

"Okay, why are telling me?" I repeated my earlier question. "I've already told you I'm not hitting the road again right now."

"I know, but haven't things changed since then?" he asked, no judgment in his tone. He wasn't trying to convince me either. He was simply asking as a matter of fact. "You came here to get your head clear and your shit together, but your head's all fucked up again, and your shit seems even farther flung that it was before."

"Can't argue with that."

He rested his forearms on the table. "It might do you some good to get out of here, even if just for a little while. I know Winter loves her school, but you can always come back. Hell, you don't even need to sign on for the whole tour. You can just do whatever shows you want to and come back when you're sick of being on the road."

I squeezed the back of my neck hard. The hollow space in my chest burned. A million objections raced through my head, but I couldn't grab hold of any of them.

What Clark was offering me felt like a lifeline. I'd been feeling like I was being tossed around in a turbulent ocean and a lifeguard had just yanked me up by the arm right before my head went under.

If we stayed here, we'd keep seeing Tiffeny. In my current frame of mind, I was going to end up hurting her. I didn't want to, even though it was kind of inevitable now that it was going to happen, no matter which choice I made here.

If we stayed here, Winter was going to see her whether I did or not. She went to Winter's day-care at least once a week. What that meant was that Winter was going to keep spending time with her and feeling more and more for her.

If we stayed here, I'd keep betraying Alice's memory, and I couldn't fucking do that to her.

"You're right," I said to Clark, pulling back my shoulders and feeling clarity seeping into my brain for the first time in a whole day. "That's exactly what we have to do. I'm in."

CHAPTER 32

TIFFENY

I knocked on Callen's front door with my breath stuck in my lungs. I felt an intense urge to bolt instead of announcing my presence to them, but I waited for someone to open up. No one did.

There weren't any cars in the driveway, but they had a garage, so that didn't mean they definitely weren't home. Lifting a shaky hand, I knocked again.

While I waited for a response, I tipped my head back and let the sunlight warm my face. It was such a beautiful day. The sky was robin's egg blue with puffy white clouds floating above. I heard waves gently crashing to the shore and the cries of seagulls in the air.

To the rest of the world, it was an ordinary Monday morning, the kind of day that made you wish it was still the weekend so you could spend some time on the beach instead of going to work.

Logically, I knew I couldn't technically be the only person in the entire *world* for whom this day would change everything, but it sure felt that way. A pregnancy test had confirmed my mother's suspicions over the weekend. *Seven pregnancy tests, in fact.*

One part of my brain kept hammering out a to-do list. I didn't know much about the first trimester of pregnancy, but I did know there were steps that needed to be taken. A blood test would have to be done. An appointment would have to be made with a doctor. Those prenatal vitamins my mom had mentioned had to be purchased, and I probably had to do some research on what to eat and what to stay away from.

The part of my brain making that list was overpowered by the other, though. And that part was perfectly content to stick its head in the sand and pretend this wasn't happening. *Just like a fucking ostrich.*

I had spent all weekend at home alone, listening to the latter part, eating ice cream, and losing myself in the dystopian world created by a book I'd been wanting to read for a while, but I knew it was time to get back to the real world.

No other Monday had brought the contrast between the reprieve brought along by the weekend into such sharp focus as this one. Usually, the shop was open over weekends, for a few hours at least, so Mondays didn't bother me so much.

I'd not only *not* opened the shop this weekend but also had some pretty huge news to tell the guy I was seeing, so this Monday morning had been a rough one for me. It had taken everything in my exhausted body to heave myself out of bed to come here.

No one answered my second knock either. Sighing as I pushed my fingers through my loose hair, I bunched it up at the nape of my neck and fought back a wave of tears. *He's not here.*

Regardless of how great a father he was to Winter, Callen and I had only known each other just over a couple of months. I had no idea how he was going to react to the news, but I had to tell him. It was the right thing to do.

After taking those tests on Saturday, I'd considered calling him. My phone had even been in my hand a few times with his number up on the screen, but I hadn't been able to bring myself to do it.

Instead, I'd decided to take the weekend to come to terms with the news myself. Then I would deliver the news to him in person on Monday, which felt like the right way to do it. Now that it *was* Monday, I regretted that decision to wait.

I'd stuck to it, though, coming here to tell him the truth before I

214

went to work. Since he wasn't here, I wondered if I could just wait until I saw him again to tell him.

No, you need to get this done, whispered the small rational part of my brain that remained after the shock. *He deserves to know the truth. It's his baby too, even if he decides he wants nothing to do with it in the end.*

Sucking in a deep breath through my nostrils, I nodded to myself. I sighed as I walked back to my car and climbed in. I rested my forehead against my fingers, wrapped around the steering wheel.

Whatever Callen ended up deciding about the baby, it was still his decision to make. In order to make that decision, he needed to be told the truth.

I swallowed a lump in my throat and dug out my phone. This was the kind of news it was better to deliver in person, but I needed to find out where he was so I could do it.

At the very least, I needed to find out when I could see him if now wasn't a good time for him to talk. Clutching my phone in a death grip, I scrolled to his number and, before I could chicken out again, pressed the dial button.

The phone was pressed so tight against my ear it hurt, but I couldn't bring myself to move a muscle to relieve the pressure. Just when I thought Callen wasn't going to answer and felt this first fluttering of relief that I was getting another reprieve, his deep voice flowed through the speaker.

"Hi." One syllable only, but already I could tell something was off with him. When he didn't follow it up by asking how I was or even what I wanted, I knew I was right.

"Hi," I said, my voice smaller than I was proud of. "How are you?"

"Fine." Only one word again. Silence at his end of the line.

I cleared my throat again when the lump started to rise once more. "That's good. Uh, I need to talk to you about something. Have you got any free time today?"

"No." I thought he was going to stick to that one word again, but then a heavy sigh came through the line, and his voice became agitated. "Look, I'm actually glad you called. I was going to call you later anyway."

"Okay." I sucked my lower lip into my mouth and sank my teeth into it. Whatever was about to happen was not going to be good. I felt it all the way down to my bones. "What did you want to talk about?"

There was a pause, during which I could practically see him scrubbing his face with his hands. "Us."

One word again, but this one cut through me like the hot slice of a blade at the inside of my ribs. I inhaled a sharp breath and closed my eyes. "What about us?"

"Things between us are moving too fast for me and Winter." There was no pause this time, no hesitation. "Clark asked me to go with him on an acoustic tour for the new album, and we're going. Until we take off, I'm going to be working with him to get ready to perform these songs. I won't be able to see you again before we leave. I'm sorry, Tiffeny. We're just not ready for this."

He's not ready for this? My hand dropped to my belly, where somewhere deep inside there was a little person I sure as hell wasn't ready for either. Yet I wasn't running away.

Betrayal, fury, and unfairness burned hot and heavy through my veins at the same time that loss and pain stabbed at my heart and forced tears to my eyes. *God, my emotions are such a mess right now.*

"So, what then? You decide you're *just not ready for this*, whatever the hell that means, and you can't even give me ten minutes of your precious time to talk to me in person?" My voice came out fierce and unwavering, which I was damn thankful for.

No matter what, I wouldn't let him hear the emotional storm ripping through my insides right then. I wouldn't allow him to have the satisfaction of knowing he was leaving a broken heart in his wake.

Maybe my heart wasn't even really broken. I didn't know what was coming from me anymore and what was being thrown at me by my rampant emotions. But it hardly mattered. I felt the way I felt no matter what was causing it.

"You said you were okay with whatever this was, Tiffeny. You're the one who said it didn't have to be anything more than it was, and this was all it was. This is my life, making music, touring. It's time for me to hit the road again."

"Yeah, I did say that," I bit out, fighting to keep my voice from cracking. The fierceness had vanished. It sounded nothing but flat now. "You said you were done with touring, though. You said you just wanted to spend some quiet time with Winter until she got mean in her teens. Do you remember that?"

"Exactly. Spend some quiet time with Winter. That was all I wanted. I never meant to hurt you, Tiffeny. I never meant to do anything to or with you at all. I wish there was more I could say, but there isn't. I really am sorry."

So am I. "Break a leg on tour, Callen. Tell Winter I said goodbye."

My voice finally cracked on the last word, and with nothing left to say anyway, I hung up. Well, there was one more thing I could have said. *Oh, by the way, I'm pregnant and it's yours.*

But no.

I couldn't say that under the circumstances. Whatever his reaction would have been, I didn't want to force his hand. He was leaving, going on tour with Clark, and he might not ever come back.

Instinctively rubbing my hand over my belly again, even though I couldn't feel anything there yet, I bowed my head. *We're in this together, you and I.*

Memories of Winter telling me she didn't have a mother flooded my brain, conjuring images of another little person with Callen's eyes saying they didn't have a father. My own eyes squeezed shut against the onslaught of tears pouring out of them.

I couldn't stop them and I didn't try. My earlier resoluteness that it was up to Callen what he did with the news flew out the window. He'd made his decision, whether or not he knew exactly what it was he was leaving behind.

He clearly didn't want me anymore, which was fine. I wasn't saddling this kid with a father who didn't want them either. Although it wasn't something I had planned for, not something I had wanted at this point in my life, at that moment, the need to protect this little person slammed into me with the force of a fighter jet in full flight.

It was up to me to do for it what Callen had done for Winter. All those things I had admired about him were now qualities I'd have to grow into myself. I could do it. I knew I could. As much as it would hurt to have to do it alone, if he could do it, so could I.

How long I sat in that driveway crying, I didn't know. When I eventually looked at the clock on my dashboard, I saw that it had been over an hour, which meant that it was time for me to stuff all these out of control emotions into a lockbox in my mind and get to work.

As it was, I'd lost out on business for the last two days. I couldn't afford to lose another day. Especially not now that there were going to be all these other expenses I had to cover.

The thought of asking Callen for child support flitted across my mind, but I banished it. My rent at the shop was paid up for six months, so at least I had some time to figure things out.

As much as I didn't want to rely on my mother for financial support, I'd rather go to her than go to Callen. I knew my mind might change eventually, but for now, that was how I felt.

I drove to my shop in a daze, wiping my tears before I got out of the car. I knew my eyes would be puffy and red, but hopefully, I wouldn't have a customer until I could get myself under control.

It turned out it wasn't a customer that caused the bell above the door to jingle first, but Julia. She took one look at me before she rushed over and enveloped me in her arms. "What's wrong, babe? What happened?"

"Nothing, I—"

"Don't lie to me, Tiff. There are literally tears streaming down your face and it doesn't look like they're the first of the day."

Well shit. I hadn't even realized the tears were still falling. "It's Callen. They're gone, Jules, and I don't think they're coming back."

CHAPTER 33

CALLEN

After a month of being back on the road, back onstage with Clark, it felt like Myrtle Beach had never happened. The only sign that those couple of months had been real was the gaping Tiffeny-shaped hole in my heart.

I hadn't even realized I'd given her a part of it until it was too late, but it *was* too late. It didn't matter that part of my heart belonged to her now because leaving hadn't been about me. It had been all about Winter and it still was.

Clark gripped his microphone and threw his head back, belting out the last lyrics of our last song of the night. The crowd waited for the last note of his voice and my guitar to fade, then went crazy.

It had been this way on every one of our stops so far. I'd been surprised at first by the amount of fans who were willing to come out for only Clark and me, but there were tons of them.

We'd talked about contacting the other guys too. Literally getting the old band back together again. They'd all moved on for now, though. All of them had signed contracts for the time Kraken was supposed to be on hiatus, and none of them were too eager to even try to get out of them.

It was okay, though. Clark and I were having a blast doing the acoustic shit we'd always wanted to do and calling all the shots on what kind of music we wanted to make. We even decided on the venues we wanted to play and chose mostly venues with natural acoustics where we could find them, opting for intimate instead of larger crowds.

All of those things had contributed to the fact that I'd lasted out this month, even though I knew Winter wasn't happy being back on the road again. Clark and I were killing it out there every night. I threw myself into the music with a fervor I'd forgotten I possessed for performing, allowing it to drown out the doubts about coming on tour, thoughts about Tiffeny and whether I'd done the right thing for my daughter.

Lights blinded me and sweat poured down my back as Clark and I took our bows. We'd already played the encore and it was time for us to get offstage.

Clark wasn't doing those last victory laps anymore. We simply both threw up our hands and waved as we made our way from the stage.

There were only a few fans waiting for us backstage, another perk of having so much more say in the tour. We got to pick shows where only a limited amount of people were allowed, so long as we paid proper attention to fans with backstage passes at the bigger venues.

I had a feeling that last condition had been written in after Clark told the label I was joining him on tour, considering I'd been known for shoving my way past fans to get to my dressing room in the past.

Clark and I both stopped for selfies and autographs now, smiling wide and making small talk while we did. Of course, Clark had always done this. It was kind of new for me.

All in all, I wasn't miserable. I just had some looming feelings that came to the fore in the dark of night when the music was quiet and the lights were off.

"How are you doing, bro?" Clark asked when we walked into the main area of the dressing room we shared at this venue. "You seemed a little preoccupied after we got offstage."

"I'm fine. I just have a lot on my mind." I twisted the top off an ice-cold bottle of water I grabbed from the fridge and drained the whole thing in one go.

Clark pulled his sweat-soaked shirt over his head, letting it fall to the floor before taking the bottle of water I offered him. "You know you don't have to fake it with me, right? This isn't an interview. You've been holding up fucking well since we left South Carolina, but don't think I haven't noticed that weight that's been settling on your shoulders again recently."

He cracked the lid off the bottle but kept his eyes on me as he drained his water. I lifted one shoulder, pulling my own shirt off before I collapsed on the couch with a fresh bottle.

"Winter isn't happy to be on the road again, as you know," I said. I dropped my head back and narrowed my eyes at the ceiling of the rocky cave that made up our dressing room tonight. "Every day, I have to face her questions about when we're going back. I have to ward off requests to call Tiffeny."

His eyes softened with understanding as he leaned his bare shoulder against the rocks. The venue we'd just finished playing was an outdoor amphitheater, and while having an actual cave of a dressing room would have probably gotten me hard a few years ago, I barely noticed it tonight.

"Have you spoken to her at all?" he asked.

He didn't need to clarify who he was talking about. I shook my head against the plush stuffing on the leather couch. "Nope. Not going to either."

"But you miss her."

I sent the ceiling a piercing glare and tightened my jaw. "I didn't say that."

"You didn't have to, man. I know you better than I know myself. You're not the type to break up with a girl you really liked over the phone, then walk away and forget about her." He smirked, jabbing a thumb at his chest. "If you were, you'd be me. And you're not."

"Maybe I've been striving to become more like you," I shot back. "You never know. Maybe I've been idolizing you all this time and I've finally gotten it right."

He barked out a laugh. "Yeah, no. Go spread your bullshit somewhere else, man. I'm not buying what you're selling."

"Didn't think you would." I blew out a breath. "It doesn't matter if I miss her. What matters is why we left, and it hasn't been long enough for that to change."

"It's been a month," he said. "You sure Winter's still that hung up on Tiffeny?"

I nodded. "She asks about her all the time. I've been in contact with the day-care center. They send me the lesson plans for each week so Di can keep Winter caught up. Every time I speak to them, Winter asks me to ask about Tiffeny."

Di was a godsend at this point in time. She was a tutor hired on for Winter by the label, another example of Clark's excellent negotiating skills. Although she didn't know who Tiffeny was, she'd grown used to the questions and had gotten good at fielding them.

Although I supposed too, she was in her fifties and had supposedly tutored hundreds of kids who were in Winter's situation. She'd reassured me plenty of times that Winter wouldn't fall behind and that a short tour wasn't detrimental to her overall, but I just wasn't sure I believed her.

Either way, we were on tour now, and in the next few weeks, we had our biggest shows so far coming up. They were all sold out and there was no way I could ditch Clark or even the fans now, no matter what he said.

Come what may, I had three more weeks on this tour. After that, I might reassess, but I just didn't know what I was going to end up doing.

"Winter will be okay, dude," Clark said, cutting into my thoughts. "In another month, she won't be asking as often anymore."

"I hope you're right." But I didn't really think he was. I pushed down on my palms and stood up, jerking my head in the direction of the bathroom. "I'm gonna go grab a shower. Then I'm out of here."

"There's an after-party at that bar on the other side of the amphitheater, just so you know, but I think you'd better get back to the hotel."

I raised both brows at him. "You're not going to try to convince me to come out with you?"

"What was the definition of insanity again?" he asked, touching the side of his mouth with his index finger before snapping it with his thumb. "Oh, right. Doing the same thing over and over again and expecting a different result. Besides, I don't think you'd be much fun tonight, even if you did decide to come."

"Well, thanks for letting me off the hook anyway. I appreciate it."

"No problem." He dragged a hand through his hair and got a beer out of the fridge before going to spread out on the couch I'd vacated. "Just don't jerk off in the shower because I know you've still got Tiffeny on your mind. I still need to use it after you."

I flipped him off, considered doing exactly what he'd asked me not to, just because he'd asked, but eventually finished up in the shower without doing anything to spite him. I just wasn't in the mood. Hadn't been since the last time I'd been with Tiffeny.

In a way, being on this tour was bringing back a lot of memories of the last tour I'd been on. The important difference was that I didn't feel dead this time. I wasn't numb to the music or to the future. I was just in limbo.

I was figuring things out, not ignoring them. The tour was giving me the time and space I needed to clear my head, and while it was slow going, I was actually managing to make some progress.

When I got back to the hotel, I knew Winter wasn't really asleep, but I kept quiet anyway. If she *fake* slept for long enough, she'd *real* sleep soon enough. Instead of calling her out on it, I went into the bathroom to brush my teeth and change into sweatpants. Then I climbed into bed with her and just held her until eventually, I drifted off as well.

CHAPTER 34

TIFFENY

"I'd say you're about thirteen weeks along," the doctor said as she moved a white-plastic wand along the cool gel she'd squeezed out on my belly.

Dr. Malone was difficult to get an appointment with, but my mother had insisted that she was the best of the best. Surprisingly, Mom had been calling to check in on me from time to time since she found out I was pregnant, and when I told her I hadn't gotten an appointment at an OB/GYN yet, she'd gotten one for me.

In all our conversations over the last month, she hadn't attempted to patronize me once. She wasn't mean or rude, didn't put me down or condescend to me. It was damn weird, but it felt like our relationship was finally, slowly, growing into something resembling a real mother-daughter relationship.

I hadn't seen her yet, since she'd been away for work a lot, and frankly, I'd been wanting to keep my distance until I could be sure she wasn't about to go say something callous and hurtful. I was feeling fragile enough as it was, even if I was getting by.

When Mom had found out I was seeing Dr. Malone today, though, she'd asked me if I wanted her to come. I said no, obviously, but then she'd told me she would be at home once I was done if I wanted to come by after.

This was my first ultrasound, and I was suddenly very, very grateful that I could go home to my mother after. A mother who actually felt like she cared about me for once.

Because seeing that little gray, black, and white, lanky yet blobby thing on the screen that was my baby was an experience that was transcendent. It was like nothing I'd ever experienced before, and I didn't think any feeling I'd ever had did or could rival it.

It was the kind of experience that was meant to be shared, and in my case, I didn't have anyone but my mother to share it with. But I did have her, and I couldn't wait to show her my baby.

I fell in love with that little lanky-looking blobby thing instantly, and when Dr. Malone fiddled with something on her machine and the sound came on, I gave my entire heart to Blobby in the same second I heard its heartbeat.

It was only the first picture I was seeing of the baby, but I was unequivocally, irrevocably in love with that little thing. I knew in that moment that life would never be the same again. As much as I was in shock at the strength of my emotions, I was also in awe of the little life growing inside me.

Dr. Malone smiled. "We've got a nice, strong heartbeat, which is good. All the measurements I've taken so far tell me you're well on your way to having a healthy baby in a few months."

My breath caught at that. *A few months.*

On the one hand, it felt like way too long before I got to meet him or her for the first time. On the other, I *only* had a *few freaking months* left before I met my baby for the first time. I practically started hyperventilating, and the doctor frowned at me.

"Are you feeling okay, sweetie?"

"I'm fine, but I guess I'm just… overwhelmed," I admitted.

Dr. Malone had kind brown eyes and graying hair pulled back in a tight bun. She gave me a smile filled with understanding and patted my hand.

"That's completely natural. I was just asking to make sure, but most girls react that way when they first do the math at how much and how little time they have before the baby comes." She grabbed a wad of paper towels from a box on the metal table beside her. "Here. You get cleaned up. Then we'll talk in my office. Do you need an extra picture printed out for your husband? Sometimes, the dads get sensitive if they weren't able to come to the appointment and don't have a picture of their own."

"I'm not—I don't—" I stammered. "No, that won't be necessary."

"Okay, then. Let me print out a set for you and I'll see you in my office in a minute." She hit a button on her fancy machine, gave me another smile, and then cracked the door open between her office and her exam room.

I lay there for another minute, dazed as I rubbed the sticky gel off my belly and glanced down at it. It still looked soft, just like it always had, but when I pushed on it, there was significantly less give.

It was like a rock underneath there now, but I was glad it was so hard. My body was helping me to protect my baby, and for that, I had a newfound rush of appreciation for it.

Despite being on the bigger side, I'd never had a problem with my body. In fact, I kind of liked having fuller curves, even if I had taken some flack for it back at school.

Those curves meant something different to me now, though. They were providing extra space and padding for my baby, and I loved the thought of that.

Smiling to myself as I got up off the exam table, I wondered if any other woman had ever smiled while getting off that table in my situation. I dressed quickly and slid into the doctor's office.

"Okay, let's get started," she said, sitting behind a large glass-topped desk.

The wide window behind her had a view of the city and the ocean beyond. There were pictures of babies on her walls and informational pamphlets on her desk, but I only noticed all of this in my periphery.

My attention was firmly fixed on the doctor. She folded her hands in her lap, a serene expression on her face and a seemingly permanent upward tilt to her lips. I'd liked her the minute I'd met her earlier, and

I was glad she was going to be the one there with me when the time finally came.

Calmness and capability seemed to seep from her pores, making me feel the same way.

"First things first. We're going to need to set up an appointment schedule. Some of your appointments will be with one of my nurses, while others will be with me. You can speak to Cassie at reception before you leave."

She clicked a pen and passed it to me, along with a stack of forms. "Those are consent forms for some standard bloodwork we'll need you to do. There are also some other forms in there. Take your time to read through them and bring them in next time you come. Cassie will keep them in your file."

Item by item, she worked through a checklist of things to keep in mind. By the end of the appointment, my brain was filled to the brim with new information, and I had her forms in my hand, along with my pictures of Blobby.

Everything seemed surreal to me at the moment, but whenever I glanced down at the pictures, the world came into sharper focus. It felt like Dr. Malone had stripped my being to its very core before putting me back together again by showing me what my baby looked like.

Driving to my mother's house, I felt like I was existing on a new plane, one I'd never been on before. It was the weirdest, most unbelievable yet terrifying drive of my life.

I had tears in my eyes when my mother opened her front door. She opened her arms to me, for the first time I could remember, and when I walked right into them, she pulled me into the tightest hug I'd gotten from her in a long time.

"How did it go?" she asked, her voice surprisingly soft and soothing. She even stroked my hair as she hugged me, letting me linger in her arms before she released me.

"It went well." I took the pictures out of my purse and showed them to her. "There he is. Or she. I guess we'll find out in a few more weeks or so."

"Oh, baby." She took the string of pictures from me with one trembling hand and brought the other to her lips. "My first grandchild."

She breathed the words almost reverently, which shocked me almost as much as her eyes misting over with tears did. *What the hell is going on with her?*

Before I could ask, she linked my arm with hers and gently guided me to the kitchen. "Let me make us some green tea and get you some water."

My jaw practically hit the ground. "You're going to get it yourself?"

She waved me off with an almost mischievous smile touching her lips. "I do know how to make tea, you know? I'm also able to open a faucet, although I'll get you a bottled water instead. You shouldn't be drinking tap."

I arched a brow at her. "Tap is fine, Mom."

Pursing her lips, she held my gaze for a beat. "Sure. Of course. Your body, your baby. Tap, it is."

Surprised by how fast she had relented, I sat down on one of the chairs around the large kitchen table and folded my arms. "What's going on with you?"

"What do you mean?" she asked, tinkering around the kitchen as she made our drinks.

I cocked my head. "You know what I mean. I don't think you've ever been this nice to me, but definitely not since I told you I was dropping out of school."

A soft sigh fell from her lips. Her head dropped forward and she braced her palms against the counter as she closed her eyes.

I watched as her chest rose and fell with several deep breaths. Then she opened her eyes again, and when they landed on me, I nearly gasped at the depth of the remorse shining from them.

"There is no denying I haven't been the perfect mother," she said. She didn't wait for me to object. I guessed she knew she wasn't getting any objections from this side of the kitchen. "But I've only ever wanted what's best for you."

She took a breath and poured the tea, carrying it over on a tray, even though it was just across the kitchen. Before she sat down, she fetched my water and passed both drinks to me.

"Here's the thing about parents, Tiffeny. Most of us have no clue what we've gotten ourselves into when our children are born, but we swear we'll always do right by them anyway. One day soon, you'll be making those promises too, and then you'll start learning that it's not always easy to keep them."

She sighed but a soft smile tipped the corners of her lips up. "Sometimes, those promises we made lead us to making mistakes, such as thinking we know what's best for our children even when we don't. All I ever wanted was for you to be happy, to be successful at what you did because I knew you wouldn't be happy if you weren't."

"I am happy," I said quietly.

"I know that now." Her eyes dropped to her cup and stayed on the steaming liquid for only a beat before coming back to mine. "You're a tough woman, darling. I'm so proud of you. I know I haven't said either of those things enough, but they're both true."

"You think I'm tough?" My brows pulled together. "Also, since when are you proud of me?"

"I've always been proud of you," she said. "I just didn't tell you because I didn't want you to think I was approving of your choices."

I touched my belly, my thumb stroking the spot beneath my belly button where I'd seen my baby lying earlier. "Are you only saying this now because I'm pregnant?"

"In a way." She held up a finger when I opened my mouth to reply. "No, hear me out first. For a long time, I was worried about you. I thought you were making a mistake and that you'd regret it someday."

"But not anymore?" I could hardly believe what I was hearing.

"Not anymore," she confirmed. "After you left here that day I told you I thought you were pregnant, it hit me that I was going to be a grandmother and you were going to be a mother. My baby was having a baby of her own. While that doesn't mean you're not my baby anymore, because you always will be, it made me realize you really are a grown woman now. A businesswoman in your own right and one who was going to start making choices for her own child soon enough."

"You don't have to be a grown woman to get pregnant," I pointed out.

She giggled, a delicate, feminine sound I didn't think I'd ever heard from her before. "I suppose that's true, but you are. You've grown into an incredible, beautiful young woman with a strong sense of independence and self. You were brave enough to stand up for yourself and you had the courage to defy our expectations in order to pursue your own happiness. I'm truly proud of who you've become, darling. I can't wait to see you instill those values into your own child."

"You're serious right now?" I pinched myself, ninety-nine percent certain I was dreaming. When I didn't wake up, I could only stare at her.

"Serious as I've ever been," she said, then linked her fingers together on the table. "That being said, my grandbaby is on the way and there are certain practical things that need to be taken care of."

"I know." I set my purse on the table and pulled out a pamphlet I'd been given, outlining prenatal care. "I never knew having a baby would involve so much work before they're even born."

She nodded, her voice still calm and gentle as she continued. "Yes, but we'll get all that done in time. What I meant to get to was whether or not you're going to tell Callen."

I sucked my lips into my mouth and lifted a shoulder as I stared at the long list of stuff I had to get ready before the baby arrived. "I don't know. I think he's still on tour, but I don't even know that for sure. I haven't heard from him, and after the last conversation we had, I don't think he'd take my calls even if I tried to get ahold of him."

"Okay then." She sat up straighter in her chair, her shoulders pulling back as she lifted her chin. "We'll take care of the baby without him. Don't worry, honey. I know I've made a lot of mistakes as a mother, but I don't plan on doing the same as a grandmother."

CHAPTER 35

CALLEN

"How long before we can go home, Daddy?" Winter's blue eyes pierced a hole in what was left of my soul as she looked up at me before our show. "I want to go home."

She wasn't pouting, crying, or complaining. It was an honest question, but one asked with such sadness in her eyes that I could barely stand to look at her without feeling my heart cracking in my chest.

We were in the dressing room of the venue Clark and I were playing tonight. It was the last big show that had been sold out for this tour, and even though we were backstage, I could hear the din of the gathering crowd trickling in.

She sat next to me on an overstuffed black couch and I slung my arm around her shoulders, pulling her close to my side. "We've only got a few more weeks of shows to do, baby. We'll go back to Myrtle Beach after that."

When Winter said *home*, she meant Myrtle Beach, even though she'd spent only a few months there compared to her years in Los Angeles. As I'd gone back and forth over the last seven weeks since we'd left, I'd often wondered if we should go back to Myrtle Beach at all.

Getting a moving company to pack our stuff and a realtor to sell the house wouldn't be too hard, but in my heart of hearts, I knew I couldn't do that to Winter. Over the weeks, she'd become more and more despondent.

Di assured me that she was keeping up to date in her lessons, but she'd also picked up on the same thing I had. Winter was not happy.

She had grown quiet and withdrawn, and despite nearly two months having passed since we left, she still talked about Tiffeny all the time.

"No, Daddy." She stomped her foot on the wooden floor as she wrenched herself free from my grip, her bottom lip jutting out as tears welled in her eyes. "I don't want to wait more weeks. I want to go home now. Why can't we just go home?"

A sob broke free then, her entire body convulsing as she gave into emotions she must have been keeping bottled up for weeks. Seeing her like this felt like I'd gotten shot in the heart. *By a cannonball. One that was on fire.*

Sliding off the couch, I dropped down on my knees and held her shaking body close as I ran my hand up and down her back. "I'm sorry, baby. I'm so sorry."

She didn't say anything, which broke my heart even further. *I fucked up. I fucked up big time.*

Movement in the doorway caught my eye, and I looked up, ready to take out all my rage and frustration with myself on the poor, unsuspecting soul who had accidentally stumbled in on us like this.

When I lifted my gaze and it landed on Clark, the urge to lash out fizzed out and only guilt remained. This was *my* fault. I'd done this to Winter. No one else.

"We're on in three," he said, his voice so quiet I could barely hear it.

I nodded my understanding and stroked Winter's hair. "I have to go, baby. I'll be back soon though, okay? We'll talk about it then."

Di popped her head in around Clark and smiled until she saw the state Winter was in. Rushing into the room, she sat down on the couch and opened her arms. With my daughter crawling into her lap, I sighed and walked to join Clark at the door.

"How long have you been standing there?" I asked him under my breath, loud enough for only him to hear as I caught Di's eye and she waved me off, mouthing, "I've got this."

"Long enough," he replied. Light green eyes filling with an emotion I couldn't quite name, he lifted a hand and clapped my shoulder as we left the dressing room together. "We'll talk later. Let's just get through this one, okay?"

"Okay." I agreed as a roadie handed me my guitar. Clark bounced on the balls of his feet, cracking his neck as he got his game face on.

The crowd was screaming our names, their voices mingling with Clark's as the venue played footage of the live performances we'd done on the tour so far. The screens they were airing it on would soon be filled by the image of Clark and his trademark smirk running onstage while I once again watched, amazed, at how fast he could transform into a true fucking rock star.

A minute ago, I'd have sworn I saw tears forming in his eyes, maybe even regret over having offered me this opportunity, but looking at him now, it was like he was a different person. Gaze filled with mirth, cocky smirk tugging on his lips, and his entire body moving with swagger.

I shook my head and wished, not for the first time, that I had the ability to do the same. Instead, I fixed what I was sure was my trademark scowl to my features and took to the stage after him.

It was only once my fingers touched the fretboard and my head dropped as I started the intro to the first song that all the troubles in my life seemed to fade into the background. *God, I love this fucking instrument.*

Strangely enough, I'd learned I was actually fine without the performing part of this life. My time in Myrtle Beach had proven that. I'd missed it a little bit, errant thoughts here and there, but I'd realized I didn't *need* it the way I'd once thought I did.

What I couldn't live without was my guitar and my songwriting. Professionally anyway.

Personally, I couldn't live without my daughter, and I didn't want to live with her being as unhappy as she was now. She was turning four soon, but she was still only three years old.

Her biggest worry at the moment should have been trying to come up with a reason why she shouldn't have to wear pants to school in the middle of winter. She shouldn't be having to beg her father to take her home so she could go back to school, back to her life. Back to the woman she loved and had started thinking about like a mother.

I fucked up. I fucked up. I fucked up. Clark might have been singing the actual lyrics to our songs, but those three words kept reverberating through my head. Somehow, I made them fit into any rhythm, and as the crowd screamed along with him, I screamed at myself.

Witnessing Winter's heartbreak and having my own break for her had shaken something loose in me, made me feel like I was floating around above myself in the memories I had on those last couple of weeks with Tiffeny.

It was like I could finally see for myself what an asshole I had been, what a coward I had been for leaving like that. At the time, it had felt like my only option. I saw now that it hadn't been.

All I'd basically done was run away, and in the meantime, I'd ripped Winter away from a stable life she'd loved. I'd also broken up with the only woman who had made me feel alive in a long, long time.

A woman with a heart of gold who I should have worshiped for loving both myself and Winter the way she did, who hadn't pushed me but had made me want to crawl out of my comfort zone all the same.

Tiffeny had accepted me just the way I was and not because I was a rock star but in spite of it. A fiery, dedicated, smart woman with the heart of a saint and the body of a sinner.

And I'd walked out on her. *No, I didn't even do that.*

Bitter laughter filled my head as I leaned back and jammed my heart out in the solo for this song. Because no, I hadn't walked out on her. Walking out would have involved seeing her face to face.

So no. I bailed on her and she hadn't even watched me walk away.

At the time, I'd been so wrapped up in preparation for the tour that I'd thought I was justified in ending things over a phone call. *What a fucking moron.*

Clark got the crowd whipped up into a frenzy and I tore up the stage to try working off some of the guilt and rage setting my insides on fire. When our set was finally done, I was dripping with sweat and my muscles were quaking.

Back in my dressing room, I still couldn't stop moving. I drank at least four bottles of water and crushed them up, pacing up and down as my mind raced.

Di had taken Winter back to the hotel, and I had to get over there soon, but I needed to talk to Clark first. He burst into the room a few minutes later, his face flushed and makeup all over his skin from the selfies he'd taken with fans while I'd stormed past everyone once again.

"It's time for you to go back to South Carolina," he said as soon the door closed behind him.

All the fight drained out of my body because he was right. And he understood. And he wanted the same thing for me as I did. I'd been struggling with how to tell him since I'd come to the realization up on that stage that I was leaving tomorrow.

"It's time, Cal," he said as he moved to the fridge and grabbed two waters for himself. He drained one after the other. "I'm glad you came out with me and I'm always happy to have you. You're welcome to join me with whatever show I'm doing whenever you feel the mood take you, but enough is enough."

"Yeah, I agree."

His head jerked back and his eyebrows jumped up. "You do?"

"Of course, I do. Why wouldn't I?"

A wide grin broke out on his lips. "Well, shit. Dude, I thought you were going to up and leave a month ago before we even did this leg of the tour. Then you told me it didn't matter that you missed Tiffeny and all that mattered was why you left."

"It was." I swallowed, then hung my head and put my hands on my hips. "Wasn't it? I had to leave. You agreed with me."

"I think it was good for you to leave when you did," he said, but his tone was careful as he picked out a chair and sat down. "Your mindset had gone back to being a minute away from imploding and ruining every good thing you had going for yourself there. I thought you needed a break and now you've taken one. I never meant for you to stay with me for the whole tour. I mean, you're welcome to, but I think your head's screwed on right again now. So to come full circle to what I said when I walked in here, I think it's time for you to go home."

"I think I ruined every good thing I had going there anyway." I didn't need to spell it out for him.

Clark stood up again, smirked, and lifted his shoulders. "You're a fucking rock star, man. If you had enough dedication and determination to make it to the level of fame we've reached, you can apply those same qualities and get your girl back."

"Maybe." I wasn't convinced she'd ever forgive me, but I had to at least apologize. Apologies didn't always need to be met by forgiveness, but it was important to make them anyway.

I realized that on the day I broke up with her, she'd been the one to call me. She'd also said she needed to talk to me. I'd never even asked her what she'd wanted to talk about.

"Thanks for understanding, bro," I said. "Thanks for everything actually."

We hugged it out for a minute. Then he clapped me on the back, wished me luck, and strode out to go party with his hordes of adoring fans. Ever the glamorous rock star I was, I took a shower and went back to the hotel.

The only difference between tonight and every other night was that I didn't crawl into bed with Winter right away. I packed our bags instead.

Tomorrow morning, we were leaving. *First thing, we're going home.*

CHAPTER 36

TIFFENY

"You're looking so cute," Julia cooed when she walked into the shop. She came right over and cupped my growing belly, stroking it with her thumbs. "Hey there, little one. It's your Aunt Julia here. Did you have a good night?"

Julia and my mom were the only ones I was comfortable with touching me, but now that I was starting to show, a lot of people sure thought my tummy was public property. A lot of them even talked to the baby, just like Julia was doing. I was trying not to let it get to me, but it was annoying to be approached by strangers all the time.

I yawned and lifted a shoulder. "The bump is making it harder to sleep now. My mother says it only gets worse from here."

"It's still such a tiny bump, though." She finally released said bump and leaned against the counter. "We'll have to get you one of those pregnancy pillows soon if you're already having trouble."

"Yeah, my mom's already on it. I spoke to her this morning and told her I couldn't sleep on my stomach anymore. If I sleep on my back, it's like there's a weight on me, and on my side, it feels like gravity just wants me to roll over."

She grimaced. "You're making it sound like so much fun to be pregnant. I think I'll wait another few years."

"Anyone who says it's fun is trying to lure you into a trap." I laughed. "Don't get me wrong. It's a miracle, and I love this little one more than life itself, but the joys of pregnancy aren't all so joyful."

"How are you feeling?" she asked sympathetically. She asked every morning, but she never made me feel like she was tired of hearing about it.

"I'm not so nauseous anymore, but my boobs still hurt, and I look like a whale, but other than that, I'm great."

"You don't look like a whale." She scoffed and bumped my shoulder with her fist. "You look adorable. These maternity clothes your mom got you are perfect. They look so comfy and they still showcase the bump so nicely."

I sighed as I looked down at the patterned cotton skirt that brushed my ankles and baby blue top. Julia was right. They were comfy. Soft and fitted to support while not being tight or clingy.

I'd tried dressing to hide the bump when my stomach first popped out, but my mom wouldn't hear of it. She said my body needed proper clothing to help keep it as comfortable as could be while still supporting where it needed support.

Therefore, my top had a built-in bra with space for breast pads to be slipped in when the time came, and the band of my skirt sat around the bump but didn't push into me at all. Truth be told, while my body was growing uncomfortable, the clothes themselves were so comfy, I had no idea how I was ever going to go back to tight jeans with a button digging into my flesh.

"Thanks," I said. "I'm glad I gave in and let her get them for me eventually. She was right about comfortable, supportive clothing making things easier."

Julia tipped her head to her side, chewing the inside of her cheek. "Your mother really has done a complete one-eighty, huh?"

"She's being super helpful," I said. "I'm so grateful to have her around right now. I don't know how I would have coped without her."

"I'm still here to help," she said. "Anything you need, you just let me know."

"Thanks, and I know. You've been amazing, too. I just..." My lungs constricted as I breathed in deeply, no longer able to expand as much as they once had. "I'm just glad my mother's there for me, too."

"You need family around at a time like this," she agreed, sadness dimming the light in her eyes. "You still haven't heard from Callen?"

"Not a word." Tears stung the backs of my eyes again. Getting randomly emotional when I thought about Callen and Winter seemed to be my thing at the moment. Another unfortunate side effect of pregnancy, making my emotions all heightened. "I miss him. I miss Winter, too. Sometimes, I think about calling, just to find out how they're doing."

"Well, I can tell you how the tour is going," Julia said hesitantly. "I haven't necessarily been following the news, but I've been following Clark on social media for years."

I sucked in a breath. I'd known she was a fan, of course. It made sense that she still got updates from him. In the last few weeks, I'd been tempted a few times to look them up myself, but I hadn't wanted to fall down that rabbit hole.

I was afraid if I started looking either of them up on social media, it'd quickly escalate to stalker level. I was desperate for news, though. Maybe this was a safer way of getting it, a small hit of information from her just to keep me going without having a link to click on for more.

"Okay, how is the tour going?"

Her eyes widened in surprise, but she didn't mention it. "Their last show was a couple of nights ago. One of the headlines I saw about it was 'An Epic Performance by Two of the Greats.' Apparently, they've been on fire since the tour started."

If it was possible, my heart both soared and fell through the floor at the same time. On the one hand, I was happy for Callen and Clark. They were both passionate about their music and they were so talented. I was glad they were doing well.

On the other, if they were doing so well, that meant Callen had probably forgotten all about his little stint in Myrtle Beach and really wasn't likely to come back.

I cleared my throat, trying to dislodge the lump growing there. "That's great. I'm glad for them. Hey, do you want some tea?"

She nodded and followed me when I headed into the back. Obviously noticing that I was getting all emotional again, she changed the topic and told me some gossip she'd learned from her clients this week.

The bell jingled just as the kettle started whistling. She waved me out to the front, stepping around me to get to the kettle. "You go serve your customer. I'll make the tea and bring it out."

My world slammed to a halt when my eyes landed on the people who had caused the bell to jingle. Callen and Winter stood just inside the door, blinking at me like they were the ones surprised to see me.

My mouth dried up and my hands flew to my belly as my eyes grew wider. Then I realized they wouldn't be able to see the bump yet. I was standing on the other side of the register and the counter was just high enough.

But they were here, which meant they were going to see it at some point. *Thanks a lot for the fitted clothing, Mom.* If I'd gone with wearing baggy clothes, they might not have noticed my belly, but in this shirt, it was clear as day.

Winter squealed then, her eyes misty with happy tears as she raced toward me with her arms open. "Tiffeny! We're back."

"I can see that." I was so overwhelmed by her joy to see me that I stepped out from behind the counter to catch her in a hug instinctively. I scooped her into my arms and held her tight, breathing in her strawberry scent and burying my face in her soft hair.

For that second, everything felt right. It felt like we were meant to be a family, like Winter was meant to be this close to her half-brother or sister.

It was only for that one moment in time, though. Then I realized I'd stepped out from behind the counter, my shield, and my eyes flew up to meet Callen's. His face said it all.

White as a sheet, he seemed torn between clenching his jaw and having it hit the floor. Eyes wider than I thought it was possible for human eyes to stretch, his body stood rigid in the same spot he'd been in when I'd first come out.

Actually, his foot was lifted off the floor like he'd been about to take a step but had then forgotten to actually to do it.

Fuck.

"How would you like a welcome home ice cream?" I asked Winter, not waiting for her answer before filling a cup with butter pecan. I always kept it on hand now, a little something to remember them by, I supposed. Julia had once pointed out to me that it was because of a spark of hope in my heart that a moment just like this one would happen and they'd come back to me, that I wanted to be ready when they did.

Now that it was happening, I felt anything but ready.

"Julia's in the back," I said as I handed over Winter's ice cream. "Do you want to go say hi to her?"

My best friend would know I needed a minute alone with Callen as soon as she saw Winter, so when the little girl nodded and skipped into the back room, I breathed a sigh of relief. It only lasted for a beat before tension ratcheted through me again.

Crossing my arms above my growing belly, I met the shocked gaze of Callen's deep green eyes. "So, um, this is what I wanted to talk to you about the day you left."

He opened and closed his mouth a few times with no words coming out, his throat working. After a solid minute when he finally managed to speak, question upon question came tumbling out of his mouth.

"How are you? Are you okay? How far along are you? Is the baby okay? Do you know what it is yet? God, Tiffeny, why didn't you tell me?"

I took another deep breath. "I'm fine. The baby is fine. I'm going on seventeen weeks now, so nearly halfway there. I don't know what it is yet. The baby was shy at my last ultrasound, so they'll check again at the next one in a few weeks."

My eyes fluttered closed as I answered the most difficult of his questions. "You know why I didn't tell you. Our relationship was what it was, remember? This wasn't something we planned and I'm not looking to have you come back into my life because you feel forced to do it now. I'm fine, really."

Pain and hurt flashed in his eyes, but he didn't argue. Winter and Julia came out from the back before he could say anything.

He held his hand out to her and jerked his head in the direction of the door. "Come on, baby. We should go. Hi, Julia. Bye, Julia. Tiffeny, we'll see you around."

Everything in me burned as pain rocked me back on my heels when he turned around and left without a backward glance. Winter waved, smiled, and followed him. Then they were gone. Again.

A sob broke free as soon as they were out of sight, but I refused to give in to the grief wanting me to fold in on myself for losing them once again.

"Are you sure that was what you wanted?" Julia asked quietly, winding her arms around me from behind.

"I don't want a relationship when the person I'm with doesn't want to be there. I don't want to force him into being with me, with us. It isn't what I wanted, but what other choice did I have?"

CHAPTER 37

CALLEN

"Thank you for watching Winter for me," I said after watching her disappearing into Julia's house.

Tiffeny's best friend gave me a much kinder smile than I deserved, her hand coming up to rest on my bicep. "No problem. You're doing the right thing, Callen. Just do me a favor and fight for her, okay? Don't let her push you away. Not if you really want to be with her."

"You think I still stand a chance?" Shame threatened to drown me as I stood in front of the woman who had been there for my girl when I should have been. "Thank you, by the way. I assume you've been supporting her while I've been out there, acting like a fucking coward."

"I've been there as much as I could, but I'm glad you're back. As for you still standing a chance, I think you do, but you're going to have to convince her that you're doing this for the right reasons."

"Yeah? What reasons are those?" I shoved my hands into the pockets of my jeans to hide the anxiety that was making me fidgety.

Julia cocked an eyebrow. "If I have to tell you, then maybe you're not doing this for the right reasons after all. I hope you figure it out, Callen. I really want both of you to be happy."

"Me too," I said, my voice growing thick.

It had been a week since my life had been thrown upside down when I walked into that ice-cream shop to see an unmistakable baby bump I really hadn't been expecting. Thrown for such a loop that I could only stand there like an idiot, I only managed to bite out the first few of the hundreds of questions barreling through my head.

Then when she'd said what she had, I just didn't have the mental capacity to formulate any kind of argument, to tell her any of the things I'd actually gone by to tell her.

All I could do was recognize that I would only do more harm than good if I tried to push the issue while trying to process the shock I'd just gotten. So I'd done the only thing I felt I could. I swallowed my pride, my questions, and the burning need to take her into my arms and promise her I'd never leave again, and I'd left.

All I'd thought about the last week was how I could make this right. It had taken me all week to come up with the most obvious answer. It was time to tell her the truth. All of it. No holds barred.

It had taken me one look at that bump to know that I couldn't hide in the past anymore, couldn't let it dictate my decisions or actions any longer. The past could hold me back and ruin the future for all of us, or I could take the lessons it had taught me and apply them to grab life by the balls and make a better future.

The past didn't have to be an anchor keeping me stuck in place any longer. Alice wouldn't have wanted it to be either. My past could be the fresh ocean breeze filling the sails of my future as I embarked on a new leg of my journey.

I was choosing for it to be just that.

Just as Tiffeny flipped the sign on her door to closed, I jogged up to her. She paled when she saw me, pain piercing through her clear blue eyes.

Her black hair tumbled past her shoulders, a perfect contrast to her smooth, pale skin. She had on another soft but fitted shirt, a deep purple one that brought out the color of her eyes.

Flat leather sandals adorned her feet and a gray and white skirt skimmed her ankles. She looked damn good. Then again, I always thought that.

Our gazes caught through the glass separating us. Then I saw her chest rise and fall on a sigh as she unlocked the door again. She stepped back and opened it, then motioned for me to come inside.

"Callen," she said, her voice strong but her arms folding across her chest like she needed to protect herself. *From me.*

Seeing it sent a searing pain through me, burning all the way to my bones. Because I knew I had caused this need she had to protect both herself and *our* baby from *me*.

The worst thing was knowing that I deserved it. The knowledge made it difficult to speak, but I also knew I had to. It was now or never.

"Hey, do you have time to talk?"

She flicked her hand toward the shop, her words light but her tone flat. "Well, I don't seem to have any customers, so I guess I have a bit of time."

After shutting and locking the door behind me, she led the way to the booth in the corner. Arms folded on the counter, she linked her fingers together and leaned forward when I sat down.

"Look, I'm actually glad you came by. You need to know that I don't expect anything from you. I—"

"No, don't. I'm sorry, Tiffeny. I'm so fucking sorry. Sorry for leaving, sorry for not asking you what it was you wanted to talk to me about that day." Emotion tightened my throat, but I kept going, even though my voice was on the verge of cracking. "I wouldn't have left if I'd known. Or at least, I like to think that I wouldn't have."

"That's the thing, Callen." Her eyes were hard, but the expression in them was sincere. "I don't want to hold you back and I don't want the baby too, either. You left to go do your thing. Like you said, it's your life. You don't owe us anything. You don't have to change for us. Don't worry."

"But I want to worry," I protested, then reached across the table and took her hand, holding it tightly as I kept my eyes on hers and implored her to see the truth in them. "I want you, Tiffeny. I want the baby. I want us all to be family. I don't want you to expect nothing from me. I want you to expect everything. I want to give you everything."

She yanked her hand away and dropped it in her lap, her eyes shutting as she shook her head fast. "No, you don't. You didn't. You made it perfectly clear we didn't have that kind of relationship before, and that's fine. I don't need you in my life—in our lives—if you only want to be there out of some misplaced sense of obligation."

I opened my mouth to protest, but she cut me off. "I'd never keep this child away from you, Callen. If you want to be in its life, you can. I'm not the type who's going to tell him or her lies or use them against you, but don't spin this like you want us all to be together when you don't. Don't turn this into some fairytale where we get to live happily ever after as a family. This is real life. It's not perfect and not everybody gets a happily ever after."

Determination and belief were laced into every one of her words, while I was lost for any of my own. Nothing came to me at first. I'd fucked up, and now she believed, truly believed, I didn't want her. She wasn't going to let me in again unless I could make her see I *wanted* to be with her, that the mistake had been what I'd done before and not now. *How can I make her understand?*

"Alice was my wife," I said finally, closing my eyes as I braced myself for telling the truth I hoped would save me. Tiffeny blanched but didn't interrupt me. "Winter's mom, her name was Alice. We were married."

"Oh," she breathed but let me continue.

"She had cancer. We found out shortly after Winter was born." Piece by piece, I gave her my past until my soul was stripped bare and every ugly thought and doubt I'd had lay on the table between us.

I swallowed hard. "The morning after you first stayed over, Winter asked me if you were her mother. When I said no, she said she wished you were."

Tiffeny's eyes were so wide, it looked like they were in danger of falling out. Silent tears fell down her cheeks as she listened to me.

"I freaked out. I got flung back into a deep pit of doubt and uncertainty. I felt like I was betraying Alice and I didn't know what to do.

Clark offered me a spot on the tour as a way to get some space and time to clear my head, and I took it."

I was breathing deeply now. "I never stopped thinking about you, never stopped missing you. Neither did Winter. At some point, it hit me that I was in love with you and I finally admitted it to myself shortly before leaving the tour. I was so scared to love someone again, struggling so much with how it would affect Alice's memory. Fuck, I didn't even know if I was allowed to love again."

With my elbows coming down on the table, I buried my head in my hands and fought to get my breathing under control. I felt Tiffeny's warmth before the seat dipped when she sat down beside me.

Her fingers closed over mine, prying them gently away. I didn't try to stop her.

One of her hands held both of mine, the other reaching for my chin and, with the lightest of touches, urged me to turn my head toward her. I expected to see pity in her eyes, maybe anger over getting involved with her in the first place.

What I hadn't been expecting to find there—never in a million years would have expected—was acceptance. But it was there. Clear as a whistle and bright as day. It was in the softened corners of her eyes and the relaxed set of her jaw, the slight tilt of her head as her thumb stroked along mine.

"How about now?" she asked. "Do you feel like you're allowed to love someone else now?"

"Yes," I said, getting lost in a sea of hope at the expression she was wearing. "It took me some time to get to the point where I could let myself, but I finally have. When I told you I wanted us to be a family, it wasn't because I felt forced. It was because that was what I came back here for, before I even knew about the baby. I came back here to make a life, a future, with you."

"You swear that's true?"

I nodded. "If you don't believe me, ask Clark. We can call him right now."

Reaching into the inner pocket of my jacket to pull out my phone, I remembered about the wad of papers I had folded in there. I pulled out the phone and tossed it on the table, but when I looked up, Tiffeny was frowning at the papers.

"What's that?" she asked tentatively. "If it's about the baby, I—"

"It's not." I reared back, dropping my chin as I pulled the papers out to show her. "I would never have anything drawn up about the baby without your knowledge and consent. These are the papers for this mall. I bought it from Nicholson."

"You... what now?" She blinked at the words she read as she unfolded the paperwork.

While she read, I told her what I'd been up to this week. "I figured out what I wanted to do with the touring money, and it was to buy the mall. I couldn't stand the thought of that Nicholson guy creeping around. I've been trying to come up with a way to keep him away from you once and for all, and this is what I came up with."

"You bought the entire mall?"

"Yep." The first stirrings of a smile started tugging at my lips. "I guess this is kind of our shop now, huh?"

She groaned and clapped a hand over her face. "If you start with that, I'm chucking you out right now."

I chuckled softly, flipping the hand she was still holding over to fit her palm against mine while lifting the other to her cheek. "I was kidding. It's all yours, baby. I told you I want to give you everything. I want everything with you. If you're willing to give me a second chance, I won't fuck it up again."

"You sure about that?" She didn't sound like she was.

I injected some steel into my voice. "I'm sure. Sometimes, some-thing might trigger me, but I promise you that next time, I'll work through it with you. You know everything now, so if you're willing to throw your baggage in with mine, I'll buy us a fucking cargo container to keep it all in. As long we get to keep it together."

For a long couple of minutes, she didn't say anything. Her eyes darted between mine, her mouth moving from side to side as if she was trying to decide.

Finally, she nodded. "I'll give you a second chance, Callen, but I'm going to need you to be honest with me when it gets hard. No more running away or shutting me out. I promise I won't push, as long as you promise to tell me what you're going through instead of pushing me away."

"I promise, but I'm doing better. I swear it. I've come a very, very long way in the last six months. Further than I thought I ever would. I'm not just saying this, Tiffeny. I'm in love with *you* and I want to be with *you*. I even wrote a song about you."

"Well, good," she said, a hint of a smile playing at the corners of her lips. "Because I'm in love with you, too. You really wrote a song about me?"

"I did. I'll play it for you sometime.." There were more pressing issues right now, like finally giving in to the urge to wrap her up in my arms and kissing her until it finally felt like there was no more distance left between us.

When we broke apart, we were both breathing heavily. She looked unsure of what to do next, so I took her hand and slid off our seat, pulling her with me. "How do you feel about dinner at my place?"

"Where's Winter?"

"At Julia's. She agreed to watch her for me."

"I miss her, but okay. I guess I'll be seeing a lot more of her again soon, assuming that you're really sticking around."

"We're sticking around," I said firmly. Then I spun around to face her and looked into her eyes as I squeezed her hands. "I love you. I mean it. I know I have a lot of making up to do, but I'm willing to do the work, Tiffeny."

"I was kidding, trying to lighten the mood, but I'm glad to hear you saying you're willing to do the work because it's going to take me some time to trust that this is really what you want. I also really want to hear that song."

"Then you'll hear it. This is really what I want." I brought my hands to her face. "I love you. I'll keep saying it until I'm blue in the face if that's what it takes. I'm sorry, Tiffeny. I never should have left. I know that now."

Her hands covered mine as she took a step closer to me. "You came back. That's what matters. I can't even imagine how difficult it must have been for you to lose Alice and then to have to work through everything after by yourself. I wish you'd told me sooner."

"Me too. I don't even really know why I didn't."

"But you've told me now. I know it isn't always going to be easy, but I'm here for you, Callen. I love you, and I want to support you in any way I can, but I couldn't take it if you walked out on me again."

"I'm not going to," I said firmly, my eyes blazing and locked on hers. "The only way I can prove it to you is to show you every day, and that's going to take time, but I swear to you that I will prove it to you. I'm in this with you, Tiffeny, and I'm not going anywhere."

"Have I mentioned that I love you?" The corners of her mouth tipped up and she leaned in to press a chaste kiss to my lips.

I smiled against hers. "You might have, but I don't think I'll ever get tired of hearing it, so tell me again."

"I love you."

"I love you, too." I brought a hand to the back of her neck and cupped it, bringing her mouth back to mine to kiss her deeply. "Now come on. Let me take you home so I can feed you."

She planted a kiss on my chin before stepping away from me. "Now that you had to go and mention food again, I'm starving."

We walked to my car and Tiffeny climbed in without any arguments about taking her own. I guessed she really was giving this a chance, or at least giving dinner with me a chance.

When we got to my house, however, food seemed to be the furthest thing from her mind. She wound her arms around my neck and played with the hair at the nape of my neck, pressing herself flush against me.

She kissed my jaw, my neck, and then pushed herself up on her tiptoes to suck my earlobe between her teeth. "If Winter isn't here and you're really in love with me like I am with you, how about helping me out with some of these pregnancy hormones?"

I groaned and hauled her even closer to me, loving the feel of the hard bump against my abdomen. "I thought you'd never ask."

CHAPTER 38

TIFFENY

Hearing Callen's story had been really difficult for me. It wasn't hearing that he'd once loved another woman that got to me, though. Of course, he had a past. Most people did.

No, it wasn't that. It was hearing the awful pain he'd been through, the gut-wrenching horror that his life had become.

I hadn't even known him for a year, and I knew that if I lost Callen in that way now, I'd be beyond devastated. I didn't even want to think about it because it hurt too much.

To have lost his wife to a disease he couldn't help her fight, regardless of how much money he threw at it, to have been left behind with a baby girl who would never remember the person who had carried her, to have to navigate parenthood and life by himself after making vows to do it alongside someone he loved. I didn't even know how he'd gone on.

That was the kind of trauma that altered a person to the very fabric of their being. As soon as I'd heard the truth, followed by the revelation of what had happened after I'd left that morning, I'd understood why he'd done it.

Sure, there were other ways he could have handled it. Maybe

better ones, but I couldn't honestly tell myself that I would have acted or reacted any differently if I'd been in his position.

It had hurt like hell when he'd left. All those weeks I hadn't heard from him didn't just go away now that I understood why he'd left, but understanding the reasoning was like a balm to my soul.

Because he hadn't left because he didn't want me or didn't feel the same way about me. He'd left because he did, and didn't know how to deal with it. He'd left because he'd been trying to protect his daughter, and now that I was carrying my own baby, I had more of an idea of how one would go to the ends of the earth to protect their kids.

Did all that mean that everything was magically fine between us? No. Not by a long shot.

It was going to take me some time to learn to trust him again, time to come to terms with the depths of the scars he would always carry with him. Needing that time didn't change the way I felt about him, though.

It also didn't change the fact that I really did love them both and I wanted them in my life and in my future. I wouldn't let his past stand in the way of that.

Callen deserved a second chance at happiness, at love. I deserved to give my first chance the best possible shot I could.

So when he kissed me like he was afraid I would change my mind at any moment, I kissed him back. I tried to show him that I wasn't going anywhere.

I was strong enough not to run from his past, to stand beside him when grief overtook him, and not to be jealous of a ghost. I would never try to compete with Alice because I didn't have to.

What Callen and I had was between us. Our love had grown despite his grief, and I knew that he had to love me deeply if he'd let it take root in his heart enough to want a second chance with me.

It was a glorious thing to have the man I loved in my arms again, and I wasn't going to ruin that by letting his past weigh us down. Instead, I was going to grab every opportunity I could with both hands and live my life to the fullest now that I'd been reminded how desperately short it really was.

It wouldn't always be easy. I knew that, but nothing worth having ever was. Moments like this were the ones I would cling to when life got hard.

Because in this moment, there wasn't a single doubt in my mind that Callen loved me, that he wanted me as much as I wanted him. Which was *a lot*.

Pregnancy hormones were no joke, and so far, I'd been alone in trying to scratch the itch. It was comforting to know I wouldn't be alone in that anymore, nor would I be alone in anything else.

"Callen," I moaned into his mouth, my body aching for his. It had been too long, and after the emotional day we'd had, all I really wanted was to feel him, to make love to him, and to solidify the bond between us now that everything was out in the open. "Bedroom, please."

"With pleasure." He pulled his head back slowly and ran his nose along the length of mine as he breathed in deeply. "Anything you want, Tiffeny. Always. All you have to do is name it, and it's yours."

"All I want is you," I whispered.

"You're in luck then because you have me. All of me. For as long as you want me." He folded my hand into both of his, then led me through his dark house to his bedroom.

Once there, he flicked on the lamp on his nightstand but left the main lights off. He stood me in front of his bed, looking at me like he still couldn't quite believe I was really there.

Slowly, like he was giving me time to stop him if I suddenly decided I didn't want him, he started taking off his clothes. His eyes never left mine as he took off his shirt first. Then his shoes followed.

They were still locked on me when his hands dropped to his shorts, lifting the waistband over the erection I'd felt against my stomach when we'd been kissing and letting them fall to the floor along with his underwear.

When he reached for me, he paused. "Are you sure?"

"I'm sure." I lifted my arms when he touched the hem of my shirt, then peeled it off me. Since it was another tank with a built-in bra, my top half was now completely exposed to him.

He sucked in a sharp breath, and for a second, I was worried he didn't like what he saw anymore. My body had changed a lot since he'd last seen me naked and it wasn't all good. My areolas were bigger, my nipples darker.

Obviously, my belly was hard and protruding. There were a few hairs leading down below my navel and a slightly darker line beneath them.

"Fuck, you're beautiful with my baby in you," he breathed as he raked his eyes down the length of my upper body. When they came back to mine, there was a wildness in them I'd never seen before. "All I want to do right now is fuck you, but I'm not going to do that."

"You're not?" My heart raced, and disappointment dipped in my lower stomach. I was so wet, my panties were damp, and I could feel how swollen and ready I was. "Why not?"

"Because I'm going to make love to you." He grinned, but his muscles were tight as he reached for my skirt and pulled that off too, along with my wet panties. He licked his lips as his eyes dropped again. "But first, I'm going to taste you."

"Can't complain about that," I said as I lay down on the bed, my legs spreading as wide as they could go. "I'm blaming my actions on the hormones, just so you know."

"Blame it on whatever you want. Just don't stop. I love it that I can see how much you want this, want me."

"So much," I moaned as he knelt between my legs and blew cool air across my heated core. "Callen, please."

He gave me a wicked grin and gripped my thighs with his big hands. "Hang on to the sheets, my love. I don't plan on stopping once I get started."

Thankfully, he got started right away. It didn't take long before I learned that one of the articles I'd read about sex during pregnancy had been one hundred percent correct. I really did feel the orgasms right through to my gums.

Screw toes curling. My entire damn body curled as he drove me to climax after earth-shattering climax with his mouth, and when he finally sank into me, completely bare for the first time, I was so sensitive that I came before he even started thrusting. Just the feeling of him inside me was enough to push me over the edge.

"God, baby. You feel so good. So fucking tight. Tighter than before, even."

"It's the pregnancy," I gritted out before he started moving and the stars came closer yet again.

He placed his elbows next to my ears and propped himself up, careful not to put too much weight on the bump. His eyes were on mine as he moved with slow, sure strokes that drove me out of my mind twice before he finally let go.

It was only once he reached the point of no return that he finally broke eye contact, and that was only so he could rest his forehead against mine as he shuddered above me. He kissed me ferociously then, making me feel loved and safe and like I was some kind of miracle.

When the last of his spasms subsided, he rolled off me so as not to collapse on top of my stomach and then he tucked me into his side.

I peered up at him. "You don't think it's weird to do this while I'm pregnant?"

"Nope. I plan on doing it as often as you'll let me while you're pregnant and every chance I get after."

"I can live with that." I smiled against the skin of his shoulder and pressed a light kiss to it. "Do we have to go get Winter in a bit?"

"No, Julia said she could stay over. I wanted tonight to be just the two of us. We'll go get her in the morning."

Both of us dozed off after that, but it wasn't long before Callen woke me up with his tongue between my legs and we started all over again. In between rounds of making love and drifting off, we talked.

We talked about the baby and what we wanted for it. We talked about us and Winter and what we thought our future might look like. Callen also finally got around to playing me the song he wrote about me, and while hearing him sing about me in his low, gravelly voice reduced me to a blubbering mess, it also convinced me that I'd made the right decision.

Even before he was willing to admit that he loved me, he'd pored the depths of his confusing feelings for me into his music and the result was as touching as it was beautiful. By the time we fell asleep, for a few hours this time, I knew in every part of my being that I'd made the right decision.

Callen was not only the father of my child. He was also the love of my life. And though he hadn't asked me to marry him, I had a feeling he would one day, and I couldn't wait to spend the rest of my life with him.

CHAPTER 39

CALLEN

"Dr. Malone, this is Callen," Tiffeny said as we walked into the doctor's examination room. "And this is Winter."

"The baby's father and sister, I assume?" she said with a soft smile as she held out her hand to each of us in turn. "It's wonderful to meet you both. I bet you're excited to find out if you're getting a baby brother or sister, huh?"

Winter nodded, her eyes wide as she looked around the room but shining with the same excitement that had been there since we'd sat her down and explained to her what was going on.

Actually, excitement was an understatement. Thrilled, exhilarated, or over the moon might have described it better.

"I can't wait for the baby to come," Winter said shyly. "Daddy said we're going to see him or her inside Tiffeny's tummy today."

"You sure are." Dr. Malone smiled and gestured at the two chairs on the opposite side of the bed from where her machine was. The chairs for any family members who wanted to come along that had remained unused during Tiffeny's visits so far but would never be empty for another one of them ever again. "Why don't you two take a seat, and we'll take a peek at the baby?"

She turned her attention on Tiffeny. "How are you feeling?"

"I'm good. Starting to get more and more uncomfortable, but I suppose that's normal."

"Very much so. It shows the baby is growing well, so it's good news." She patted the bed. "Hop on up. Let's see if we can get baby to show us what's going on between those legs today."

Already used to the drill by now, Tiffeny lifted her shirt and tucked it into her bra before pushing down the soft waistband of her maternity jeans. She looked so damn beautiful with that bump, I got choked up at times when I looked at her.

Tiffeny said a nurse named Beth had taken care of her at her previous couple of visits, but I was glad the doctor was here for this one. She'd been researching and asking me questions since we'd gotten back together last month, and I knew she'd been looking forward to asking the doctor some of them.

Of course, she'd pointed out that I'd been through this before and, as such, should have been the one able to answer the questions myself. It had felt like a kick to the stomach. I'd grown quiet after that comment, sitting out on the deck strumming my guitar for about an hour after as I worked through the sting.

As she'd promised, she hadn't pushed me for answers immediately. She'd settled on the couch with a book and waited for me to come to her. It couldn't have been easy for her to wait, and I knew she'd questioned whether I would keep up my side of our bargain, but I had.

When I was sure I wasn't about to say something that might fuck it up again and only after I'd reminded myself it would be different this time, I went back inside the house, lifted her feet, and took a seat before setting them down in my lap.

While lightly massaging them, I told her the truth, that I hadn't been very involved or present during Alice's pregnancy with Winter.

The band had been on tour, and while she had been with me, it had been our first big tour, and our days had been jam packed. There had been days that went by when I hadn't even gotten to see her while she was awake.

I told her about how I'd sworn it would be different next time, that I would be at every appointment and how disappointed I was in myself that I hadn't kept that promise. Tiffeny had listened patiently, just like she always did. Then she told me I couldn't blame myself for not being at appointments I didn't know about, and she made me make her a new promise.

So I promised again that I'd be there for every appointment, with the important addition of the words "that I know about."

I practically saw her heart break for me all over again. I knew my story had moved her to tears more than once, which I hated, but she'd assured me that it had placed things in perspective for her, had explained so much about my behavior that she'd forgiven me almost immediately for being the jackass who left because of one question.

She'd also made it crystal clear that she wouldn't let me use Alice or my past as an excuse but that she understood what had triggered me then and wanted to help me through it now.

Tiffeny had a way of understanding me, of letting me know how she was feeling and about reasoning things out, that was almost superhuman. It was part of what made her *her* and I fucking loved her.

Once when I'd tried to apologize again, she'd put a finger to my lips and said, "If this baby had to go asking about its father when I'd gone through all you had, asking if another man was you, Callen... I get choked up just thinking about it."

She'd continued on by saying, "Grief is complicated. I've been doing some reading on it so I'll be able to support you, both of you, and the more I read, the more I realize exactly how complicated it really is. I love both of you enough to face it with you, though."

Both of us knew we were in for tough times when Winter finally really did start asking questions, but we'd be ready. Or at least, we'd be as ready as we could be.

Gel being squeezed onto Tiffeny's belly jerked me out of my head. *Here we go.*

Dr. Malone gave her an apologetic smile. "Sorry, sweetheart. I know it's a bit cold, but trying to warm it up between my hands and then smearing it on is always a mess."

"It's fine, I'm okay," she reassured her. Then I slid my hand into hers to do the same for her.

When I glanced over at her, her eyes were fixed to the screen. The doctor picked up her wand and brought it to her belly, dipping the end in the gel before she let it glide. "There we are. Hello, darling baby. Are you going to show us what you are today?"

Apparently, there were other big things she had to look at today, which was why she was performing the scan herself, but I hadn't wanted to look it all up. I'd discovered the internet was not my friend during pregnancy.

Whatever she found—or didn't find—freaking out about the possibilities beforehand wasn't going to help anyone. She took some more measurements, her lips twitching into a smile as she noted whatever it was she was looking at.

I felt tears sting the backs of my eyes when I looked at that monitor and clearly saw my baby for the first time. Releasing Winter's hand for a minute, I curled my hand into a fist and bit down on my knuckles to keep myself from breaking down into a bawling wreck right there. *I can't believe I'm getting this opportunity. That's my baby in there.*

Winter was just as captivated as I was by the screen, but she was bouncing lightly in her seat instead of wanting to break down and cry.

"Everything is looking good so far. Just the way it should be." She slid the wand farther. "Come on now, baby. Show us what you are."

She gave the bump a gentle prod, and suddenly, a brilliant smile lit her face. "Good boy. Oh, dear. I guess that gave it away. Congratulations, family. It's a boy."

"You hear that, baby?" Tiffeny whispered to me. "Your firstborn son."

I could only squeeze her hand back, my heart swelling to a size I'd previously had thought to be unhealthy or impossible. *A son. I'm having a son.*

"I'm guessing you'd like some pictures of your son to take home?" the doctor asked, holding the wand in place as she pushed some buttons on her machine. The printer whirred a second later and she handed the roll of pictures over before removing the wand. "Do you have any names in mind?"

Tiffeny shook her head while I took the pictures from her and just kept staring at them. I couldn't take my eyes off my son. "We'll have to start thinking about it now."

"Exciting times." She winked at us, then motioned to her office. "I'll be in there when you're ready."

Standing up once the doc left, I leaned over to kiss Tiffeny's lips, my voice the barest whisper as I tried to hold it together. "Thank you, Tiffeny. Thank you for taking such good care of our son while I was off getting my head together."

"I'm just glad you got it together eventually," she said, then smiled. "Thank you for being here. It means the world to me."

Winter threw her arms over her legs as Tiffeny wiped her stomach down. "I'm having a baby brother. We should name him Duncan."

"Duncan, huh?" I asked, waiting until she withdrew her arms before scooping her into mine. "I like it, but we'll talk about it."

"No, I like it, too." Tiffeny wadded up the paper towels and sat up after releasing her shirt. Pulling her waistband back up, she accepted my hand to help her upright, then slid off the bed. "It was actually one of the ones I had on my shortlist if it was a boy."

"Seriously?" My eyebrows were high, my heart pounding. "Because it's one of my all-time favorite names, which is probably why Winter thought of it. She had a male doll once and I called it Duncan."

"He was my baby," she added. "Just like this will be."

"Well, I think that's settled then." She smiled at us both and took my hand, leading us into Dr. Malone's office. Just before we closed the door behind us, she added, "Duncan Clark, I think. If you still want to."

I raised an eyebrow but smiled as we dropped into chairs across from the doctor's desk.

While she answered all of Tiffeny's one hundred and one questions, I reflected back on the reasons why we'd decided about a week or so ago that if the baby was a boy, Clark's name had to be in there somewhere.

Over the last few weeks, I'd told her more about everything Clark had done for us while Alice had been sick and after her passing. I told her how he'd stuck up for me when I'd gotten into trouble for missing practices or interviews, how he'd been right there by my side every painful step of the way, and how he'd eventually been the one to make me feel like I was allowed to move on.

Tiffeny had then come to the conclusion that without Clark, I wouldn't have been anywhere near ready for us to happen when I met her, and even then, I probably would have left her for good if Clark hadn't been there to talk me through it when I finally had.

I didn't completely agree with that last bit, considering that I decided to come back by myself, but I hadn't argued with her. She was pregnant and everyone knew you didn't argue with a pregnant lady.

She also knew Clark had been my rock and, as such, was the reason why I could be hers now. Again, I didn't completely agree, but I couldn't really disagree either. The point was that we both figured he deserved to be honored for that.

After we walked out of the doctor's office, I swept her up in my arms and my lips brushed against her ear when I talked. "A boy. I never thought I'd see the day I'd get to be there to find out what we were having. I love Clark as a middle name, and I love you."

"I love you, too." Her smile couldn't be wider. "But you might love me a little bit less when I tell you we have to go to my mother's now. I promised her we'd come right over after the appointment."

My eyes drifted to Winter, who was carefully inspecting a butterfly perched on a flower nearby. "We never told your mother about her."

"I know, but I don't think she's going to hold it against us. She's been different. We had a talk just after I found out I was pregnant, like I told you, and she's been a different person since."

"Well, I guess we're going to see." I took her hand, ushered Winter over to the car, and drove to Tiffeny's mother's house.

Neither of us were expecting it, but she took to Winter even more than she had taken to me. She hadn't seen me since I'd come back but spent her time playing with Winter first. Only after that did she spend some time with us.

She cooed over the pictures of Duncan Clark, gave her seal of approval for the name, and by the time we left, it felt like we'd just taken another big step forward as a family. One which her mother was going to be part of. Her father? Well, we'd have to see.

"I'm so happy for you two," she said when she walked us out, embracing each of us in turn. "And for the big sister, of course."

I turned to her when we left her mother's house, my hand on my leg, and a smile on my face. "You know, I think today is going to go down in history as one of my ultimate favorite days."

EPILOGUE

TIFFENY

"See, you have to hold his neck," Callen said, helping Winter cradle her brother on her lap.

He was on his knees in front of the armchair beside my hospital bed, and she sat in it, carefully trying to hold Duncan the way Callen was showing her to. My heart burst with pride as I watched the three of them together.

My body felt like it had been run over by several freight trains, but my soul was so happy, it could burst. Duncan had blue eyes like mine, but the nurse had informed us they were likely to change color within the next few months.

I was secretly hoping they'd turn into Callen's forest green. Other than that, the little man was already the spitting image of his handsome father.

Once Winter was settled with her brother, Callen sat down on the armrest of her chair and gazed down at them, then up at me. His eyes were misty, but a mischievous grin spread on his lips. "Right, so how many more of these do you want? I'm thinking we should have at least four more. Six feels like a good number."

"Six?" My eyebrows jumped as I bit back an incredulous laugh.

"You've got to be kidding me. That means I'll have to be pregnant four more times."

His grin widened. "I'm happy to do my part in making that happen. All you need to do is say the word."

"I don't even want to think about that word right now." I groaned, lifting the arm with the plastic hospital bracelet around my wrist. "Besides, given that this only happened this morning, I'm pretty sure we should take some time to see how it goes before deciding on having four more."

"It's going to go incredibly well," he said firmly. "Plus, Duncan was your first child and he was screaming fifty-two minutes after your water broke. I think that means we owe it to your body to give it as many more kids as it wants. You're a champ."

My head fell back against the pillow as I laughed. Then I winced because laughing hurt. "Keep telling yourself that. My body definitely doesn't want any more children right now."

"It will, but there's plenty of time for that," he said, gazing at me with this stupid, adoring look in his eye that made me want to give him anything he wanted. The man was sexy as hell, but man, could he be adorable when he wanted to be.

"What do you think of your brother, Winter?" I asked, curious to know her answer.

If anyone had been a champ throughout this whole process, it was Winter. She wasn't even five yet, but when my water broke this morning, she was first to notice, and then she'd even grabbed Callen's wallet to yank a bill out to pay for our breakfast.

Apparently, she paid a hundred dollars for two cups of tea and some pancakes, but hey, at least one of us had remembered to pay in our dash to get out of there.

I'd been worried she was going to feel like we were replacing her, but based on the expression of absolute pure love shining in her eyes right then, I didn't think we had anything to worry about. "He's so small and perfect."

"He is, isn't he?" I smiled and rubbed my chest, wondering if it was possible to explode from feeling way too much.

It had been an overwhelming day but in the best way possible. Callen had asked me to move in with them several weeks ago. Then he'd had me totally moved before the sun set the same day I agreed.

I'd taken charge of the kitchen and usually made breakfast, but both of them had insisted on going out for breakfast this morning. They'd said they wanted to treat me.

Duncan must have decided he didn't want to miss another family breakfast because Callen and I had still been waiting for our food when he'd decided he was ready to come out. Between Winter pointing out there was a puddle on the floor and then crying out that my water had broken, getting pulled over for speeding, and then having the same policeman escort us to the hospital, and Duncan being born shortly after, the day was a bit of a blur.

Callen had gone outside a while after Duncan's birth to thank the policeman, who'd told him he wanted to stay until he heard the news. It was sweet really, a very eventful birth story for our little man to tell someday. It seemed fitting, somehow.

"Is my mother on her way?" I asked Callen. She'd been very involved in our preparations for Duncan's arrival and had even set up an entire nursery at her house for when she babysat Duncan, which she insisted she would be doing often.

Winter had her own room at my parents' house now, too. It was beyond weird to see my mother in all her *granny glory*, as I'd started calling it in my head. My father's *grampy glory* was a bit more toned down, but my mother's new attitude seemed to extend to him, and things were going better with them as well.

Callen nodded, holding up his phone. "She's been hounding me for updates, but she's also been giving me some of her own. They've just landed. She had to charter a plane because she refused to wait until tonight, but they'll be here within the hour."

"My dad is with her?" I was surprised. As much as things were going better, he was still a workaholic, and the meeting they'd been in was a big deal. Something about getting their new line of baby products, which they'd named *For Duncan*, into stores nationwide.

"Yeah, I guess so," he said, coming over to plant a kiss on my forehead. "I'm glad he's coming."

"So am I." For my mother as much as for myself. "What about Clark and Julia?"

"Clark's flight will be in tomorrow morning. He's got that show in Dallas tonight. Then he's heading right over to the airport to catch a red-eye. He offered to cancel the show, but I told him we didn't want him to do that."

"Definitely not." Although I truly believed he would if we'd asked him. The man was already as crazy for his godson as he was for his goddaughter.

He hadn't been thrilled about the prospect of sharing said godson with Julia, but eventually, he'd agreed. Only after Julia had called him and threatened his balls if he tried to take her godson away from her.

Those two as godparents were our obvious choices, but they truly were going to need God to help them if anything were to happen to us. Callen seemed to be thinking along the same lines I was.

"Jules will be here in about two hours. She said she'd leave her client in the booth again, but I told her your parents were on their way. She wanted to give them some time with Duncan before she came barreling in."

"That's considerate of her." I smiled. "It's probably only because she knows she'll still get to meet him before Clark does."

"When did they become so competitive anyway?" he asked, a confused frown furrowing his brow. "One morning, they were all giggles, and the next time they saw each other, they were all giggles and competition."

I sighed, arching an eyebrow at my boyfriend and baby daddy. "She never mentioned it, but I'm not the only one who got left behind when you guys went on tour. They really hit it off, and I think she was hurt he left without saying goodbye."

There was no more hurt in Callen's expression when I mentioned them leaving. His eyes darkened momentarily because I knew it would always bother him that things had gone down the way they had, but he also knew I'd forgiven him fully, so it didn't necessarily hurt him anymore.

The past four months had been like something out of a dream. Callen had been absolutely perfect and reminded me how much he loved me every day. He was also well on his way to proving to me that he wasn't just going to leave again.

Kraken's hiatus had gotten extended indefinitely, thanks to him and Clark, but he assured me that even if they did get back together one day, it wouldn't be for touring. It remained to be seen, but it wasn't even on the horizon at the moment.

Callen was still writing songs every day and he'd been contacted by quite a few other artists to write for them. His career as a song-writer was taking off and he was deliriously happy about it. He claimed it was the best of both worlds.

"Yeah, I guess I never thought about it that way," he said. "Any-way, they'll all be here soon, so we'd better make the best of this last hour of family time. We're only going to get it again in a couple of weeks once Clark leaves, your parents move out of our house, and—"

"Did you say my parents are only moving out of our house in a couple of weeks?" I blinked, my eyes widening. "When exactly did they move in?"

He laughed and leaned over to iron out my frown. "I wish you could see your face right now, but no, they haven't moved in officially. I just think they're going to be around constantly until their grand-maternity and grand-paternity leave wears off."

I rolled my eyes but smiled as I thought back to the day they told me they were implementing that at the company. I thought it was ridiculous, but my mother was deadly serious.

She insisted that grandparents played such an important role in grandkids' lives, they deserved special leave of their own. She claimed it was to support their own kids as they journeyed into parenthood too, so I kind of understood where Callen was coming from with the being around constantly thing.

"Speaking about making the best of our family time," he said, turning to Winter and giving her a small nod before lifting Duncan off her lap. "I think it's time we gave Tiffeny her present, don't you?"

She nodded excitely, jumping to her feet. Waiting for Callen to lay Duncan down in the bassinet beside the bed, she formed a little shield with her side pressed tightly against his and both their backs to me.

When she turned around, it was with a blue-velvet box open in the palm of her hand. She presented it proudly to me, holding it out as she walked up to the bed carrying the most exquisite ring I'd ever seen.

The silver band was made up of the finest, detailed filigree that wrapped around it all the way to where it disappeared into the black-velvet cushion. In the center of the band was one ridiculously large diamond with a trio of smaller diamonds around it.

"That's you in the middle." Winter dipped her eyes to the largest diamond. "Because you're the bright spot in the darkness and the one we all orbit around. The other three are for me, Daddy, and Duncan, because we will always be right with you. I love you, Tiffeny, and my Daddy does too. Will you be my second mommy?"

"And my wife?" Callen added, lowering himself to one knee as Winter took the ring out of the box and held it ready to slide onto my finger.

My hands flew to my mouth. I knew Callen would have told her what to say, but I also knew the significance of the question she'd asked me and, obviously, the significance of what she'd asked.

Callen and I had been trying to explain to Winter that she had a mommy, but that I was there for her too. At some point, she'd asked if that meant I was her second mommy. He'd said that maybe, hopefully, one day, I would be.

It had already felt like I was, but I knew what he meant, so I hadn't said anything. "In my heart, I've always been your second mommy, sweetheart. I'd love to make it official."

And then I finally looked into those deep green eyes, the ones I'd once thought belonged to the sexiest man I'd ever seen and now knew there was so much more behind them than just good looks.

He was the best man I'd ever known, as well as still being the best-looking one, and honestly, there was nothing I'd like more than to finally claim him as mine. Forever this time.

"Yes, Callen. I'll be your wife, but only because Winter here asked so nicely." She laughed and slid the ring onto my finger, and as simple as that, we were engaged.

Callen pushed up from the floor and claimed my mouth in a kiss that would've made my knees buckle if I hadn't already been lying down. Then he rested his forehead against mine and smiled. "I love you, Tiffeny. Thank you for believing in second chances, and thank you for not giving up on us. I promise to spend the rest of my life making it up to you."

"I love you too, future husband."

The road to getting there had been bumpy—pun intended—but we'd made it. Now it was time for our happily ever after. When my parents burst into the room, all smiles and hugs and love for us all, I knew were well on our way to it.

The End.

ABOUT THE AUTHOR

Hey there. I'm Weston.

I'm a former firefighter/EMS guy who's picked up the proverbial pen and started writing bad boy romance stories. I co-write with my sister, Ali Parker as we travel the United States for the next two years.

You're going to find Billionaires, Bad Boys, Mafia and loads of sexiness. Something for everyone, hopefully. I'd love to connect with you. Check out the links below and come find me.

OTHER BOOKS BY WESTON PARKER

Hot Stuff

Doctor Feelgood

Captain Hotness

Mister Big Stuff

Debt Collector

Worth the Risk

Worth the Distraction

Worth the Effort

Deepest Desire

Ryder

Axel

Jax

Sabian

Aiden

Rhys

My Last First Kiss

My First Love

My One and Only

Made for Me

Air Force Hero

Light Up the Night

Love Me Last

Take A Chance On Me

Brand New Man

We Belong Together

Good Luck Charm